KEN BEGG

Fenton's Winter

FONTANA/Collins

First published in Great Britain by
Fontana Paperbacks 1989

Copyright © Ken Begg 1989

Printed and bound in Great Britain
by William Collins Sons & Co. Ltd Glasgow

A sad tale's best for winter.

WILLIAM SHAKESPEARE
The Winter's Tale

PROLOGUE

THE POWER-DRIVEN DOOR of the sterilizer swung slowly shut. Its side shields clamped it in an airtight embrace and a vacuum pump began sucking out the air until, four minutes later, the automatic controller stopped the pump and opened up a valve. Scalding steam from the hospital's main supply-line flooded in to raise the internal temperature to 126° centigrade. The vacuum ensured that the steam found its way into every nook and cranny of the load, giving up its latent heat and in doing so destroying all vestiges of microbial life. The smallest virus hiding in the remotest corner of a crease would be sought out and exterminated by the relentless steam. There would be no hiding place, no escape, no reprieve. An orange light flicked on as the target temperature was reached and triggered an electric timer. A relay clicked on and off as it held the temperature steady on 126°.

Half-way through the cycle Sister Moira Kincaid returned from lunch and furrowed her brow. She walked over to the unattended sterilizer and took down a clipboard from the side of the machine, checking through the one-line entries with her forefinger and frowning even more. Last entry: nine-fifteen; eight packs of surgical dressings, fourteen instrument packs, gloves, gowns; Cycle normal; Emptied eleven-thirty; Signed J. MacLean. There was no further entry, no indication of what the present load might be or who had commissioned it. Two sins had been committed and Moira Kincaid was annoyed. As sister in charge of the

7

Central Sterile Supply Department at the Princess Mary Hospital it was her job to know everything about everything in her domain. She was a stickler for order and routine. Someone had upset that routine and that someone, she decided, was going to have a very uncomfortable afternoon.

Sterilizer Orderly John MacLean was whistling as he returned from his lunch break, but the off-key rendition died on his lips as he saw the vinegar stare that welcomed him.

'Is something wrong?' he asked tentatively.

Moira Kincaid tapped the edge of the clipboard against the side of the sterilizer and paused for effect. 'This autoclave is running, yet there is no entry on the board.'

MacLean sighed slightly with relief. 'Not me,' he said. 'It was empty when I went for my break; besides, there was no load for it.'

Moira Kincaid looked puzzled. 'That's what I thought,' she said quietly.

'Might be MacDonald, Sister.'

'MacDonald?'

MacLean looked uncomfortable. 'Harry sometimes sterilizes his home-brewing equipment in it,' he said sheepishly.

'Ask him to come and see me when he gets back,' said Moira Kincaid as she turned on her heel and walked across the tiled floor to her office.

She closed the door behind her and leaned back on it for a moment before letting her breath out in a long sigh. She was glad to have these few moments before MacDonald arrived. It would give her time to calm down and get things into perspective. She would give MacDonald a dressing-down but it would go no further than that for, facing facts, MacLean and MacDonald were the best orderlies she had had since taking over the department. She would be loath to lose either of them. Running the Sterile Supply Department was very different to ward work. There was no chain of command, simply because none was required. The work of preparing sterile dressings and instruments did not

8

demand qualified nursing personnel, only the application of average intelligence. As a result her staff of seven – five women and two men – were all of equally unqualified status. Keeping harmony among them was a prime consideration; petty niggles and jealousies had to be stamped out as soon as they occurred, while the vital nature of the work had constantly to be stressed. An unsterile instrument-pack in theatre would almost certainly mean infection and death for an innocent patient, and should such an event occur there would be only one head on the chopping block: hers. A knock at the door interrupted her thoughts 'Come.'

'You wanted to see me, Sister?'

Moira Kincaid swivelled round in her chair. 'Come in, MacDonald. Close the door.' She held the man's gaze till he broke eye contact and looked briefly at the floor. 'Now understand this,' she began. 'I personally have no objection to you sterilizing your brewery in the autoclaves but one thing I do insist on, as you should well know by now, is that every sterilizer run should be properly logged and signed for by the operator.'

'I'm sorry . . . I don't understand,' said the man.

Moira Kincaid was irritated. 'Number three autoclave. Your home-brewing utensils, man. You didn't log the run.'

'But I'm not using the autoclave,' protested the man.

'Then who . . .' Moira Kincaid's voice trailed off and she got to her feet to follow MacDonald out into the main sterilizing area. They joined MacLean in front of number three sterilizer.

'How long to go?'

'Two or three minutes.' They waited in silence while the machine's safety systems sent reports to its silicon brain about conditions inside the chamber. They saw the pressure gauge drop to zero and traced the painfully slow descent of the temperature gauge until a buzzer began to sound and the green open-door light flashed on.

'Right then, let's have a look. Open it up.'

MacLean pressed the door release and the steel shrouds

9

slowly relaxed their grip on the seal. With a slight sigh the airtight joint broke and the heavy door swung open, allowing a residual cloud of steam to billow out.

'Well, John, what is it?'

MacLean was silent. His eyes opened wider and wider until they stopped seeing and he collapsed on to the tiled floor in front of the sterilizer. There was a sickening crack as he hit his head on the corner of the door-shield, and blood welled up from a gash on his forehead to spill on to the tiles. Together, Moira Kincaid and Harry MacDonald went to his aid, but as the steam cleared all concern for their colleague evaporated, for there, in the chamber of the sterilizer, sat the pressure-cooked body of a man.

MacDonald stumbled to the nearest sink and brought up his lunch. Moira Kincaid's nails dug into her cheeks in a subconscious attempt to divert attention from the horror before her eyes, but there was no denying the fact that she recognized the man. Despite the flesh peeling off the cheek-bones and the congealing of the eyes she knew that she was looking at the body of Dr Neil Munro from the Biochemistry Department.

ONE

Small groups of people were discussing the tragedy in nearly every room of the Biochemistry Department but Tom Fenton did not join any of them. He cleared his work bench, washed his hands and put on his waterproof gear.

The big Honda started first time and, switching on the lights, he pulled out into the early-evening traffic. As he neared the city centre a double-decker bus drew out sharply in front of him, causing him to brake hard and correct a slight wanderlust in the rear wheel, but he remained impassive. He weaved purposefully in and out of the rush-hour traffic in Princes Street, not even bothering to glance up at the castle; it was the first time he had failed to do so in the two years he had worked in Edinburgh.

The flat felt cold and empty when he got in. 'Jenny!' he called out as he pulled off his gloves. 'Jenny!' He looked into the kitchen, then remembered that she was on late duty and cursed under his breath. Without pausing to take off the rest of his leathers he poured himself a large Bells whisky and walked over to the window. He revolved the glass in his hand for a moment as he watched the hurrying figures below, then tossed the whisky down his throat in one swift, sudden movement, taking pleasure in the burning sensation it provoked. On impulse he turned and threw the empty glass into the fireplace; he couldn't bear the awful silence. But almost immediately he felt ashamed at what he had done and began picking up the pieces, cursing softly as he did so. When he had finished he took off his leathers and poured himself a fresh drink before sitting down in an armchair and hoisting his feet on to the stool that lurked round the fireplace. Half-way through the bottle he fell asleep.

Just after nine-thirty Fenton was aroused to a groggy state of wakefulness by the sound of keys rattling at the lock and the front door opening. A blonde girl in her mid-twenties, her nurse's uniform showing beneath her coat, came into the room and stood in the doorway for a moment before saying, 'God, Tom, I've rushed all the way home and now I don't know what to say.'

Fenton nodded.

'It's just so awful. I keep thinking it can't be true. How could anyone . . . Isn't there a chance it could have been some kind of freak accident?'

'None at all. It was murder. Someone pushed Neil into the autoclave and pushed the right buttons,' said Fenton.

'But why? What possible reason could they have had?'

'None. It had to be a lunatic, a head case.' Fenton swung his feet off the stool and sat upright in the chair.

'Have you had anything to eat?' asked Jenny.

'Not hungry.'

'Me neither but we'll have coffee.' Jenny leaned down and kissed him on the top of his head. As she straightened up she removed the whisky bottle from the side of his chair. A few minutes later she brought in two mugs of steaming coffee. Fenton took one in both hands and sipped it slowly till the act of drinking coffee with her had re-established a sense of normality.

'Do the police have any ideas?' asked Jenny.

'If they did they didn't tell me.'

'I suppose they spoke to everyone in the lab?'

'At least twice.'

'What happens now?'

'We just go on as if nothing . . .' Fenton stopped in mid-

12

sentence and put his hand up to his forehead. Jenny reached out and took it. She said softly, 'I know, Neil was your closest friend.'

Tom Fenton was twenty-nine years old. After graduating from Glasgow University with a degree in biochemistry he had joined the staff of the Western Infirmary in the same city as a basic-grade biochemist. One year later he had met the girl who was to become his wife, Louise. In almost traditional fashion, Louise's parents had disapproved of their daughter's choice, frowning on Fenton's humble origins, but they had been unable to stop the marriage which was to give him the happiest year he had ever known. Louise's gentleness and charm had woven a spell which had caught him up in a love that had known no bounds, a love which was to prove his undoing when both she and the baby she was carrying were killed in a road accident.

Fenton had been inconsolable. He had fallen into a seemingly endless night of despair which had taken him to the limits of his reason and threatened to push him beyond. Time, tears and a great deal of whisky had returned him to society, but as a changed man. Gone was the happy, carefree Tom Fenton. His place had been taken by a morose, withdrawn individual, devoid of all drive and ambition.

After a year of being haunted by the ghost of Louise Fenton, he had taken his first major decision. He had applied for a job abroad, and, four months later, he had been on his way to a hospital in Zambia.

Africa had been good for him. Within a year he had recovered his self-confidence and could think of Louise without despairing; he could sometimes even speak about her. He had enjoyed the life and the climate and renewed his contract twice, bringing his stay to three years in all before he suddenly decided it was time to return to Scotland and pick up the threads of his old life. The prevailing economic climate and the perilous state of the National

Health Service had made it dificult for him to find a job quickly and he had spent a year at Edinburgh University in a grant-aided research assistant's post before securing his current position at the Princess Mary Hospital.

The sudden return to the demands of a busy hospital laboratory after a year of academic calm had been a bit of a shock but he had weathered the storm and established himself as a reliable and conscientious member of the lab team. The fact that the Princess Mary was a children's hospital and the lab specialized in paediatric techniques pleased him. Working for the welfare of child patients seemed to compensate in some way for the child he had lost.

After a year he had scraped together the deposit for a flat of his own in the Comely Bank area of the city, and on a bright May morning, assisted by Neil Munro and two of the technicians from the lab, he had moved in. The flat was on the top floor of a respectable tenement building that had been built around the turn of the century and featured high ceilings with cornice work that had particularly attracted him to it. It had south-facing windows which, on the odd occasion that the skies were clear in Edinburgh, allowed the sun to stream in from noon onwards. The reward he reaped from having to climb four flights of stairs up to the flat was the magnificent view. As autumn had come around he had watched the smoke from burning leaves hanging heavy in the deep yellow sunshine and felt he understood what Keats, who had once lived in the same area of the city, had meant by 'mists and mellow fruitfulness'.

During the last year Fenton had met Jenny, a nurse at the hospital. She was very different from Louise but he had been attracted to her from the moment they met. Their relationship was easy, undemanding and good. Marriage had not been mentioned but Jenny had moved into the flat and they were letting things take their course.

Jenny Buchan was twenty-four. She had been born in the small fishing village of Findochty on the Moray Firth, the youngest of three children. Her father was George Buchan, who had been a fisherman all his life. He had died in a storm at sea when she was fourteen, leaving her mother Ellen to fend for the family, but luckily it had not been long before her two older brothers, Ian and Grant, had reached working age and had followed their late father into the fleet fishing out of Buckie. They had their own boat, the *Margaret Ross*, and between them they had provided Jenny with three nephews and two nieces. Jenny herself had travelled south to Aberdeen after leaving school and had trained as a nurse at the Royal Infirmary before moving still further south to Edinburgh and the Princess Mary. She had spent her first year in the Nurses' Home before moving into a rented flat with two other nurses and living in traditional but pleasant chaos.

She had met Tom Fenton at a hospital party and been drawn to him in the first instance because he seemed genuinely content just to sit and talk to her. His dark, sad eyes intrigued her and she resolved to find out what lay behind them. After their third date, he had told her about Louise and alarm bells had rung in her head. If Tom Fenton had decided to dedicate his life to the memory of a dead woman then she didn't want to know any more. She need not have worried for, after an idyllic picnic in the Border country, Fenton had taken her home and made love to her with such gentleness and consideration that she had fallen head over heels in love with him. Despite this she had decided to make her position clear. One night as they lay together in the darkness she had turned to him and said, 'I'm Jenny, not Louise. Are you quite sure you understand that?' Fenton had assured her that he did.

The rain, aided by a bitter February wind, woke them before the alarm did. 'What's the time?' asked Fenton.

'Ten past seven.'

'What duty do you have?'

15

'Start at two.'

'You mean I've got to get up alone?'

'Correct.'

'Good God, listen to that rain.'

Jenny snuggled down under the covers.

Fenton swung himself slowly over the edge of the bed and sat for a moment holding his head in his hands. 'I feel awful.'

Jenny leaned over and kissed his bare back. 'The whisky,' she said.

'Coffee?'

'Please.'

Fenton returned to sit on the edge of the bed while they drank their coffee.

'Are you on call this weekend?'

'Tomorrow.'

Jenny put down her cup on the bedside table and put her hand on Fenton's forearm. 'You will be careful, won't you?'

Fenton looked puzzled. 'What do you mean?'

'You said yourself it must have been a lunatic who did that to Neil. Just take care, that's all.'

Fenton was taken aback. 'You know,' he said, 'I hadn't even thought of that.'

The rain drove into Fenton's visor as he wound the Honda up through the streets of Edinburgh's Georgian 'New Town', streets crammed with the offices of the city's professional classes. The road surface was wet and the bike threatened to part company with the cobbles at every flirtation with the brakes. The infatuation with two-wheeled machinery that most men experience in their late teens and early twenties had proved in Fenton's case to be the real thing. Apart from a brief period when he had succumbed to the promise of warmth and dryness from an ageing Volkswagen beetle, his love for motor-cycles had remained undiminished. There was just no car remotely within his price range that could provide the feeling he got when the Honda's rev counter edged into the red sector. Tales of being caught doing 45 in the family Ford paled into insignificance when compared with Fenton's one conviction for entering the outskirts of Edinburgh from the Forth Road Bridge at 110 miles an hour. The traffic police had shown more than a trace of admiration when issuing the ticket but the magistrate had failed to share their enthusiasm and had almost choked on hearing the charge of 'exceeding the speed limit by 70 miles per hour'. His admonition that a man of Fenton's age should have 'known better' had hurt almost as much as the fine.

Fenton reached the hospital at two minutes to nine and edged the bike up the narrow lane at the side of the lab to park it in a small courtyard under a canopy of corrugated iron. The Princess Mary Hospital, being near the centre of the city, had had no room to expand over the years through building extensions and had resorted, like the university, to buying up neighbouring property instead. The Biochemistry Department was actually one of a row of Victorian terraced villas that the hospital had acquired some twenty years before. The inside, of course, had been extensively altered but the external façade remained the same, its stone blackened from years of passing traffic.

Fenton pushed open the dark-blue door and took off his leathers in the outer hall before a row of steel lockers. Susan Daniels, one of the technicians, saw him through the inner glass door and opened it. 'Dr Tyson would like to see you,' she said. Fenton buttoned his lab coat as he climbed the stairs to the upper flat, then knocked on the door bearing the legend 'Consultant Biochemist'.

'Come.'

As Fenton entered, Charles Tyson looked up from his desk and peered at him over his glasses. 'What weather.'

Fenton agreed.

'We're going to have the police with us for most if not all

of the day,' said Tyson. 'We'll just have to try and work round them.'

'Of course.'

'I've requested a locum as a matter of priority but until such time . . .'

'Of course,' said Fenton again.

'I'd like you to speak to Neil's technician, find out what needs attending to and deal with it, if you would. I'll have Ian Ferguson cover for you in the blood lab in the mean time.'

Fenton nodded and turned to leave. As he got to the door Tyson said, 'Oh, there is one more thing.'

'Yes?'

'Neil's funeral. It'll probably be at the end of next week, when the fiscal releases the body. We can't all go; the work of the lab has to go on. I thought maybe you, Alex Ross and myself would go?'

'Fine,' replied Fenton without emotion.

He walked along the first-floor landing to a room that had once been a small bedroom but in more recent times had been Neil Munro's lab. He sat down at the desk and started to empty out the drawers, pausing as he came to a photograph of himself holding up a newly caught fish. He remembered the occasion. He and Munro had gone fishing on Loch Lomond in November. They had left Edinburgh at six in the morning to pick up their hired boat in Balmaha at eight. The fish, a small pike, had been caught off the Endrick bank on almost the first cast of the day, and Munro had captured the moment on film.

There had been no more fish and the weather had turned bad in the early afternoon, so they had been soaked to the skin by the time they returned to MacFarlane's boatyard.

Fenton put the photograph in his top pocket and continued sifting through the contents of the desk. He was working through the last drawer when Susan Daniels came in. 'I understand you'll be taking over Neil's work,' she said. 'Can we talk?'

'Give me five minutes and I'll be with you.'

A system involving three piles of paper had evolved. One for Munro's personal belongings, one for lab documents and one for 'anything else'. The personal pile was by far the smallest: a scientific calculator, a University of Edinburgh diary, a well-thumbed copy of *Biochemical Values in Clinical Medicine* by R. D. Eastham, a few postcards, and a handful of assorted pens and pencils. Fenton put them all in a large manila envelope and marked it 'Neil's' in black marker pen. The 'anything else' pile was consigned mainly to the waste-paper basket; it consisted of typed circulars advising of seminars and meetings and updates to trade catalogues. Fenton started to work his way through the lab-document pile while he waited for Susan to return. Much of it was concerned with a new automated blood analyzer that the department had been appraising for the past three months. Neil had been acting as liaison officer with the company, Saxon Medical, and the relevant licensing authorities, and from what Fenton could see in copies of the reports there had been no problems. The preliminary and intermediate reports that Munro had submitted were unstinting in their praise.

Fenton turned his attention to Munro's personal lab book and tried to pick up the thread of the entries but found it difficult, for there was no indication of where the listed data had come from or what it referred to. Munro, like the other senior members of staff, had been working on a research project of his own, something they were all encouraged to do, although, in a busy hospital laboratory, this usually had to be something small and relatively unambitious. Fenton stopped trying to decipher the figures and went to look out of the window. It was still raining although the sky was beginning to lighten. He turned round as Susan came in.

'Sorry. The police wanted to talk to me again.'

Fenton nodded.

'It all seems a bit pointless really. Who would want to kill Neil?' said the girl.

Fenton looked out of the window again. 'The point is, somebody did kill him.'

'I'd better brief you on what Neil was doing,' said Susan.

'Do you know what his own research project was on?'

'No, I don't. Is it important?'

'Maybe not, I just thought you might know.'

'He didn't speak about it, although he seemed to be spending more and more time on it over the past few weeks.'

'Really?'

'Actually he seemed so preoccupied over the last week or so that I asked him if anything was the matter.'

'And?'

'He just shook his head and said it probably wasn't important.'

Fenton nodded. That was typical of Munro. Although he had had friends, Neil Munro had been a loner by nature, never keen to confide in anyone unless pressed hard. Fenton himself had not seen much of him over the past few weeks; in fact since Jenny had moved into the flat, they had seen very little of each other socially although that would have changed when the fishing season opened in April.

'You've been running the tests on the Saxon Blood Analyzer, I see,' said Fenton, picking up the relevant papers.

'In conjunction with Nigel. He's been showing us how to use it.'

Nigel Saxon was the chief sales rep from Saxon Medical who had been attached to the department for the period of the trial. Like most reps, he had a pleasant, outgoing personality which, combined with a generous nature and the fact that he was the boss's son, had made him a popular figure in the lab.

'Neil seemed to like the machine,' said Fenton, looking at Munro's intermediate report.

'We all do,' said Susan.

'What's so special about it?'

20

She opened one of the wall cupboards and took out a handful of what appeared to be plastic spheres. 'These,' she said. 'These are the samplers. They're made out of a special plastic. You just touch them against the patient's skin and they charge by capillary attraction. All you need is a pinprick, no need for venipuncture.'

'But the volume?'

'That's all the machine needs to do the standard values.'

'I'm impressed,' said Fenton. 'What stage are the tests at?'

'They're complete. It just requires the final report to be written up and signed by Dr Tyson.'

'Is all the information here?'

'I've still got the data from the last set of tests in my notebook. I'll bring it up after lunch.'

'I'll come down; I'd like to see the machine in action. Anything else I should know?'

'Neil was running some special blood tests for Dr Michaelson in the Metabolic Unit. Perhaps you could contact him and have a chat.'

Fenton nodded and made a note on the desk pad. 'Anything else?'

'There are a couple of bypass operations scheduled for next week. Neil was supposed to organize the lab cover.'

Fenton made another note. He looked at his watch and said, 'Why don't you go to lunch? If you think of anything else you can let me know.' He got up as Susan left the room and returned to the window to check on the weather. It had stopped raining.

Fenton pulled up his collar as he felt the icy wind touch his cheek. He decided to give the hospital canteen a miss, knowing that it would still be buzzing with talk of Neil's death and a new day's crop of rumours. He walked off in the opposite direction, not at all sure where he was going. He paused as he came to the entrance to a park and wandered in to find himself alone beneath the trees. The wide expanse of grass that would be crowded with lunch-time picnic makers in July was utterly deserted this cold February day.

A bird wrested a worm from the wet, windswept grass and flew off with it in its beak. That's the awful thing about death, thought Fenton, life goes on as if you had never existed. He reached the far end of the park and let the iron gate clang shut behind him as he returned to the street and looked for inspiration. He saw the beckoning sign of the Croft Tavern and crossed the road.

A sudden calm engulfed him as he went in, making him aware of the windburn on his cheeks. He ran his fingers ineffectually through his hair as he approached the deserted bar to pick up a grubby menu. The barmaid tapped her teeth with a biro.

'Sausage and chips, and a pint of lager.'

'I'm only food; you get your drink separately,' said the sullen girl with an air that suggested she had said the same thing a million times before.

Fenton looked to the other barmaid. 'Pint of lager, please.'

'Skol or Carlsberg?'

'Carlsberg.'

A plume of froth emanated from the tap. 'Barrel's off.'

'All right, Skol.'

Fenton looked behind the bar at a poster on the wall which proudly announced, 'This establishment has been nominated in the *Daily News* pub of the year competition.' By the landlord, thought Fenton.

'Hello there,' said a voice behind him. He turned to find Steve Kelly from the Blood Transfusion Service. 'Didn't know you came here for lunch.'

'First time,' said Fenton.

'Me too. I'm sitting over there by the fire. Join me when you get your food.'

Fenton and Kelly sat on plastic leather seats in front of a plastic stone fireplace. They watched imitation flames flicker up to plastic horse brasses.

'The breweries really do these places up well,' said Kelly

without a trace of a smile. Fenton choked over his beer. Kelly smiled.

Fenton's fork ricocheted off a sausage, causing chips to run for cover in all directions. One landed in Kelly's lap and he popped it into his mouth.

'You can have the rest if you want,' said Fenton, putting down his knife and fork.

'No thanks, I've just tasted it.'

'What brings you here?' asked Fenton.

'I was looking around for a nice quiet wee place to bring that nurse from Ward Seven to one lunchtime.'

'You mean somewhere where the wife wouldn't be likely to find you?'

'You've got it.'

'Well, this place seems quiet enough.'

'Aye, but it wasn't exactly food poisoning I was planning on giving her.'

'Point taken.'

They sipped their beer in silence for a few minutes before Kelly said, 'So who's the loony, Tom?'

Fenton kept his eyes on the flames. 'I wish to God I knew.'

'Munro was a friend of yours, wasn't he?'

Fenton nodded.

'I'm sorry.'

Fenton sipped his beer.

'Who'll be taking over his projects?' asked Kelly.

'I will for the moment.'

'Then you'll be wanting the blood?'

Fenton was puzzled. 'What blood?'

'Munro phoned me on Monday; he wanted some blood from the Service.'

'Better hold on to that till I find out what he needed it for.'

'Will do.'

'Another drink?'

'No.'

They got up and moved towards the door. 'Would you mind returning your glasses to the bar?' drawled the lounging barmaid.

'Aye, we would,' said Kelly flatly. They left.

Fenton waited while Kelly finished buttoning his coat up to the collar. He hunched his shoulders against the wind. Kelly said, 'So you'll let me know about the blood?' Fenton nodded and they parted.

Fenton was grateful that the wind was now behind him, supporting him like a cushion, as he walked slowly back to the hospital. This time he avoided the park and opted instead for the streets of Victorian terraced housing; black stone houses that looked cool in summer but dark and forbidding in winter. The bare branches of the trees fronting them waved in the wind like witches in torment. As he reached the lab he had to pause to let a silver-grey Ford turn into the lane beside it. One of its front wheels dipped into a pot-hole, splashing water over his feet. He raised his eyes to the heavens then saw that the driver was Nigel Saxon, who stopped and wound down the window, looking apologetic. 'I say, I'm most frightfully sorry.'

Fenton smiled, for it was hard to get angry with Saxon. He waited while he parked his car then watched him attempt to side-step the puddles as he hurried to join him. Saxon was everyone's idea of a rugby forward running to seed, which indeed he was. He had played the game religiously for his old public school until, at the age of twenty-five or so, he had discovered that it was possible to have the post-match drink and revels without actually having to go through the pain of playing. Now, at the age of thirty-two, he was beginning to look distinctly blowzy, a fact of which he seemed cheerfully aware. He had managed to scramble a poor degree in mechanical engineering before joining his father's company, Saxon Medical, where his engineering skills had been completely ignored in favour of the amiable personality and self-confidence that made him invaluable in sales and customer liaison. Saxon would never appreciate the fact that his greatest talent lay in making customers feel superior; Fenton found this ironic.

'You've got lipstick on your cheek,' said Fenton.

Saxon pulled a handkerchief from his pocket, scattering loose change over the pavement. Fenton helped pick it up and paused to look at something that turned out not to be a coin. It appeared to be a silver medallion with a tree engraved on it. 'Very nice,' he said, and as he handed it back he was surprised at the intense way Saxon was looking at him. It was as if Saxon had asked him a question and was waiting for an answer.

Saxon dabbed absent-mindedly at his cheek.

'Other one,' said Fenton.

There were three policemen in the hallway when they entered the lab. 'Mr Fenton?' said one. Fenton nodded. 'Inspector Jamieson would like to see you again, sir, if that's convenient?'

'Of course. I'll be in one-oh-four.'

'You know, I still can't believe it,' said Saxon as he and Fenton climbed the stairs to the first floor, 'I keep expecting to see Neil.' Fenton nodded but managed to convey to Saxon that he did not want to talk about it.

'I was wondering if we might have a talk about the Blood Analyzer,' said Saxon.

Fenton said that he was about to suggest the same thing and told Saxon that he had arranged with Susan to see the machine working that afternoon. Saxon said that he would join them and asked when.

'As soon as I finish with the police.' As Fenton closed the door he heard the rain begin to lash against the windows once more. The sky was leaden. Mouthing a single expletive he turned to Munro's personal research book and started to go through it again. He wanted to know why Munro had asked the Blood Transfusion Service for a supply of blood and what exactly he had planned to do with it. Kelly had not said how much blood Neil had asked for and he had neglected to ask. He picked up the internal phone and asked the lab secretary to check the official requisition.

As he waited for a reply, there was a knock at the door. It was Inspector Jamieson and his sergeant, whose last name Fenton could not remember. He motioned them to come in and said that he would be with them in a moment.

'What day did you say?' asked the secretary's voice on the phone.

'Monday.'

'That's what I thought you said. There isn't one.'

'Are you quite sure?'

'I've checked three times.'

'Perhaps I misunderstood,' said Fenton thoughtfully. He put down the phone. So Neil had made the request privately, without going through the usual channels. Curiouser and curiouser. He became aware of the policemen looking at him and put the thought temporarily out of his mind.

Fenton had taken a dislike to Jamieson after their first meeting but had been unable to rationalize it, thinking perhaps that he might have taken a dislike to anyone who appeared to be asking so many pointless questions.

'I thought we might just go through a few of these points again, sir,' Jamieson began.

'If you insist.'

'I'm afraid I do, sir.' It was said with an ingratiating smile.

So, thought Fenton, the dislike was mutual.

At five foot ten Jamieson was small for a policeman in the Edinburgh force, but what he lacked in height he made up for in breadth. His shoulders filled his tweed jacket, providing a firm base for a thick neck and a head that appeared to be larger than it actually was because of a thick mop of grey hair. He sported a small clipped moustache and this, together with the twill trousers and checked shirt, gave him the appearance of an English country gentleman in weekend wear. The voice, however, belied the image. It was both Scottish and aggressive.

As the interview progressed Fenton was convinced that he was answering the same questions over and over again. It irritated him but, not knowing anything of police procedure, he concluded that this might be a routine gambit: annoy the subject until he loses his temper then look for inconsistencies in what is being said. It irritated him even more to think that he might be being treated as some kind of laboratory animal. His answers became more and more cursory, while privately he became more and more impatient. Of course Neil hadn't had any enemies. He had no earthly idea why anyone should want to kill him. Wasn't it obvious that some kind of deranged psychopath had committed the crime? Why were they wasting time asking such damn fool questions? Did the police have no imagination at all?

'Miss Daniels tells us that Dr Munro seemed very preoccupied, to use her word, over the last week or so. Do you have any idea why?' asked Jamieson.

Fenton said that he did not.

'Miss Daniels thinks it may have had something to do with his personal research work.' There was a pause while Jamieson waited for Fenton to say something. When he did not Jamieson asked, 'Would you happen to know what that was?' Again Fenton said that he did not. 'But you were a friend of the deceased, were you not?' Jamieson turned on the smile which Fenton could see he was going to come to dislike a great deal. 'Yes I was, but I don't know what he was working on.'

'I see, sir,' said Jamieson, smiling again. 'I understand from Dr Tyson that you'll be tidying up the loose ends of Dr Munro's work?'

Fenton said that was so.

'Perhaps if you come across anything that might indicate the reason for Dr Munro's state of mind you would let us know?'

* * *

Fenton came downstairs to join Susan in the main laboratory, a large bay-windowed room that had once been a Victorian parlour. He apologized for being late. Nigel Saxon was already there, making an adjustment to the machine in response to something that Susan had mentioned.

'Well, impress me,' said Fenton.

Susan picked up one of the plastic spheres that Fenton had seen earlier and held it over a blood sample. 'In normal times we would be doing this at the patient's bedside after a simple skin prick with a stylet, but for the moment we're using samples that have been taken in the conventional way.' She touched the sphere to the surface of the blood and Fenton saw it charge. 'That's all there is to it,' she said, removing the sphere and introducing it into the machine. She pressed a button and the analyzer began its process.

'Amazing,' said Fenton, 'but what happens when the temperature varies and the sampler takes up more or less blood? The readings won't be accurate.'

'That's where you're wrong, old boy,' said Saxon with a smile. 'The plastic is special. It's thermo-neutral; it doesn't go soft when it warms up and it doesn't go hard when it's cold. It's always the same. Well, what do you think?'

Fenton admitted that he was impressed. Saxon beamed at his reaction.

'I suppose this stuff costs a fortune,' said Fenton.

Saxon smiled again. 'Actually it doesn't. It costs very little more than conventional plastics.'

'But the potential for it outside medicine must be enormous.'

Saxon shook his head and said, 'We thought so too at first, but the truth is it's just not strong enough to be useful in the big money affairs like defence and space technology. For medical uses, of course, it doesn't have to be. We've manufactured a range of test-tubes, bottles, tubing, and so on, which will cost only a fraction more than the stuff in use at present. We think the advantages will outweigh the extra cost and hospitals will start changing to Saxon equipment.'

'I take it you have a patent on the plastic?'

'Of course,' smiled Saxon.

'It sounds like a winner,' said Fenton.

'We think so too. We're so confident that we have gifted a three-month supply of our disposables to the Princess Mary.'

'That was generous,' conceded Fenton.

'Well you were kind enough to put our Blood Analyzer through its paces for the licensing board; it seemed the least we could do.'

The printer started to chatter and Susan removed a strip of paper from the tractor feed. 'All done,' she said.

Fenton accepted the paper and looked at the figures. 'Normal blood,' he said.

'A control sample,' said Susan.

'How do the figures compare with the ones given by our own analyzer?'

'Almost identical, but the Saxon performed the analysis on one-fifth of the blood volume and in half the time.'

'Maybe Saxon will gift us one of their machines as well as the Tupperware,' said Fenton, tongue in cheek.

Nigel Saxon smiled and said, 'There has to be a limit even to our generosity.'

Susan handed Fenton a sheaf of papers. 'These are the results of the final tests. You'll need them for the report.'

Saxon said to him, 'I hate to press you at a time like this but have you any idea when the final report will be ready?'

'End of next week, I should think.'

Fenton left the room to return upstairs but paused at the foot of the stairs when he saw a small puddle of water lying in the stairwell. He looked up and saw a raindrop fall from the cupola and splash into the puddle. 'All we need,' he muttered, going to fetch a bucket from the glassware preparation room. He placed the bucket under the drip

29

before calling in on the chief technician. 'The roof's leaking, Alex.'

'Again?' said Alex Ross with a shake of the head. 'It's only two months since they repaired it.' He made a note on his desk pad and said he would inform the works department.

When he got back to his own lab Fenton found Ian Ferguson, one of the two basic-grade biochemists on the staff, hard at work. He looked up as Fenton entered and said, 'Dr Tyson asked me to cover for you.'

'He told me. Thanks. How's business?'

'Brisk,' smiled Ferguson. 'But I think everything's under control. There are a couple of things I think you'd better look at, but apart from that it's been largely routine.'

Fenton picked up the two request forms that Ferguson had put to one side and nodded. 'I'll deal with them,' he said. 'You can go back to your own work, if you like. I can manage now.'

Ferguson got up and tidied the bench before leaving. As he turned to go Fenton said to him, 'Did Neil mention anything to you about requesting blood from the Transfusion Service?'

Ferguson turned and shook his head. 'No, nothing.'

Fenton tried to phone Dr Ian Michaelson for the third time. This time he was successful. He asked about the special blood monitoring that had been requested and Michaelson explained what he had in mind. 'We could postpone the tests for a week or two if you can't cope after what's happened,' said Michaelson.

'But it would be better for the patient if they were done this week?'

'Yes.'

Fenton did some calculations in his head, translating the required tests into man hours. 'We'll manage,' he said. Next he contacted the cardiac unit about the proposed bypass operations and learned that there were now three on the schedules instead of two. 'This is not good news,' he said. Once again he was asked if the lab could cope. 'Some of us won't be going home too much,' he replied, 'but we'll manage.'

Despite the fact that Ferguson had cleared most of the morning blood tests Fenton found himself busy for most of the afternoon. He found this therapeutic, for it made it impossible for him to dwell on anything other than the work in hand, but at four-thirty he was disturbed by the sound of raised voices coming from downstairs. He looked out from his room and asked one of the junior technicians what was wrong.

'It's Susan,' the girl replied. 'She's been taken ill.'

TWO

Fenton ran downstairs to find Susan Daniels lying on the floor outside the ladies' lavatory. She was surrounded by people giving conflicting advice. Help her up! No, don't move her! Loosen her clothing! Keep her warm!

'What happened?' he asked.

'She fainted when she came out of the toilet,' said a voice.

'She's bleeding!' said another voice.

'I've sent for Dr Tyson,' said Alex Ross. Tyson was the only medically qualified member of the staff; the others were purely scientists.

Fenton knelt down beside the prostrate girl and felt her forehead; it was cold and clammy. 'Who said she was bleeding?' he asked.

Liz Scott, the lab secretary, knelt down beside him and said qiuetly, 'There's blood all over the floor in the toilet.'

Fenton reached his hand under the unconscious girl's thigh and found her skirt wet and sticky. 'She *is* bleeding,' he said. 'Get some towels!' The crowd dispersed. 'Was Susan pregnant?' Fenton asked Alex Ross.

'If she was she never said,' replied the chief technician.

'She seems to be having a miscarriage,' said Fenton.

'Poor lass.'

Someone handed Fenton a bundle of clean linen towels. He folded one and pushed it up between Susan's legs, then followed it with another. He was relieved when Charles Tyson arrived on the scene to take over. He stood up and noticed one of the juniors wince at the sight of his blood-soaked hand.

'She's lost a lot,' said Tyson. 'We'll have to get her over to the main hospital.'

Responsibility passed from Tyson to two nurses in Casualty who wheeled Susan into a side room leaving Tyson and Fenton waiting in the long corridor outside. They sat on a wooden bench in silence. Fenton leaned his head back against the wall and turned to look along the length of the corridor. An orderly was buffing the linoleum with an electric polisher in a steady side-to-side motion some forty metres away at the other end. A nurse, dressed in the pink uniform of a first-year student, flitted briefly across his field of view. Distant sounds of children's voices echoed along the high Victorian ceilings. He turned his attention to the posters of Disney characters which had been stuck up at intervals along the walls to lighten the atmosphere. The sheer height of the walls swamped them, making them seem pathetic rather than effective.

A figure hurried towards them, white coat billowing open. His eyes fell on Tyson. 'Sorry sir, couldn't get here any sooner. We've got a minibus accident to contend with.'

Tyson nodded non-commitally. 'She's in there,' he said.

Fenton saw Tyson swither over whether or not to join the registrar in the treatment room and decide not to. It had been over twenty years since he had been involved in direct patient care.

A heavy trolley pushed by two porters swung erratically to the side as it passed them and made them draw in their feet. Each porter blamed the other. Tyson looked at his watch and displayed uncharacteristic irritation. 'Come on, come on,' he muttered. Another two minutes had passed before a nurse accompanied by an orderly appeared. They were carrying transfusion equipment, the orderly weighed down on one side by a green plastic crate containing six blood packs. They almost collided with the registrar, who chose that moment to emerge from the room. He ignored the new arrivals and came directly towards Tyson. Fenton thought he looked embarrassed and had a sense of forboding.

'I'm sorry,' said the registrar, as if unable to believe what he was about to say. 'We've lost her.'

Fenton felt a prickle of sweat break out all over his skin. 'We've lost her.' That's what they had said that awful night when Louise had died. The words echoed inside his head, rekindling every emotion of that hellish moment. After the phone call he had run through the streets in the pouring rain desperately trying to wave down a taxi, but the weather had made sure that they were all occupied. He had ended up running the entire three miles to the hospital, had stood there, dripping wet under the daylight glare of the lights in Casualty, to be told that his wife and child were dead. He remembered every pore on the face of the house officer who had told him, the way he had touched the frames of his glasses, the way he had looked at his feet. Now he waited for the next line, 'We did all we could,' but it didn't come. Instead, Tyson's voice broke the spell. 'What do you mean, "lost her"?' he asked hoarsely.

The registrar had gone a little red in the face. 'I'm sorry,' he said, making a gesture with open palms. 'We couldn't stop the bleeding in time. It's as simple and as awful as that.'

'But why not?' insisted Tyson.

The registrar made another helpless gesture with his hands. 'I'm afraid we really won't know the answer to that until after the post-mortem.'

Tyson got slowly to his feet and walked past the registrar into the treatment room; Fenton followed. The nurses melted back from the table to reveal the body of Susan Daniels, very still and very white. Fenton thought that she looked more beautiful than he had ever realized, like a pale delicate flower that had been cut and left lying on its side. Soon it would wither and fade. He was filled with grief and looked for some mundane object to focus his eyes on while he regained control of his emotions. He settled his gaze on a steel instrument-tray and kept it there.

On looking up he saw tears running down the face of one of the nurses. He squeezed the girl's shoulder gently and indicated to her that she should leave the room. He himself followed a few moments later. He pretended to look at one of the Disney posters while he waited for Tyson.

In the background Fenton could hear Tyson and the registrar discussing the post-mortem arrangements; then he had the feeling that he was no longer alone. He looked down to see a little boy dressed in pyjamas staring up at him. The child's nose was running. He did not say anything but had a questioning look on his face. Fenton said, 'Now where did you come from?'

The child continued to stare at him, then said, 'I want my mummy.'

Fenton gently asked the boy his name but before he could answer, a distraught nurse appeared on the scene. 'Timothy Watson! So there you are!' She swept the child up into her arms and said to Fenton, 'You just can't turn your back on this one for a moment or he's off.' The boy put his thumb in his mouth and snuggled down on the nurse's shoulder.

'Goodbye, Timothy,' said Fenton as the nurse walked away. He decided to walk back to the lab on his own without waiting any longer for Tyson, who was still deep in discussion with the Casualty registrar.

It was already dark outside, and reflections from the sodium streetlights glistened in puddles of rainwater as he walked back towards the old villa. As he drew nearer he saw three figures standing in the bay window of the main lab and knew that they were waiting for news of Susan. One of them, Ian Ferguson, came to the door to meet them. 'How is she?' he asked. Fenton stepped inside the hallway and saw everyone standing there. 'Susan's dead,' he said softly. 'She bled to death.'

Ferguson and Alex Ross, the chief technician, followed Fenton into the front room, closing the door and leaving the others out in the hall. Fenton crossed the floor and put his hands on the radiator by the window. 'God, it's cold.'

'Did they say what it was?' Ross asked.

'No, I don't think they know. They're going to do a post-mortem on her.' Fenton sensed that his answer had failed to satisfy Ross; he turned round to face him.

Ross said, 'It was natural, wasn't it? I mean, she wasn't murdered like Neil?'

Fenton was shocked. 'Christ, I hadn't even considered that. I assumed it was some gynaecological thing.'

'Me too,' said Ferguson.

'You're probably right,' said Ross. 'It was just a thought.'

'What a thought,' said Fenton, turning back to look out at the rain that had just begun again.

On Saturday the lab staff finished at 1 P.M., leaving Fenton as duty biochemist till Sunday morning. He picked up the internal phone and gave the hospital switchboard his name and bleep number, adding that he was about to go to lunch. He hurried up to the main hospital, leaning forward against a fiercely gusting wind, and climbed the stairs to the staff restaurant; it was half empty. He looked around for a familiar face but recognized only Moira Kincaid from the Sterile Supply Department, who was just leaving. He nodded to her as she passed.

Fenton paid for a cellophane-wrapped salad and took it to a table by a window where he could watch the trees bend in the wind, which seemed to be blowing more strongly than ever.

'Want some company?' asked a voice behind him.

Fenton turned to find Jenny and smiled.

Jenny laid down her tray and Fenton held the edge of it steady while she extracted her fingers. 'What a morning,' she complained. 'The ward's going like a fair.'

Fenton smiled, paying scant attention to what she was saying but thinking that Jenny Buchan was the best thing that had happened to him in a very long time. 'I didn't hear you leave this morning,' he said.

'You were asleep. It seemed a shame to wake you.'

Jenny too looked out of the window at the rain as it lashed against the blackened stone in windswept frenzy. 'Do you think you'll manage to get home tonight?' she asked.

Fenton shrugged his shoulders without taking his eyes off the rain, and was about to reply when the bleeper in his jacket pocket went off. He shrugged again and Jenny nodded as he got up to leave. Outside in the corridor he picked up the phone and called the switchboard.

Although the biochemistry lab was primarily concerned with the patients of the Princess Mary Hospital, it also carried out paediatric work for other hospitals in the city. Fenton had been informed that a blood sample was on its way from the maternity unit at the Royal Infirmary, a sample from a jaundiced baby for bilirubin estimation. He sat in the front room until the clatter of a diesel engine outside told him that it had arrived. He took the plastic bag from the driver, signed the man's book and carried the sample upstairs for analysis.

With the blood sample in the first stages of assay Fenton turned on the radio and tuned it to Radio Three. The sombre music seemed appropriate to a grey Saturday afternoon in February. He changed the settings on the analyzer for the next stage and, with a fifteen-minute wait in prospect, went along the corridor to Neil Munro's lab to collect Munro's research notes. He settled down to read them as the rain hammered on the windows. The sound made him appreciate the warmth of the lab. He wondered for a moment if the house had ever been this comfortable when it had been home to a well-to-do Victorian family. No trace of a fireplace could now be seen along any wall; the only original fitting left was on the ceiling, where a plaster repair job had failed to conceal the rose from which a chandelier had once hung.

Fluorescent lights were now bolted to the ceiling, incongruous against the cornice.

The bilirubin result chattered out of the printer. Fenton looked at it and compared it with the standard graphs on the wall. 'Well, young' – he checked the name on the request form – 'John Taylor, aged three days, you won't be going home for a while yet.' He called the maternity unit with the result and asked the nurse who took the call to read it back to him. 'Check.'

Finding that he was making little or no progress with Munro's book, Fenton decided to make some coffee and went down to switch on the electric kettle in the common room. The front door rattled in the wind as he came down the spiral stairs and crossed the hallway. He paused in front of one of the lockers to look at a photograph stuck up on one of the doors. 'Summer '86', said the caption in Dymo tape. It had been taken on the lab staff picnic in July, one of the few occasions Fenton could remember when a planned outing in Scotland had coincided with a dry sunny day. The good weather had made all the difference to the party, as the smiles on the faces in the photograph testified.

Fenton looked at Neil Munro, relaxed, smiling, and now dead; at Susan Daniels in T-shirt and shorts, young, carefree, and now dead. He thought about Susan's death and what Alex Ross had said. Surely it couldn't have been murder. But the idea had been voiced; it would not go away. Two people in the lab murdered? Considering the notion, albeit briefly, spawned another thought that was even colder than the icy wind that sought entrance to the hall through the cracks round the door. If two people in the lab had been murdered, did that not suggest that the killer was one of the lab staff? One of the people in this photograph? Impossible.

The phone rang as Fenton drank his coffee; he swivelled in his chair to pick up the receiver. Four blood samples were on their way. The phone was to ring twice more that afternoon for the same reason, keeping him busy till a little after seven when things seemed to quieten down. He began to toy with the idea of going home, deciding finally to give it until seven-thirty before committing himself. At twenty to eight he phoned Jenny to say that he was on his way, then called the switchboard to say where he would be should his bleep fail.

The smell of cooking greeted him as he opened the door of the flat, making him think how nice it was to come home to a warm bright apartment instead of the cold, dark silence that he had been used to in the days before Jenny.

'How was it?' Jenny asked.

'Busy,' Fenton replied, grunting as he pulled off his motor-cycle boots. 'You?'

'It quietened down a lot this afternoon but we had one admission for the bypass op.'

Fenton washed his hands and joined Jenny at the table.

'I've got some bad news, Tom,' said Jenny.

'What?' asked Fenton.

'I'm going on night duty soon.'

Fenton made a face. 'What does that involve?'

'Four nights on, three off.'

'Well, at least the bed will never get cold,' said Fenton. 'There'll always be one of us in it.'

Jenny came towards him and put her arms round his neck. 'And we'll make sure that there are still plenty of times when there are two.'

They finished their meal and shared the washing-up before sitting down in front of the fire to drink their coffee. 'Did you manage to make anything of Neil's research notes?' Jenny asked.

Fenton replied that he hadn't, but that he hadn't had very much time yet to look at them.

'Do you think that Neil was on to something important?'

Fenton shrugged and said, 'There's no way of knowing until we decipher the notes, but I wish I knew what he wanted the blood for.'

'Blood?'

39

Fenton told her about the request Munro had submitted to the Blood Transfusion Service and how the requisition had not gone through normal channels.

'Why would he have done that?' asked Jenny.

'Another question without an answer.'

'I suppose when you think about it, that was quite like Neil. He kept things very much to himself, didn't he?'

Fenton agreed and gave a big yawn. Jenny smiled and said, 'Was that some kind of hint?'

Fenton kissed her lightly on the forehead. 'Early night?'

'Nice idea.'

Fenton was taking off his second sock when his bleeper sounded from the chair his jacket was stretched over. He put his head in his hands before looking at Jenny, who was already in bed. 'God, you'd think they knew.'

Fenton fastened the strap of his crash helmet and looked out of the window, shielding his eyes from the glare of the lights in the room. The look on his face when he turned round told Jenny that it was still raining.

'Take care.'

It was six in the morning when Fenton returned. Jenny was already out of bed and putting on her uniform; she stopped buttoning her dress when Fenton came in and walked over to him. 'Bad night?' she asked, putting her arms round his neck.

'One thing after another.'

Despite his tiredness Fenton felt aroused by Jenny's nearness. He kissed her hard on the lips and felt her respond after her initial surprise.

When they parted Jenny said, 'At six in the morning on a cold, damp winter's day?'

'Any time and any day,' said Fenton, drawing her close again.

Jenny giggled and Fenton slipped his hand inside the top of her uniform to feel the warm swell of her breast. Pushing

40

her back on to the bed he felt the muscles of her face relax as he pressed his mouth down on hers. Her lips parted to let his tongue probe the soft warm inside. 'I want you,' he murmured.

'I believe you, I believe you,' Jenny giggled, struggling with his trouser zip to free him. She raised her bottom slightly to let him pull her panties down half-way then raised her knees as he knelt over her to take them off. He let his erection rest between her calves as he looked down at her. 'I love you, Jenny Buchan. God knows how I love you.' He ran his hands gently up the insides of her thighs.

Jenny looked at her watch. 'Duty calls,' she said. There was no reply from Fenton. She raised herself on her elbows and looked at him; he was fast asleep. She got up quietly from the bed and smoothed her uniform, then, looking down at him again, she smiled and bent down to kiss him lightly on the forehead before she left.

Tyson called a meeting of the lab staff on Wednesday afternoon in the common room. The wind and rain that had lashed Edinburgh for the past week had still not abated, and the windows rattled as he looked around to see if everyone was present. Fenton was missing, delayed by an urgent blood test, but he arrived before anyone had been sent to fetch him. He came in to find Tyson and Inspector Jamieson looking grim.

'We are now in possession of the post-mortem report on Susan Daniels,' said Tyson. 'Inspector Jamieson obtained it from the fiscal's office this morning. Susan did not suffer a miscarriage as some of us had imagined. She wasn't pregnant. She died because the normal clotting mechanisms of her blood were no longer functional. She had received a massive dose of some, as yet undetermined, anticoagulant

41

drug, so that when she contracted a minor internal bleed there was no way of stopping it. It seems unthinkable that she administered the drug to herself, which leaves us with the unpleasant but inevitable alternative that she was murdered.' Tyson paused to let the hubbub die down. Fenton looked at Ian Ferguson who returned his glance. The nightmare was coming true.

Jamieson rose to put everyone's fears into words. There had been two murders in the hospital and both victims had been members of the Biochemistry Department. As both killings were apparently without personal motive, the possibility that there was a psychopathic killer at large in the hospital with a particular grudge against the lab had to be faced. Jamieson concluded by saying, 'I'm sure I don't have to tell you, but if you have the slightest suspicion, the vaguest notion, of anything not being quite right, tell the police. We shall be here in the hospital. Nothing is too trivial.'

The possibility that the killer might actually be one of the lab staff was not mentioned but it ran through everyone's mind. The staff of the lab was small: sixteen in all including the two women who washed the glassware. There were no convenient strangers to suspect. Everyone knew everyone else, or so they thought.

Another day passed and the work of the lab went on as usual. It had to; but the atmosphere had changed dramatically. The light good humour which had made it such a pleasant place to work disappeared overnight. Neil Munro and Susan Daniels had gone, and in their place had come fear and suspicion. The comings and goings of the police as they returned to ask the same questions time and time again only served to heighten the tension.

Fenton's spirits hit a new low on Friday at Neil Munro's funeral. Unrelenting wind and rain swept through an unkempt cemetery as they lowered Munro's coffin into the ground. Their prayers were carried away on the wind and the handful of earth that spattered irreverently on the lid turned almost immediately to mud. Tyson, Ross and Fenton, the three representatives from the lab, went to a nearby pub afterwards and drank whisky without speaking, water still trickling down the backs of their necks and wet grass from the graveside clinging to their shoes.

Fenton got home at six to find Jenny already there. 'It was that bad?' she asked, reading his face.

'That bad,' Fenton quietly agreed.

'Do you want to stay home and brood about it or shall we go out?'

Fenton thought for a moment, then said, 'We'll go out. Somewhere noisy.'

They had no trouble finding a noisy pub in Edinburgh on a Friday evening. They picked one near the west end of Princes Street that proclaimed 'Live Music Tonight' and pushed their way through the throng to the bar. Jenny watched the changing expressions on Fenton's face as he tried unsuccessfully to attract the barmaid's attention. He had the most expressive face of anyone she had ever known. His eyes could sparkle with good humour one moment and turn to dark pools of sadness the next. His mouth, wide and generous, always searched for a reason to break into the boyish grin she loved so much. As he turned away from the bar she smiled quickly to conceal the fact that she had been watching him. 'Hey, look,' said Fenton, pointing with his elbow, 'They're just leaving.'

Jenny saw the couple who were about to rise and led the way over to the table. Fenton followed, holding their drinks at shoulder level to avoid being bumped and saying 'Excuse me' at appropriate intervals. He sat down and gazed round at the Friday-night people. Groups of girls, groups of boys, all pretending to be engrossed in their own conversations but betraying themselves by constant sidelong glances; the occasional loner, more interested in alcohol than company; couples old, couples young.

Intermittent and discordant tuning noises suddenly coalesced into a solid wall of electric noise, wiping out conversation like a shell burst. 'Release me!' demanded a spotty youth through his over-amplifying microphone as he gyrated inside black leather trousers. 'Satan's Sons', proclaimed the Gothic script on the bass drum. Fenton exchanged pained glances with Jenny, his head reeling against the sheer volume. He saw her mouth move but could not lipread the comment. The song ended, leaving their ears ringing in the sudden quiet. 'I feel a hundred years old,' said Fenton.

'Let's go,' said Jenny. They finished their drinks and got up to leave as the spotty youth prepared to launch his second front.

The wind had dropped and the air smelled fresh and sweet as they emerged from the smoke and noise on to the still-wet street. 'I think a trifle more sophistication is called for at your age,' said Jenny with a smile.

They walked for a while before turning off along a wide, sweeping Georgian terrace where most of the houses had been turned into hotels, each engaged in a neon struggle with its neighbour to attract attention. They decided on the Emerald Hotel, where the bar was uncrowded and, more important, quiet. Green-shaded table lamps and oak panelling on the walls suggested a country-house library.

'How are things in the lab?' Jenny asked.

'Terrible,' said Fenton. 'Nothing is said but suspicion is rife. One of the juniors brought me a cup of coffee this morning and I actually toyed with the idea of pouring it down the sink when he'd gone, just in case.'

'But surely the killer could be an outsider?'

'I suppose so, but it's obvious that the police are concentrating on the lab.'

'What do you think?' asked Jenny.

Fenton shook his head. 'I have no idea, no idea at all.'

* * *

On Monday the secrecy contrived by the police and hospital authorities came to a sudden dramatic end. 'Mystery Hospital Deaths' in the *Scotsman* became 'Maniac Stalks Hospital Corridors' in the *Daily News*, and the hospital switchboard was jammed all day with calls from anxious relatives seeking reassurance. Tyson called the lab staff together to warn them against talking to reporters and making things worse. The official line was to be that two members of staff had died in suspicious circumstances and the police were investigating. No details were to be divulged. But too many people in the hospital knew the details. Tuesday morning brought 'Sterilizer Horror' and 'Girl Dies In Pool of Blood'.

The idea of a psychopathic killer at large in a city hospital fired the imagination of every newspaper editor in the country. Radio and television reporters interviewed anyone who had even a remote connection with the Princess Mary, and the Chief Constable of Edinburgh appeared on television in full dress uniform, to assure a worried public that matters were well in hand and a speedy arrest could be confidently expected.

In private, Inspector Jamieson could not share his superior's optimism. With no obvious logic or motive behind the killings, police routine was largely useless. Their best hope lay in the possibility that the killer might get overconfident and reveal himself in the process. Of course there was always the chance that the murderer, like Jack the Ripper, might just stop, but he wouldn't be betting his pension on that. Special passes were hurriedly printed and issued to staff and relatives to allow them to cross the police picket at the gates, which had been mounted to keep the morbidly curious at bay.

Fenton was speaking to Nigel Saxon about the enforced delay in completing the paperwork for the Saxon Blood Analyzer when Ian Ferguson came into the room. Ferguson was obviously surprised to find Saxon there and said, 'Sorry, I just wondered if I might have a word.'

Saxon got to his feet, 'No problem. I was just going anyway.'

Ferguson stood to one side to allow Saxon to pass, then closed the door. He seemed embarrassed.

'What can I do for you?' Fenton asked.

'Fact is,' faltered Ferguson, 'well . . . I've decided to apply for another job. Can I put you down as a referee?'

Fenton stared at him for a moment, for it was the last thing he had expected to hear from Ian Ferguson. 'What's the problem?' he asked.

Ferguson looked at his feet. He said, 'There's a job going at the Western General. I quite fancy a change. More experience and all that . . .'

'And you're scared,' said Fenton.

Ferguson looked as if he were about to argue but then he simply sighed and said, 'Aren't you?'

'Yes,' said Fenton.

An uneasy silence reigned for a moment before Ferguson said, 'You must think I'm a right coward.'

Fenton turned to face him. 'I don't think that at all. I'll even give you a good reference, but what I won't give you is a round of applause. There are three hundred children in this hospital, and if you leave we'll be three under strength. We'll manage but it'll be that much harder on those of us who stay.'

'Well,' sighed Ferguson. 'I hadn't quite thought about it that way. You don't beat about the bush, do you?'

The question was rhetorical but Fenton chose to reply anyway: 'No, I don't.'

Charles Tyson put his head round the door as Ferguson left. 'What was all that about?' he asked, feeling the atmosphere in the room.

'Ian is thinking of applying for another job.'

'That would be a pity,' said Tyson. 'He's one of the best we have.'

'It would also leave us up shit creek without a paddle,' added Fenton.

46

Tyson grimaced at Fenton's expression and said, 'A fact I'm sure you managed to convey to him with admirable clarity.'

Fenton grunted.

'Did Nigel Saxon see you about the report?' Tyson asked.

'Yes, but I'm still up to my eyes. It'll have to wait.'

'Fair enough,' said Tyson. 'The patients come first.'

It was after seven when Fenton got home. He arrived to find Jenny in a particularly attentive mood. 'Do I have to guess what you're going to ask or are you going to tell me?' he said.

'It's Mrs Doig's fan heater. I said that you'd have a look at it. There's a smell of burning.'

'Sure,' said Fenton.

'I love you.'

Mrs Doig was their next-door neighbour, a woman in her seventies who lived alone with two cats and her memories. Jenny had adopted her as a personal responsibility and Fenton provided the technical back-up, changing tap washers, mending fuses and the like.

They finished their meal and went next door, Fenton carrying a screwdriver and pliers. The old woman was clearly pleased to see them. 'You'll have a cup of tea?' she asked. Fenton was about to decline when Jenny nudged him, knowing how much the old woman liked to feel she was doing something for them. Fenton was removing the back of the fan heater as the women chatted, but he still found time to observe Jenny in action. Whereas he himself would adopt a cheerful air and make forced conversation about the weather, Jenny was quite sincere in her care and concern for the old woman. She would joke with her, tease her, cajole her into laughter until her spirits rose visibly and she began to speak freely. Fenton felt a lump come into his throat. He knew that Jenny would like to get married and have children. If only he could get over the awful mental block of associating marriage with the agony of losing Louise, the unreasonable but undeniable feeling that he would be tempting fate.

He found the fault in the heater and repaired it. Like everything else in the flat, it was old; like the black, coal-fired grate, the dark, varnished wallpaper, the five-amp wiring. It was all just waiting for the old woman to die before it could be stripped out. 'All done,' he said.

Fenton poured out a couple of drinks when they got back to their own flat and they sat in front of the fire nursing their glasses. He mentioned his conversation with Ian Ferguson.

'Ian Ferguson?' exclaimed Jenny. 'You surprise me.'

'Why so?'

'He's a public-school product. I thought that all that emphasis on character-building would make him the last person to run away from an unpleasant situation.'

'Maybe "character" has to be innate after all,' said Fenton drily.

'You know what I meant,' smiled Jenny, soothing Fenton's socialist hackles. 'We have the same problem on the wards. There's been a sudden outbreak of flu, so we're about a third under strength. In fact, I may have to go on nights sooner than I thought. Flu seems to have hit the night staff worst of all.'

'People associate darkness with danger,' said Fenton.

Jenny got up to switch the television on. 'Anything in particular you want to see?' she asked.

Fenton said not. He was going to make another attempt to decipher Neil Munro's notes.

'You're working too hard,' said Jenny. 'You'll make yourself ill and that will do the lab no good at all.'

'Just an hour or so, I promise.'

Fenton collected Munro's book, a notepad and some pencils, and took them to another room where he would have quiet. His immediate problem was that the front room of the flat was so cold. He switched on the electric fire and crouched down in front of it till it made some impression on the still, icy air.

Just as before, the stumbling block in Munro's notes lay in the fact that he had given no indication of what units his figures referred to. Temperature? Volume? Time? Without that information the notes comprised several neat columns of meaningless figures interspersed with occasional letters. Fenton tried fitting the figures to various biochemical parameters but had no success. After an hour he kept his word to Jenny and put the book aside. He went to watch the news on television.

THREE

In Ward Four of the Princess Mary Hospital, Timothy Watson was not having a good day. It had started badly when he had not been allowed any breakfast and got worse when a man in a white coat had pricked his arm with a needle after personally assuring him that it was not going to hurt. Grown-ups were not to be trusted. Shortly afterwards the protests had died on his lips as the drowsiness of premedication had stolen over him, and the world had suddenly become lighter, warmer, fluffier, fuzzier, until suddenly it wasn't there any more. Now his bed lay empty, its covers turned down, and his teddy bear sat on the pillow with limbs askew, patiently awaiting his return.

The plastic name-tag on Timothy's wrist provided his only introduction to many of the green-clad figures who now hovered over him, intent on freeing him from the breathlessness that had plagued him from birth. The comforting blip of the heart monitor sounded regularly as synchronous spikes chased each other across the green face of an oscilloscope and the muted sound of classical music emanated from concealed speakers in Theatre Two.

James Rogan looked up at the theatre clock and gave a satisfied grunt. 'Going to knock three minutes off my record, eh, Sister?'

'Yes, sir,' answered Theatre Sister Rose Glynn without moving her eyes. Dutiful laughter added to the already relaxed atmosphere round the table, an atmosphere not left to chance. The green smocks, the smooth pastel walls, the shadowless light, the perfect temperature and the surgeon's own choice of music conspired to produce perfect conditions for the surgical team.

'How's he doing?' Rogan asked the anaesthetist.

'Steady as a rock.'

'Money for old rope, eh, Sister?'

'Yes, sir.'

'Spencer-Wells!'

Rose Glynn slapped the forceps into Rogan's gloved hand as he carried on a commentary for the benefit of his two assistants. He asked for instruments in mid-sentence, without pausing, and Rose Glynn slapped them into his hand. She never missed a request; she had worked with Rogan so often before.

'All right, Allan, sew him up,' said Rogan to his chief assistant. He stepped back from the table and stripped his gloves off in dramatic fashion before saying, 'Thank you, everybody,' and turning on his heel to make an exit through both swing doors.

'Who was that masked man, Mummy?' asked one of the assistants, under his breath but loud enough for everyone in the theatre to hear. Eyes met above masks and twitching ears signalled smiles hidden behind gauze. A student nurse giggled and Rose Glynn froze her with a stare. 'Can we start the count, sir?' she asked Rogan's assistant.

'Yes, Sister, thank you.'

Rose Glynn and her student nurse ran through the swab and instrument count, ensuring that all were accounted for. The tally was agreed, the stitching completed and the patient wheeled out into the recovery room. Two hours later he was back in bed with his teddy bear, sleeping soundly. His parents, who had spent an anxious day at the hospital, were able to leave for home and enjoy their first good night's sleep for many weeks.

* * *

At eight-fifteen, Staff Nurse Carol Mileham noticed that Timothy Watson had become restless in his sleep and went over to him. She smoothed the hair back from his forehead and found that he was very hot. Half turning to go and call the duty houseman, she was stopped by a gurgling sound from the boy's throat; she bent down to listen and a cascade of bright-red blood erupted from his mouth, drenching her apron and splashing silently on to the sheets.

The surgical team and Timothy Watson had their unscheduled reunion in Theatre Four, and this time the atmosphere was very different. There were no smiles, no jokes and no music. The irregular blip of the heart monitor probed the team's nerves like a dentist's drill, the spikes constantly dodging anticipation. Rogan had come directly from home on getting his houseman's call. 'Massive internal bleed' had been the message that had brought him racing to the hospital still in carpet slippers.

Timothy's chest was reopened and the flesh held back with retractors. 'Ye gods,' murmured Rogan, 'he's awash . . . Suck, please!'

Rogan's assistant started clearing the blood with a vacuum suction tube while he himself dabbed with cotton swabs. A nurse changed the transfusion pack for the second time.

'Mop!' Rogan inclined his head for Rose Glynn to wipe away the sweat from his brow, but it reappeared almost immediately. Rogan was losing the battle, and the tension in his voice conveyed that fact to everyone. Tension, like laughter, was infectious.

'He's leaking like a sieve.' Exasperation took over from anxiety, as Rogan realized there was nothing he could do. 'There's something wrong with his blood, damn it. I can't stop it.'

Four minutes later the heart monitor lapsed into a long, continuous monotone. The tension evaporated, leaving silence in its place. 'Thank you, Sister,' said Rogan quietly. He lowered his mask and took off his gloves, this time slowly and deliberately. 'Get some blood to the haematology lab, will you.' His assistant nodded. Rose Glynn looked at her student nurse and saw that her eyes were moist. She had planned to have words with the girl about her giggling earlier. She resolved not to bother.

Malcolm Baird, consultant haematologist at the Princess Mary, phoned Rogan personally next morning, but only to say – rather cryptically, Rogan thought – that there was to be a meeting of all consultants at eleven-thirty in the medical superintendent's office to discuss the Watson case. He should bring his case notes.

Charles Tyson was last to arrive at the meeting and got the least comfortable seat as his just desert. He apologized for his lateness but did not offer any reason. Cyril Fenwick, medical superintendent at the Princess Mary for the past seven years, opened the meeting with a short history of Timothy Watson's illness leading up to his admission. Rogan was invited to follow and duly gave his account of the operation and the subsequent tragic, and ultimately fatal, internal haemorrhage. He sat down again and Baird got to his feet to make his report. 'A thorough haematological examination of the blood sample taken from the boy Watson has shown conclusively that all coagulation potential had been lost, just as in the case of Daniels, in fact. A massive dose of an anticoagulant drug is indicated.'

Tyson leaned forward, putting his elbows on the table to support his head. 'So the bastard has started on the patients now,' he said.

Anger vied with gloom and despondency around the table.

'What the hell are the police doing, anyway?' demanded George Miles from Radiology.

'Running round in circles, if you ask me,' said Rogan.

'It's not easy in a case like this,' said orthopaedic surgeon Gordon Clyde.

'I didn't say it was,' snapped Rogan.

Fenwick intervened to prevent further disharmony. 'Gentlemen,' he said, 'we have one overriding and immediate problem to discuss.' All eyes turned to him. 'We have to stop the press from finding out about the Watson boy. If the papers get hold of this there will be blind panic amongst patients' relatives.'

'And people would be right to panic,' said Tyson.

'Would you mind explaining that remark?' asked Rogan.

Tyson said calmly, 'Let's not pretend that we're taking steps to prevent *unnecessary* panic. The truth is that we are quite powerless to prevent another killing. This hospital is at the mercy of a lunatic.'

The desire to argue was stillborn on the lips of Tyson's colleagues; it was left to Fenwick to break the silence. He said, 'We have, of course, discussed the option of closing the hospital with the police and local authorities, but we simply cannot do it. We're too big, there are too many patients to transfer and, as the police point out, the staff who went with our patients would almost certainly include the killer. We'd just be transferring the problem.'

'So we sit tight and do nothing?'

'Yes, and hope the police come up with something,' said Fenwick. The frown on Rogan's face suggested a feeling shared by the others.

'What about the Watson boy's parents?' asked Tyson. 'They're bound to talk to the press.'

Fenwick looked uneasy. He fidgeted with his pen before saying quietly, almost inaudibly, 'They don't know.'

'What?' exclaimed Tyson and Clyde together.

'They are not in possession of the full facts surrounding their son's death; they just know that the boy died after post-operative complications.'

'But that's . . .' Rogan was interrupted by Fenwick.

'Don't lecture me on ethics, Mr Rogan,' he said firmly. 'The police suggested this course of action and I agreed. There is no way we could expect the parents to suppress their anger and keep this matter quiet. Just how much you tell your own staff I leave to your discretion.'

'I suggest we tell them nothing,' said Clyde.

'I think Tyson might disagree with you,' said Fenwick.

Tyson looked over his glasses and nodded slowly. He said, 'So far, my department has taken the brunt of the strain in this affair. We've lost two people and we've had to live with the fear that this psychopath has a particular grudge against the lab, or, worse, that he might actually be one of our number. This latest death makes both these possibilities less likely. I think that at least some of my people should be told to lessen the tension.'

A murmur of agreement filled the room.

'Sorry Tyson,' said Clyde, 'I didn't think.'

Tyson left the meeting and walked back along the main corridor past the room where Susan Daniels had died. Two nurses were standing talking outside it, laughing about some idiosyncrasy in one of their colleagues. Tyson excused himself and squeezed past. The voices dropped to a whisper as he did so, making him reflect on how often this had happened in the past. It was part of being a hospital consultant; people tended to stop speaking when you came near.

By the time he had battled back to the lab against the wind and spitting rain, he had decided to tell Alex Ross, Ian Ferguson and Tom Fenton about the Watson boy's death.

The relief that Fenton felt on hearing that the killer had struck somewhere else was followed almost immediately by a wave of guilt at having found a child's death any cause for relief. His guilt was redoubled when he remembered that Timothy Watson had been the child who had spoken to him in the corridor the day Susan had died.

Before Tyson left the room Fenton asked him a question about Neil Munro's personal research project. Did he know what it was? Tyson replied that he did not. Fenton opened

Munro's notes and pointed to a page heading: 'CT'. 'It's just that I thought this might stand for Charles Tyson,' he said.

There was a long silence while Tyson looked at the page. 'Doesn't mean a thing,' he said and left before Fenton had time to ask anything else.

Ian Ferguson came into the room and put some keys down on the desk. 'These were Neil Munro's lab keys. Alex Ross asked me to give you them. He said something about a locked cupboard.'

Fenton thanked him. He had asked Ross about a locked cupboard in Munro's room for which he had been unable to find a key.

'If you find an electric timer in it, let me know, will you? Neil borrowed mine and I haven't been able to find it since,' said Ferguson.

'I'll check right now, if you like,' said Fenton and got up to lead the way to Munro's lab.

Ferguson looked on while Fenton tried the keys; he was successful at his third attempt. 'There's no timer here,' he said.

'Damn.'

Fenton sifted through the contents of the cupboard: test-tube racks, plastic tubes and beakers, and several brown glass bottles with chemicals in them. He examined the labels. Potassium oxalate, sodium citrate, heparin, EDTA, warfarin. 'What do you make of that?' he asked Ferguson.

'They're all anticoagulants,' replied Ferguson quietly.

Fenton nodded. 'Indeed they are.'

'I don't understand,' said Ferguson.

Fenton did not reply, for his mind was working overtime, trying to work out why Munro had been using anticoagulants at all and why they had been locked away out of sight. They must have had something to do with his research project, he concluded, but what? He needed time to think, time to ponder the frightening fact that Munro had apparently been working with the same sorts of drugs and chemicals that had been used to murder two people in the

56

hospital. He looked at Ferguson, who was obviously thinking the same thing but waiting for him to say something
first. Fenton said, 'I think it might be best if we didn't say
anything about this for the moment.'

'Of course,' said Ferguson. 'Whatever you think.'

Fenton took out the one remaining bottle in the cupboard
and looked at the label. Dimethylformamide.

'What's that?' asked Ferguson.

'A powerful solvent,' said Fenton.

Jenny came to the lab at five-thirty hoping for a lift home.
Almost as soon as she entered the downstairs hallway she
became aware of the absence of Susan Daniels, who in the
past had always come out of her lab to chat to her. A junior
went to find Fenton, leaving her looking at the notices on
the general information board by the staff lockers. Ian
Ferguson saw her standing there and stopped to say hello,
just as Fenton appeared at the head of the stairs to say he
would be another ten minutes.

'She can come and talk to me until you're ready,' said
Ferguson.

Jenny sat on a swivel stool in Ferguson's lab while he
continued to add small volumes of a chemical to a long row
of test-tubes. She was about to ask what he was doing when
Ferguson opened the conversation by asking how things
were going on the wards. 'We're busy,' replied Jenny.
'We're at least a third under strength. People are frightened.'
Jenny remembered what Fenton had told her about Ferguson applying for a new job and felt embarrassed at what she
had said. As casually as possible she said, 'I understand from
Tom that you're applying for an exciting new job?'

'I was,' replied Ferguson, 'but I've changed my mind.
Tom made me realize just what it would mean to the
department.'

'But if it was a good opportunity . . .'

'There'll be others.'

'I see,' said Jenny, although she was not sure that she did. She hoped that Fenton had not been too hard on him, had not embarrassed him into changing his mind, for in many ways Ferguson was very like Tom Fenton. He was tall and dark and very intelligent. She supposed that he was more classically handsome than Fenton. Fenton's face was too open, too frank, too honest to be considered handsome, whereas Ian Ferguson had the dark, brooding quality beloved of women's magazines. There was an air of introversion about him, but it was certainly not bred of shyness and there was nothing in his eyes to suggest any lack of confidence.

Fenton and Jenny had missed the worst of the rush-hour traffic and were home in under fifteen minutes, both feeling that they had had a hard day.

'Let's eat out,' said Fenton.

'Where?'

'Somewhere nice. We haven't been out for a meal for ages.'

'Queensferry?'

'Why Queensferry?'

'I want to be near the sea,' said Jenny. 'There is one thing . . .' she added tentatively.

'I know. No bike. We'll get a taxi.'

Fenton got out of the shower and towelled down. His body still bore signs of the tan he had acquired during the summer, and frequent exercise in the form of squash and running had kept the flab of a sedentary occupation at bay. Wrapping the towel round his waist he padded through to the bedroom and opened the sliding wardrobe. He laid out his clothes on the bed: plain blue shirt, navy socks, black shoes, dark-blue tie, dark-blue suit. He shrugged his shoulders as he put on the jacket and looked in the mirror to straighten his tie. He flicked at his hair with his fingers but there was little he could do about it. It was curly and unruly and that was that. Dark curls licked along his forehead, taking five years off his age. Fiddling with his cufflinks, he walked through to join Jenny.

She was sitting at an angle on the sofa, her stockinged legs crossed, her elbow resting on one knee, her hand supporting her chin. She was wearing a close-fitting dress in royal blue, the very plainness of which accentuated her smooth skin and high cheekbones. Her silky blonde hair was swept back from her face and held tightly in a dark-blue clasp. Round her neck she wore the gold peardrop locket that Fenton had given her for Christmas.

'You look good,' said Fenton.

'You're no slouch yourself, Mr Bond. Did you call the cab?'

A thick sea mist lay on the still water of the Firth of Forth as they got out of the taxi in the village of South Queens-ferry, some eight miles from the heart of Edinburgh. The lights of cars high above them on the Forth Road Bridge twinkled in and out of the fog while the huge, red-painted spans of the famous old railway bridge towered silently up into the damp air. Only the regular drone of foghorns broke the silence as they crossed the road to look over the sea wall.

'It's creepy when it's like this,' said Jenny, looking down at the unbroken surface of the water.

'But nice,' said Fenton.

They entered the bar of the restaurant to find it practically deserted. 'Thursday night,' said the barman by way of explanation. 'Nothing happens on Thursdays.'

'Except elections,' said Fenton, as he and Jenny were drawn to a large coal fire like moths to a flame.

They finished looking at the menu and ordered before lapsing into silence for a few moments. Jenny held her drink between her palms. She said, 'A child died in theatre yesterday, did you hear?'

'I heard,' said Fenton, feeling uncomfortable.

'Do you know anything about it?'

Fenton was silent.

'Oh dear,' said Jenny, 'I see that you do.'

'Jenny, I . . .'

'Don't say anything. Just listen. Today at lunch I heard Rose Glynn mention "excessive bleeding", then later I heard someone else say that the haematology report wasn't available. I put two and two together and came up with four.'

'Three,' said Fenton. 'Timothy Watson was the third victim. I felt so awful just now when you asked and I couldn't tell you.'

'Relax, you didn't. I worked it out for myself. So the killer isn't someone with a grudge against the lab.'

'No, it's someone who murders five-year-olds.'

Jenny heard the bitterness in Fenton's voice and was forced to ask, 'You didn't know the boy, did you?'

'Well enough to be able to put a face to the name. He was running around in the main corridor the day Susan Daniels was murdered.'

They left the restaurant just after ten-thirty and crossed the road to take a last look at the water. Fenton picked up a handful of gravel and began to flick it idly into the water with his thumbnail. As they leaned on the railing Jenny said, 'You know, when you think about it, it's a strange way to kill people, isn't it – anticoagulants?'

'That's how they kill rats.'

'Rats?'

Fenton flicked some more gravel into the water and watched the rings spread. 'That's how rat poison works. It knocks out the clotting mechanism in their blood; one scratch in the sewers and they bleed to death.'

A ship's siren sounded out in the Forth. They peered into the swirling mist but saw nothing. Jenny said, 'I just don't see how the drug could have been administered, can you?'

'Rats have to eat it, so maybe it was mixed into the

60

victims' food or drink. I can't see anyone having an injection without knowing it.'

'Unless the victim was a patient who was having injections all the time, or a child who trusted anyone in uniform.'

'Susan wasn't a patient or a child and she wasn't having injections,' said Fenton.

'Are you sure?'

The question made Fenton think. 'No, I suppose I'm not, come to think of it. All of us in the lab get protective vaccines from time to time because we handle so much contaminated material.'

Jenny said, 'Just suppose Susan had been given a large dose of anticoagulant instead of, say, an antityphoid injection. She wouldn't have known, would she?'

'That would make our killer a doctor or a nurse, someone with access to the wards and the staff.'

'Can you find out if Susan did have any innoculations shortly before her death?' Jenny asked.

'It will be in the lab personnel files.'

'I could try to find out who's been on duty in the staff treatment suite over the past few weeks.'

'I've just had another thought,' said Fenton, pausing for a moment to see if it made sense before committing himself. 'The staff treatment suite is next to the Central Sterile Supply Department, where Neil was killed.'

'And anticoagulants are not on the restricted drugs list; they're not kept under lock and key . . .'

'. . . So they'd be readily available and the killer wouldn't have to account for them . . .'

'Let's suppose some more,' said Jenny, the adrenalin flowing fast now. 'Suppose Neil went to the Sterile Supply Department to see Sister Kincaid and found that she wasn't there. We know she wasn't; she was at lunch. He went next door to look for her and stumbled on the killer messing with injection phials.'

'So the killer murdered Neil to keep him quiet? Makes sense.'

61

'It must have been a man,' said Jenny. 'I can't see a woman overpowering Neil, can you?'

'No, and there was no sign of a weapon having been used. You're right: it had to be a man, and a powerful man at that. Neil was no seven-stone weakling.'

At seven-fifteen next morning Jenny left for the hospital, leaving Fenton still in bed. They had arranged to meet at lunch time to discuss the information they had agreed to obtain. Fenton rose at eight, washed, dressed and sat down at the kitchen table with orange juice and coffee to read the *Scotsman*, which had popped noisily through the letter box while he was shaving. He scanned the front page for mention of the hospital and was relieved to find only a few lines near the bottom to the effect that inquiries were still continuing into the sudden deaths of two members of the Biochemistry Department.

Fenton waited until ten o'clock, when he knew that Liz Scott, the lab secretary, would be at her busiest, then went downstairs to the office. 'Good morning, Liz. I just want to check when my next TAB is due . . . Don't worry, I can find it myself.'

'Thanks, I'm snowed under at the moment.'

Fenton took the keys that were handed to him and approached the filing cabinet by the window. The sound of rain against the grimy barred window all but obliterated the noise of the top drawer being pulled out. He flicked through the index cards till he found what he was looking for. Daniels, Susan . . . Age . . . Weight . . . Height . . . Blood Group . . . X-Ray Record . . . Inoculations. Last entry: TAB vaccine given on — Fenton's heart missed a beat — 15 February! Two days before she died! He steeled himelf to present a calm exterior when he turned round and handed the keys back to Liz Scott. 'Find what you wanted?' she asked without looking up.

Instead of going back to his own lab, Fenton went into

Neil Munro's room and sat down for a moment. Should he tell someone what he had discovered? If so, who? Tyson? Jamieson? It was too soon to say anything, he decided; he needed more to go on. He would wait until he had seen Jenny at lunch time.

Fenton took out the chemicals and equipment he had removed from Munro's locked cupboard and spread them out on the bench in front of him. He rearranged a number of plastic test-tubes into a symmetrical pattern on the desk top and idly balanced two small beakers in the centre while he considered what he knew. Munro had requested blood from the Transfusion Service and he had been working with anticoagulants. These two facts made him feel very uneasy. But what else was there to go on? A meaningless series of figures in a notebook and the letters CT which Charles Tyson said were nothing to do with him. So what did they stand for?

Fenton was balancing a third beaker on top of the other two when the door opened and the pile collapsed. Nigel Saxon stood in the doorway. 'Sorry, did I do that?' he asked.

Fenton reassured him and admitted that he had just been playing with the tubes.

'I see,' said Nigel Saxon, sounding as though he didn't. 'I hate to keep pressing you like this but . . .'

'I know, the report on the analyzer,' said Fenton.

'Have you managed to look at Susan's final figures?'

'I've been through them. They seem fine apart from one failure, a patient named Moran. Susan wrote that no analysis was obtained. Were you with her when this test was performed?'

'Neil Munro and I were both there,' said Saxon. 'We decided that the ward must have sent the sample in the wrong kind of specimen container.'

'It happens,' agreed Fenton.

'Was that the only thing?'

'Everything else seems fine.'

63

Saxon smiled broadly and said, 'Good, then we'll still get our licence by the end of the month.'

'That soon?' exclaimed Fenton.

Fenton's surprise took Saxon aback and he flushed slightly in embarrassment. 'Sometimes the wheels of bureaucracy can turn quite smoothly, you know,' he said.

'Saxon Medical must have a magic wand.'

'A plastic one.'

As Saxon turned to leave Fenton said, 'The Moran sample – it *was* run through the conventional analyzer, wasn't it? I mean as well as the new one?'

'I presume so.'

'Same result?'

'As far as I know.'

Fenton met Jenny at one o'clock. She was standing at the main gate as he walked up to the hospital from the lab. She smiled as she saw him but had to wait to allow an ambulance to pass before crossing the road to link her arm through his. 'Where shall we go?' she asked.

'Let's walk for a bit,' Fenton replied. They didn't speak until they had left the noise and bustle of the main road and turned down a side street. 'How did you get on?' Jenny asked.

'Susan Daniels had a TAB inoculation two days before she died,' said Fenton. 'It looks as if you could be right.'

'I don't think I really want to be,' said Jenny. Fenton asked her if her own researches had come up with anything.

'Sister Murphy has been in charge of the staff treatment room for the past three months.'

'Old Mother Murphy?'

'The very same.'

'Doesn't sound too hopeful,' said Fenton.

'There's more.' Jenny had to pause for they had rejoined the main road and a bus was roaring past them. 'The doctor doing the staff inoculations is one of the new residents, Dr

David Malcolm. He's been doing it for about a month and he's the resident on Ward Four, Timothy Watson's ward.'

'Do you know him?'

'By sight. He's about six feet tall and broad with it.'

Fenton halted in his stride to allow a woman pushing a pram to pass. 'Do you know any more about him?'

'Only that it's his first residency and that he hasn't asked any of the nurses out.'

'Maybe he's married.'

'No.'

'Gay?'

'If he is he's not the effeminate type, I'm told.'

The sky darkened and Fenton felt the first spot of rain on his cheek as another brief respite from the weather came to an end. The man in front of them stopped walking in order to put on a plastic raincoat. An old woman threatened Jenny's eyesight as she struggled to put up her umbrella. Fenton pushed it gently out of the way, getting a dirty look for his trouble. They took refuge in a small café where the air was already dank with condensation from wet clothing. The coffee was lukewarm and instant. 'What do we do now?' Jenny asked.

'Tell the police,' replied Fenton.

'I'm glad you said that. This business scares me to death.'

When they returned to the hospital Fenton left word at the administration block that he would like to see Inspector Jamieson as soon as the policeman found it convenient. Jamieson duly turned up at the lab at half-past two as Fenton was loading blood samples into a centrifuge. He watched what Fenton was doing for a few moments before moving across to the bookcase and peering through the glass doors in order to read the titles while he waited. He quickly tired of this and moved to the window.

Fenton closed the lid of the centrifuge and set the timer to run for ten minutes. He crossed the room to wash his hands in the sink. Jamieson still had his back to him; he was silhouetted against the cold grey light in the window.

'Sorry about that,' said Fenton. Jamieson turned and smiled dutifully. 'How can I help you?' he asked.

Fenton told Jamieson everything. He told him how he and Jenny had come to suspect that the killer was one of the medical staff and how they had gone about gathering evidence to support their theory. Everything, he said, seemed to point to Dr David Malcolm's being implicated in the killings.

Jamieson listened carefully, fiddling throughout with his moustache, brushing it upwards with his forefinger then smoothing it down again with both thumb and forefinger. 'I see, sir,' he said when Fenton had finished. There was a long pause during which a distant clap of thunder heralded still more rain. Fenton was puzzled, for although he had not expected Jamieson to leap to his feet in excitement, he had not anticipated that he would fall into a catatonic trance. At length Jamieson got to his feet and said, 'Thank you, sir. You did the right thing in telling us.'

'That's all?'

'What did you expect?' asked Jamieson, pointedly dropping the 'sir'.

'Some comment, I suppose. Some reaction.'

'I'm a great believer in horses for courses, sir.'

'What does that mean?'

'It means that I don't tell you how to run your lab and you don't tell me how to do my job.'

Fenton saw the anger in Jamieson's eyes and was about to argue that he was only trying to help when Jamieson interrupted him.

'Give the police a little credit. We were perfectly well aware that Miss Daniels had had an inoculation shortly before her death; we also know that Sister Murphy administered it because Dr Malcolm was off duty that day. We know that Dr Malcolm wasn't here on the day that Dr Munro was murdered because he was attending a one-day seminar at Stirling Royal Infirmary. In fact, we were able to eliminate Dr Malcolm from our inquiries some time ago. We know all that, sir, because it is our job to know.'

Fenton was contrite. 'I'm sorry, I've wasted your time,' he offered.

'Not at all, sir,' said Jamieson. He left the room.

Fenton was left sitting astride a wooden lab stool, watching the rain stream down through the grime on the windows. He had made a fool of himself and now suffered his humiliation in silence. The sound of the decelerating centrifuge told him that his blood samples were ready for analysis.

Jenny was equally dejected when Fenton told her what had happened, but as was her wont she looked for something positive to derive from the experience. 'At least it shows that the police know what they're doing.'

Ferguson ignored the comment and said, 'I felt about two inches tall when Jamieson put me in my place. He enjoyed doing it too. I could tell.'

'You're probably imagining it.'

'No, I don't think so,' said Fenton, reliving the experience as he stared into the fire.

Jenny looked at him and smiled. 'Well, we can't really blame him, can we?' she said. 'We were trying to do his job for him.'

Fenton returned to the present and shrugged. 'I suppose you're right,' he sighed.

'And if we are absolutely honest with ourselves,' said Jenny, getting to her feet and ruffling Fenton's hair, 'Thomas Fenton was never one to like being proved wrong . . .'

'There's a letter for you on the hall table,' said Fenton, anxious to change the subject.

Jenny went out in search of it, and the cry from the hall told Fenton that she hadn't opened a bill. 'Tom! It's from my brother Grant. He's coming to Edinburgh next week with Jamie. Do you remember? Jamie fell off his tricycle and injured his eye a while back. He's to see a specialist at the Eye Pavilion.'

'What day?'

Jenny paused in the doorway, scanning down the letter for the answer. 'Wednesday . . . next Wednesday. They've to be at the hospital on Friday morning.'

'They can stay here, if you like,' said Fenton.

'Tom, could they?' asked Jenny, obviously pleased at the suggestion.

'Of course.'

FOUR

The following morning brought yet more wind and rain and Fenton, who had harboured a lifelong hatred of wind, found his patience strained to the limit. 'Will it never let up?' he growled as he opened the curtains to look on wet roofs and whirling chimney cowls. 'Another wrestling match with the bike.'

Jenny was about to point out the merits of four-wheeled transport but thought better of it. There was no need, she reasoned, looking at the black sky. Another couple of weeks of this and Fenton could be driving a Ford Escort by the spring.

He arrived at the lab with water running off the front of his leathers like a mountain stream. The letter box in the heavy front door of the lab rattled in the wind as he stood in the outer hall peeling them off with hands that were numb with cold. He hung them up as best he could and opened the inner glass door, blowing his fingers in an attempt to restore circulation.

'And Jack the shepherd blows his nail . . .' intoned Ian Ferguson.

'Pardon?'

'Shakespeare.'

'Oh,' said Fenton, following him into the common room, where he found Alex Ross speaking to Mary Tyler.

Mary Tyler had previously been employed on a part-time basis in the department; Charles Tyson had coerced her back into working full time since the deaths of Neil Munro and Susan Daniels. 'Good morning, Mary, back to getting up early in the morning?' Mary retorted that with three young children she was always up early. Fenton poured himself some coffee and warmed his fingers on the mug.

Charles Tyson arrived, brushing the rain from the shoulders of his overcoat as he put his head round the common-room door. He asked Fenton to come up and see him when he was ready. Fenton allowed him enough time to reach his office and take off his wet things before joining him. He waited patiently while the consultant organized his papers and settled into the seat behind his desk. 'It's about the Saxon report,' said Tyson, still rearranging piles of paper.

'I left it on your desk,' said Fenton.

'The sterilizing records are missing from it.'

'What sterilizing records?'

'We have to include details of how we sterilized the plastic samplers for the machine.'

'I didn't find any records among Neil's things.'

'Damn. He must have been aware of the fact.'

'Perhaps they're still down at the Sterile Supply Department.'

'Would you check and let me know?'

Fenton agreed to do so, adding that he was just about to go up to the administration block anyway to look at some service contracts. He would call in to see Sister Kincaid on his way back. 'Nigel Saxon told me that they were confident of getting a licence for their machine by the end of the month,' he said.

'I heard that too,' said Tyson, 'and from the number of phone calls I've been getting from the Scottish Office about this damned report I don't think he is being overly optimistic. All the stops have been pulled out for Saxon.'

'Friends in high places?'

Tyson grunted.

'It's funny when you think about it,' said Fenton.

'What is?'

'The Scottish Office with their trouser legs rolled up.'
Tyson smiled but did not say anything.

Fenton saw from a ground-floor window that the rain had slackened off and decided to sprint up to the main hospital without changing out of his lab coat. He ran up the drive and took the stone steps three at a time to reach the shelter of the main entrance. A domestic dressed in green overalls was polishing a brass plaque set in the wood panelling, placed there in remembrance of long-forgotten names. The woman looked down at his feet and the muddy prints he had just made on the mosaic floor. 'Sorry,' he said. The woman shook her head and returned to her polishing without comment. A nurse was having an argument over laundry baskets with a porter as he passed along the main corridor.

'I'm telling you! Ward Ten gets . . .' The voices trailed off behind Fenton and merged with new sounds, clangs from ward kitchens, children's yells, hurrying feet. He reached Jenny's ward just as she was crossing the corridor with a steel tray in her hand.

'What brings you out of your ivory tower?' she asked.

Fenton explained that he was on his way to sort out a misunderstanding over service contracts taken out on lab equipment.

'What's the problem?' asked Jenny.

'Archaic equipment and no money to replace it.'

'So what's new? Do you have time for a cup of tea?'

'A quick one.'

Fenton was sipping his tea in the ward side-room when an ashen-faced student nurse came in. Jenny put down her cup and got to her feet. 'What's the matter?' she asked.

Another nurse came into the room. 'It's Belle Wilson,' she said. 'She's dead. I think she killed herself.'

'The ward maid,' said Jenny in answer to Fenton's look. They followed the second nurse next door to the sluice room where a small middle-aged woman dressed in green overalls was slumped over one of the large white porcelain sinks. Her eyes were wide and lifeless; her right arm dangled limply in the sink in a pool of red.

'She cut her wrist,' said the nurse.

Jenny felt for a pulse in the woman's neck but knew that it was useless. She was quite dead.

Fenton stared at the marble-white face under its crop of recently dyed hair and thought that she looked like a clown lying over a theatrical basket.

'I'll phone the front office,' said Jenny quietly.

Fenton was left alone in the room. He looked more closely at the woman's arm. The cut was not in her wrist at all. It was in the palm of her hand. He went to find the nurse who had discovered her and asked, 'What was Belle Wilson doing before she cut herself?'

The nurse was taken aback. 'I'm not sure,' she stammered.

'Think!' said Fenton.

'Er . . . er . . . Cleaning vases. I remember now, Staff Nurse asked her to wash out the flower vases.'

'Where?' asked Fenton, looking about him. 'In here?'

'Next door,' said the nurse, 'in the broom cupboard.'

'Show me.'

Fenton followed the nurse into a small, dark, wood-panelled room that smelt strongly of Lysol. His foot struck a metal bucket before the nurse had had time to find the light switch behind a forest of brush- and mop-handles. They saw the broken glass on the floor. Fenton knelt down to gather the pieces.

'She must have dropped one,' said the nurse, still puzzled by Fenton's behaviour.

'Any more bits?' asked Fenton.

'There by the sink.'

Fenton picked up a jagged piece of glass from the draining board and saw the red stains on it. He swore under his breath.

'I don't understand,' said the nurse.

'Belle Wilson cut herself accidentally on the broken vase and bled to death. She didn't deliberately cut herself. She was murdered. She's another victim of that bloody lunatic.'

Fenton found Jenny in the sluice room and told her what he had discovered. She approached the body and bent over the sink to examine the dead woman's hand. She could see now that the river of red did indeed emanate from a deep wound on the palm, not from the wrist. 'Look at the blood in the sink,' said Fenton.

'What about it?'

'It's still liquid. It hasn't clotted.'

The police were on the scene quickly; a mobile incident room had been parked behind the administration block since the death of Neil Munro. Fenton called Tyson at the lab to explain that he was going to be delayed and why. He was still on the telephone when Inspector Jamieson came into the duty room and found him there. When Fenton put down the receiver he continued to look at him without saying anything. Fenton could almost hear his mind working.

'Well, well, Mr Fenton,' growled Jamieson, 'a bit out of our way aren't we?'

'I was just passing,' said Fenton limply.

It was another forty minutes before Fenton was allowed to leave the ward and continue on up to the management offices, an errand for which he now had little patience, knowing how far behind with his work he was slipping.

Fenton was waiting for a clerk to return with the relevant file when Nigel Saxon appeared at his elbow and read the frustration in his face. 'Trouble, old boy?'

Fenton told him the problem. Saxon was less than sympathetic. 'I love hearing about problems with our competitors. Now, if you were to buy a Saxon Analyzer . . .'

'This is the National Health Service,' said Fenton by way of an answer.

'What on earth is going on?' asked Saxon, noticing people scurrying about. Fenton told him.

'Another one? Dear God.'

Fenton asked Saxon what he was doing there.

'Lunch with the health board – their way of saying thank you for the disposables,' said Saxon.

'*Bon appetit.*'

The clerk returned with the service-contract file and Fenton flicked through the pages to find the relevant section while Saxon looked over his shoulder. 'Damnation,' he said softly. 'The company's right; there's a clause excluding the main transformer board. We'll have to pay.'

Two orderlies were loading a sterilizer with goods taken from a metal trolley as Fenton entered the Central Sterile Supply Department. They lined up the heavy cage with the rails on the floor of the chamber and slid it slowly inside, taking care that nothing tumbled off. On the other side of the room three women wearing white overalls and hairnets were sifting through a massive pile of forceps, wrapping each pair individually and placing it on an assembly tray. Fenton walked over to them. 'Sister Kincaid?'

'In her office,' said one of the women, pointing with the instruments she held in her hand.

Moira Kincaid looked up from her desk as Fenton's shadow crossed the glass panel on her door. She motioned him to enter and asked to what she owed the honour of a visit. Fenton explained. 'They're here,' said Moira Kincaid. She opened her desk drawer and withdrew a pink cardboard folder. 'I didn't know what was to happen to them, but they're all in here.'

Fenton flicked through the papers and said, 'This seems to be what's required.'

'They're just simple record sheets of the sterilizing cycles used for Dr Munro's samplers. They're all the same, just the standard run.'

'Pieces of paper to you and me, Sister,' said Fenton. 'But a career to some others not a million miles from here.' He was still angry about a contract exclusion that he felt the administrators should have picked up at the time of signing. Through the glass panel he saw a porter come into the sterilizing bay and speak to one of the orderlies. Shortly afterwards the orderly burst into the office. 'Have you heard, Sister? There's been another murder!'

Moira Kincaid looked at Fenton who nodded and said, 'A maid in Ward Twelve.'

As he left the office and closed the door behind him Fenton heard a warning buzzer sound and the ventilation fans start up. He paused to watch the orderlies he had seen earlier lower their visors and pull on heavy gauntlets. They manoeuvred a trolley into position and the door to one of the autoclaves swung open. Steam filled the white-tiled area as if it were a Turkish bath until the fans began to deal with it. They locked their trolley on to the guide rails and pulled out the load cage, grunting with the effort as one of the wheels refused to engage properly. Fenton saw the number above the autoclave and realized this was the sterilizer that had been used in Neil Munro's murder. He shivered involuntarily at the thought. Even with its huge mouth open and its insides empty, the shiny steel cavern seemed full of menace. Just a machine, he reasoned. It had no mind of its own; it was only obeying orders. Whose orders? That was the question.

Fenton walked out through the swing doors and climbed the stairs to ground level, wondering just what it was about the Sterile Supply Department that he disliked so intensely. As he reached the top of the stairs he realized what it was: it didn't have any windows. It was situated in a basement and lit entirely by artificial light, white fluorescent light that made everyone look sickly pale.

* * *

Charles Tyson was taking the news of the latest death badly. Fenton thought he had never seen him look so ill and was very much aware of the change that had come over Tyson since the start of the killings: the man had aged quite visibly. The pastel shirts that he favoured now seemed several collar sizes too large and a universal greyness had descended on him, making even the stubble shadow on his face seem grey against the winter pallor of his skin. Fenton had begun to wonder whether or not the strain was the only reason for the change or whether there might be some underlying clinical reason for it.

Fenton respected Tyson. He did not know whether or not he liked him, for the truth was that he hardly knew the man. He doubted whether anyone did, for Tyson was a very private person. As head of department he was excellent, but that was the only role anyone had ever seen him play. Neil Munro had told him once that Tyson had served in the army and seen active service in Korea, but that, together with the fact that he was not married, was about the sum total of his knowledge of the man.

'Seems fine,' said Tyson, looking through the folder that Fenton had brought him. Fenton told him about the problem with the service contract. 'How much is it going to cost?'

'Seven hundred pounds.'

'All because somebody in the office didn't read the small print. This will practically wipe out all the benefit the hospital gained from the free supply of plastic disposables from Saxon Medical,' said Tyson, shaking his head.

'You could kick up hell at the next board meeting,' said Fenton.

Tyson shook his head again. 'No, they'd only close ranks. Besides, I don't want to antagonize the management at the moment. I was thinking of trying for one of these new analyzers for the lab. Rumour has it that there's some charity money up for grabs.'

'What are the chances?'

'Who knows? Actually, I was thinking it might strengthen our case if we could reuse the plastic samplers. They work out quite expensively if we have to throw them away each time.'

'I could run some tests,' suggested Fenton.

'You've got enough on your plate at the moment.'

'It shouldn't take long. I could get the lab staff to volunteer a few millilitres of blood each, run the samples through the analyzer, autoclave the samplers a few times, then rerun the samples. Compare the values before and after sterilizing?'

'If you really think you could manage . . .' said Tyson thoughtfully.

'No problem.'

It was late in the afternoon, while Fenton was trying to cajole Mary Tyler into providing a blood sample for the new tests, that Nigel Saxon came into the lab to collect a copy of the final report on the Blood Analyzer. 'Don't give in to him, Mary, whatever he's after,' joked Saxon. 'Now, if you'd care to have dinner with me this evening . . .'

'I'm a respectable married woman,' protested Mary Tyler.

'They're always the worst,' grinned Saxon.

'As you're here, Nigel . . .' began Fenton in a tone that put Saxon on the defensive.

'What are you after?' he asked suspiciously.

'Your blood,' said Fenton. 'Quite literally.' He explained the idea for new tests on the Saxon Analyzer. It could even lead to a sale, he confided. Saxon agreed to 'volunteer', along with Mary Tyler, Ian Ferguson, Alex Ross, and four of the others.

'When?' asked Saxon.

'Before you leave, if that's all right?' said Fenton. Saxon nodded but seemed a little dubious about the whole business. He came back after collecting the report from Tyson and was led into a small side-room by Fenton. 'Slip off your jacket and roll up your sleeve.' Saxon did as he was told and sat down with his arms on the table in front of him. He looked nervous.

Fenton finished rummaging in a drawer and joined Saxon at the table holding a piece of rubber tubing in his hand. 'I'll just wrap this around your upper arm,' he said. 'Perhaps you could hold it there?' Saxon reached across and held the tubing in place while Fenton slapped the inside of his arm to make the veins stand out. He slipped a sterile needle on to the end of a disposable ten-millilitre syringe, swabbed the exposed area of Saxon's arm with an alcohol-impregnated swab, and pushed the needle smoothly into the vein. Dark-red blood flooded into the syringe until it had reached the right level, then Fenton withdrew it and pressed another swab over the site of entry. 'Just hold that there for a moment,' he told Saxon.

Once the sample was safely in the fridge, Fenton held Saxon's jacket for him while he put it back on. Saxon said, 'I hope my father appreciates what I do for our company!' He prefaced the remark with a loud laugh, but Fenton noticed the beads of sweat along his forehead. He really had been afraid.

It was nearly a quarter-past seven when Fenton finally finished his day's work. Thinking he was the last one left in the lab he was surprised to see a light on under one of the doors as he came downstairs. It made him feel a little uneasy. He crossed the hall quietly and listened outside for a few seconds. There was no sound. Cautiously he opened the door and looked in, startling Alex Ross who had been sitting writing. 'Good God, you nearly gave me a heart attack,' said Ross.

'Sorry. You're here late.'

'The monthly accounts,' said Ross. 'I didn't have time during the day.'

'Fancy a drink?'

'Good idea.' Ross put down his pen and rubbed his eyes. 'I've had quite enough for one day.'

The two men walked the short distance to the Thistle Arms and joined the early-evening drinkers. It was a grimy little pub that relied much more on the custom of regulars than on passing trade. Little or no attention had been paid to the décor and it remained essentially a Scottish man's pub, a place where the presence of a woman would still be frowned upon. The solid Victorian bar was highly polished but bore the scars of countless generations of carelessly stubbed cigarettes, while the floor was covered with linoleum that had once been green but was now an indeterminate dark shade under the inadequate lighting.

Several solitary drinkers sat at tables along a wall, their faces bearing tell-tale signs of a life that had been none too kind; escape lay in the amber fluid in front of them. A few small groups chatted at the bar; men on their way home, some still carrying the badges of their trade. A railway guard in his gendarme's cap; a security guard with his hat moulded to suggest that he was really Burt Lancaster in *Run Silent Run Deep*; an insurance agent in a grubby raincoat with a battered briefcase. A noisy group of students sat in the corner, savouring the haunts of the working man but retaining their university scarves as a badge of distance.

The two barmen were of the old school, with spotless white aprons and hands that were never idle, constantly wiping imaginary spillages from the counter, eyeing the levels in the glasses along the bar, anticipating where the next order would come from. The smaller of the two, narrow-shouldered and bespectacled, looked up as Ross and Fenton approached. 'Still cold outside?' he asked.

'Freezing,' replied Ross. He ordered whisky for them both.

As they stood at the bar Fenton ran his eye along the gantry, noting that nearly all the space was taken up by whisky, a good range of single malts and nearly every known blended variety. Other spirits were represented by solitary bottles. The contents of the glasses along the counter reflected the stock on the shelves. He took comfort from the fact that some things never seemed to change. It might be a sociologist's nightmare, but the fact remained that in certain places in Scotland drinking was still a man's game.

Ross threw back his head and drained his glass, declining Fenton's offer of a second drink and pleading 'hell from the wife' as an excuse. Fenton wished him good night and ordered another for himself. The barman handed him a copy of the evening paper to look at and said that Rangers had bought another English player.

'Really?' said Fenton, not having any interest in football but feeling obliged to display some reaction.

'Not that it'll do them any good,' said another man at the bar, taking the strain off Fenton and diverting the barman's attention.

Fenton drank up his beer and went to the lavatory. It was a dingy, brick-built cellar, and it had been painted so many times that the grouting between the bricks had all but disappeared. Rust clung to the pipework and to the old iron cisterns fixed to the wall above the urinal. He stood there, head tilted to one side to read the graffiti, and heard the door open behind him. But no one joined him at the wall.

Feeling more comfortable Fenton zipped up his fly. He turned round to see two men standing there, looking straight at him. The older of the two, a thickset man wearing leather jacket and jeans, came towards him; the other remained leaning against the door. Without saying anything the first man swung his fist into Fenton's stomach with a power that suggested he might once have done this for a living. Fenton's eyes opened wide as he doubled over, only to meet the boot that was directed up into his face. His cheekbone shattered in a haze of pain.

The whole affair was conducted in absolute silence; there were no jeers, no insults, no words, just the cold, professional application of pain. The boot swung again, this time into Fenton's ribs, overloading his appreciation of agony; he felt consciousness slip away from him. The frustration of not even being able to protest vied with the pain for his receding attention as he slid slowly down the wall, feeling the porcelain of the urinal cold against his cheek before his face came finally to rest in the gutter at the bottom. The stench that filled his nostrils made him vomit weakly, adding to the cocktail of blood and urine. The boot thudded into him again but it was by now a long way from Fenton; he had drifted off into oblivion.

Fenton emerged sporadically from the darkness to snatch an occasional sight or sound. A flashing blue light was reflected in glass somewhere, raindrops caressed his forehead, a hand touched him gently. There was a moustache; a cap; a siren that never faded into the distance, searchlight beams on a low ceiling, voices, but all far away . . . very far away.

Fenton surfaced from the blackness and opened his eyes to find everything still and bright. He stared upwards till the object he had elected to focus his attention on resolved itself into a light fitting. There were dead flies in it. He took a deep breath which attracted the attention of a nurse; she saw now that his eyes were open. Her voice was soft and gentle. 'So you're back with us,' she said.

Fenton opened his mouth to ask where he was, and a flight of burning arrows tore into his cheek. His gasp brought a gentle chiding from the nurse; the soft voice said, 'Lie still. Rest. Don't try to speak.'

Three days passed before Fenton could sit up and concern himself with the more humdrum matters of life like the itch that persisted inside the heavy strapping on his ribs, and the whereabouts of his motor-bike and his jacket with the unpaid electricity bill in its pocket. He attempted to smile when Jenny came to see him but immediately wished he hadn't when his broken cheekbone made itself felt. He had been able to give the police good descriptions of his attackers but no clue as to motive. It had seemed just a mindless act of violence.

The novelty of grapes, Lucozade and get-well cards soon began to wear thin; Fenton was soon well enough to feel bored stiff and said so with increasing frequency to the nursing staff, who had heard it all before. But his persistent badgering paid off, and at the end of the week he was allowed to go home by taxi after promising to take things easy. He was just in time to see Jenny's brother Grant, who was on the point of leaving for home with his son Jamie. Fenton asked how the boy had got on at the hospital.

'The surgeons decided that they should delay operating until he's a little older; maybe next year,' said Grant.

Fenton looked down at the little boy, who was wearing a patch over one eye and staring up at the plasters on Fenton's face. The two of them felt they had a lot in common and established an instant rapport. Fenton bent down and asked the boy about the toy fire engine that he was carrying.

Grant looked at his watch and announced that he and Jamie would have to be off. He thanked Jenny and shook Fenton's hand before ushering Jamie out of the door.

Jenny looked accusingly at Fenton. 'You should still be in hospital.'

Fenton smiled and said, 'It's good to be home.'

Jenny kissed him. 'It's good having you home.'

By the following Wednesday Fenton was climbing the wall with boredom. Still confined to the flat, he made endless cups of tea, pacing up and down between times and pausing occasionally to look out at the rain. He telephoned Charles Tyson at the lab to be told that he was out at a meeting. He did speak to Ian Ferguson for a while but ran out of things to say after being assured that the lab was coping well despite his absence.

In the middle of the afternoon Fenton answered a ring of the doorbell to find Nigel Saxon standing there.

'How's the invalid?' asked Saxon.

The conversation, like most of Saxon's conversations, degenerated into talk of women, cars and booze, but it did cheer Fenton up and made him smile for the first time in days. Saxon also announced that he was giving a dinner party for everyone in the lab to celebrate the successful conclusion to trials on the Saxon Analyzer.

'When?' asked Fenton.

'Saturday evening.'

'Where?'

'The Grange Hotel. It's not too far from the lab so the duty staff will be within bleeper-range and can flit back and forth if necessary.'

On Friday morning Fenton visited his GP and was declared fit to return to work. Having had no need of a doctor over the past year he had neglected to register with a practitioner near his home and so had to cross town to the doctor he had been listed with on his arrival in the city.

Was this really the system envied by the world? he wondered as he sat in a crowded room surrounded by peeling wallpaper and coughing people. The windows hadn't been cleaned for decades by the look of them and there was a strong smell of cats' urine. Three back copies of *Punch*, a two-minute consultation, and he was free of the system, but not of the despondency it inspired.

The return bus took an age to cross town and Fenton had to keep clearing the window with his sleeve to see where he was, for the atmosphere on the top deck was heavy and damp and reeked of stale cigarette smoke. A fat woman weighed down with shopping bags plumped herself down beside him, her face glowing with the exertion of climbing the stairs. The smell of sweat mingling with the tobacco was the last straw for Fenton. He got off at the next stop and walked through the rain; he was soaked to the skin by the time he reached the flat.

FIVE

The party at the Grange Hotel was a disaster. But then, as Fenton reasoned afterwards, it could never have been anything else. Their host, Nigel Saxon, tried his best to foster a spirit of light-heartedness and jollity, and the generosity of the company in terms of food and drink could not be faulted, but Neil Munro and Susan Daniels were just too conspicuous by their absence. In addition, the knowledge that the killer had not yet been identified was still uppermost in most people's minds. Pulling together and presenting a common front in times of adversity were all very well when you were certain of your neighbours, but when it was possible that the murderer might be sitting at the same table, circumspection became the order of the day.

Alex Ross was the exception to this rule. He drank too much whisky and, to his wife's obvious embarrassment, had quite a lot to say for himself. Jenny, of whom Ross was very fond, did her best to humour him and tried to prevent him becoming too loud in his opinions by diverting his attention to other matters. Ross's wife Morag, a large woman who was wearing a purple dress smothered in sequins and a matching hat which she kept on throughout the dinner, tried to minimize the damage to her pride by smiling broadly at everyone in turn and asking where they planned to spend their summer holidays.

Ross eventually grew wise to Jenny's intervention and decided to bait Nigel Saxon about the speed with which Saxon Medical had obtained official approval for its product.

For the first time since he had met him Fenton saw Saxon lose his good humour. Ross, despite the fact that he was drunk, sensed it too, and was inspired to greater efforts. He said loudly, 'If you ask me, the funny handshake brigade were involved.'

There was uneasy laughter and Jenny leaned across to Fenton to ask what he meant.

'Freemasonry,' whispered Fenton in reply.

Saxon managed a smile too, but Ross was still intent on goading him. 'Or maybe they weren't,' he said conspiratorially. 'They're too busy running the police force!'

There was more laughter, then Ross suddenly added, 'I think it was more like the Tree Mob.'

Fenton had no idea what Ross meant and saw that many other people were similarly mystified, but it certainly meant something to Saxon. The colour drained from his face and his hands shook slightly as they rested on the table. 'I think you've said enough, Mr Ross,' he whispered through gritted teeth.

Jenny and Fenton were mesmerized by the change that had come over Saxon, and a complete silence fell until Ross, who like many drunks seemed absolutely amazed that he had managed to offend anyone, said loudly, 'What's the matter? It was only a wee joke, man.'

Ian Ferguson quickly stepped in to defuse the situation, getting to his feet and saying, 'I've no idea what this is all about but I'm going to have some more wine. Anyone else?'

Glasses were proffered and the moment passed.

'A fun evening,' whispered Jenny in Fenton's ear.

'We'll go soon,' Fenton promised.

As the table was cleared Jenny was engaged in conversation by Liz Scott and Fenton found himself standing beside Ian Ferguson.

'Have you had any more thoughts about the stuff we found in Neil's cupboard?' asked Ferguson quietly.

Fenton shook his head and said, 'No. You?'

'No, but it's worrying me.'

'In what way?'

'I think we should have told someone.'

'Who?'

'You know, someone in authority, the police.'

'Why?' asked Fenton, knowing full well that he was being obtuse but perversely wanting to hear his own fears expressed by somebody else.

'We know that the killer is using anticoagulants and we know that Neil Munro had a whole cupboardful of them hidden away in his lab.'

'Neil couldn't have been the killer.'

'I know that, but it's an uncomfortable coincidence, don't you think?'

Fenton didn't get a chance to reply for they were joined by Tyson and Saxon. Saxon asked if they were having a good time and held up a bottle of whisky. Fenton declined but Ferguson offered his glass for topping up.

'Dr Tyson tells me you're on duty on Sunday morning, Ian — is that right?' asked Saxon.

'All too true, I'm afraid. Why do you ask?'

'I have to dismantle the Saxon Analyzer some time in the afternoon. I wondered if you might be willing to stay on to give me a hand?'

Ferguson made an apologetic gesture. 'If only you'd said sooner,' he said. 'I've arranged to meet my girlfriend in the afternoon. Maybe I could put her off if I . . .'

'I'll do it,' interrupted Fenton.

'You're sure?' asked Saxon.

'Of course. I've been idle for so long it'll be a pleasure.'

'Well, if you're quite certain . . .'

Fenton arranged to be at the lab by two o'clock on Sunday afternoon.

On the way home Jenny asked Fenton, 'What did Alex Ross mean by the "Tree Mob"?'

'I've no idea,' replied Fenton.

'Charles Tyson knew,' said Jenny. 'I read it in his face.'

* * *

Nigel Saxon was waiting outside the lab when Fenton arrived on Sunday afternoon. He was stamping his feet and throwing his arms across his chest to keep warm as he patrolled the kerb near his parked car.

'Not late, am I?' asked Fenton, checking his watch to find it had just gone two.

'Not at all,' smiled Saxon. 'I'm grateful to you for helping out. The company is a bit short of demo models and this one has to be shown at Glasgow Royal tomorrow. You can have it back afterwards for a few more days.'

The two men set about dismantling the Saxon Analyzer, Saxon concentrating on the hardware and Fenton disassembling the supply lines and removing the reagent reservoirs. Fenton came to a blue plastic container among the tubing and asked what it was.

'Be careful with that,' warned Saxon. 'It's the acid sump.'

'I'll get rid of it down the drain in the fume cupboard,' said Fenton, disconnecting the blue cylinder from its manifold and removing it carefully.

Saxon said, 'I'm just going to nip out to the car for a moment to get my socket set.'

The door banged behind him and Fenton carried the blue container slowly across the lab to the fume cupboard to place it inside the chamber. He turned on the fan motor and heard the extractor whine into life. The fan would suck any toxic fumes up through a flue and out through an aluminium stack on the roof of the building.

Fenton had unscrewed the cap of the acid bottle and was about to start pouring the contents down the drain when suddenly he froze. There was a bottle of benzene sitting inside the cupboard and he realized that he could smell it! He could smell benzene!

How could that be? The bottle was on the other side of the glass screen and the fan was running. How could the fumes escape? He put the cap back on the acid container and took a few steps backwards. Everything looked and sounded normal but there was something very wrong. He lit a piece of scrap paper in a bunsen burner and held it to the mouth of the fume cupboard. The flame did not flicker. The extractor fan was running but there was absolutely no air movement through the flue.

Puzzled as to what the fault could be, Fenton brought a step ladder across to the fume cupboard and climbed up to inspect the motor housing. It seemed in good condition. He then moved on to the filter block in the chimney stack and found the source of the problem. The fire damper had closed. Fire dampers were fitted as a safety measure to fume cupboards. In the event of a fire in the lab they isolated the chamber and prevented flames from reaching highly volatile chemicals via the flue. In this case the damper had apparently closed of its own accord and rendered the fan ineffectual.

The satisfaction that Fenton felt at discovering the cause of the problem immediately gave way to a distinct unease when he saw why the damper had closed. The retaining clips were missing. He searched the area at the base of the filter block but failed to find them. There was a chance that they had snapped and fallen down inside the flue, but there was also a possibility that they had been removed deliberately.

Fenton came down the ladder and rested his foot on the bottom rung for a moment while his mind raced to find a motive for someone's sabotaging the fume cupboard. After all, nothing drastic would have happened if he had gone ahead and poured the acid down the drain; an unpleasant whiff of acid fumes, perhaps, but nothing too serious unless . . .

Fenton's gaze fell on to the drain down which he had been about to pour the acid, and a dark thought crossed his mind like a cloud across the moon. Wondering if paranoia were getting the better of him, he squatted down and examined the pipe leading down from the drain. He was looking for signs of recent dismantling. He failed to find any, but remained uneasy. He had to know for sure. He fetched a spanner from the lab tool-box and undid the coupling at the head of the bend. Gently he slid out the curved section of pipe and looked inside. His fingers were shaking slightly as he saw signs of a chemical lying in the trap. Cautiously he sniffed the end of the pipe and recognized the smell. It was potassium cyanide.

If he had poured acid down the drain on top of cyanide crystals while the extractor was non-functional, the whole lab would have been filled with hydrocyanic gas within seconds and everyone in it would have died.

Everyone in it? thought Fenton. *He* was the only one in it, and where was Saxon? He'd been gone for ages.

Nigel Saxon came into the lab carrying a tool-box. 'Couldn't find the damn thing. It was under the back seat.'

'Really?' Fenton looked Saxon straight in the eye.

'Good God. What's happened?' asked Saxon as he caught sight of Fenton's face. 'You look as if you've seen a ghost.'

'There's something wrong with the fume cupboard.'

'Is that all?' asked a puzzled Saxon.

'There are cyanide crystals in the drain.'

'You mean the drain is blocked?'

Fenton stared at Saxon for a full thirty seconds before saying, 'If I had poured acid down it . . .'

Saxon shook his head and said apologetically, 'I'm sorry. I'm not a chemist. What are you trying to say?'

Fenton was desperately trying to appraise Saxon's behaviour. It seemed genuine enough. But did he really not know what the consequences would have been? Had it really been coincidence that Saxon had chosen that particular moment to be out of the room?

Fenton's head was reeling. Had someone tried to kill him? He searched for another explanation but all he found was a new suspicion. He faced the possibility that the accident in the pub had been no accident either, no 'act of mindless violence' as the police had called it. It appeared that someone wanted him out of the way, and whether it was temporary or permanent did not much seem to matter. But why? Whoever it was must think that he knew more than he did. He felt the irony of it: someone was trying to kill him for something he didn't know.

The flat was empty when Fenton got in, for Jenny had gone to visit her old flatmates. He was glad of the time it gave him to calm down. His hands still shook a little and his insides still felt hollow, but a stiff whisky helped fight the symptoms and prepared him to confide in Jenny when she did come in.

'But why?' exclaimed Jenny when he told her.

'I keep telling you I don't know.'

'Who knew you would be in the lab today?'

'Lots of people. We discussed it at the dinner party the other night.'

'So it has to be one of the lab staff?'

'Or Saxon. He picked that very moment to disappear.'

'What about when he came back? Did he look guilty?'

'No,' conceded Fenton.

'What other possibilities are there?'

'I suppose it's just possible that the damper failed for some technical reason.'

'And the cyanide crystals?'

'Coincidence? We use cyanide a lot.'

'I think I prefer that notion.'

Fenton preferred it too. He just didn't believe it.

Jenny was still sleeping when he left for work the next morning. She didn't stir when he kissed her, so Fenton tiptoed out of the room, taking great pains to close the door quietly behind him.

It felt good to be back on the bike again, although his ribs still hurt when anything more than light pressure was required on the handlebars. He gunned it up the outside of a long queue of cars in Lothian Road and joined the leading one at the traffic lights. They changed, and Fenton was a memory to the car's driver before the man had had time to engage first gear.

Charles Tyson arrived in the car-park at the rear of the lab as Fenton was heaving the Honda on to its stand. They exchanged pleasantries and walked into the lab together. There were two engineers from the hospital works department mending the fume cupboard and Tyson paused to ask what was wrong. He asked Ian Ferguson but it was Fenton who answered.

By ten o'clock Fenton felt as if he had never been away, for within minutes of sitting down at his desk he had picked up the threads and was back in the old routine. Hospital biochemistry kept him fully occupied until Wednesday, when he found time to chase up those who had volunteered to give blood for the Saxon Analyzer tests. Charles Tyson was the last on the list. Fenton withrew the blood, ejected the sample into two plastic tubes and took them along to his lab. He brought out the relevant rack from the fridge and placed Tyson's samples in it.

As he made to put the rack back in the fridge he noticed something odd about Tyson's specimen in the second tube. It was still unclotted. He withdrew both tubes and shook them gently. One should have remained quite fluid for the test-tube had anticoagulant in it, but the other contained nothing but blood. It should have clotted. Fenton looked at his watch and saw that ten minutes had passed since he had taken the sample. Far too long! He raced along the corridor and burst into Tyson's room, receiving startled looks from both Tyson and Liz Scott, who was taking dictation. 'Your blood isn't clotting,' he blurted out.

Tyson looked at the inside of his arm and said, 'It isn't bleeding. It stopped normally.' Fenton still looked doubtful. Tyson said, 'Probably a dirty tube . . . but just to make sure, pass me a scalpel blade, will you.'

Fenton opened a glass-fronted cabinet and removed a small packet wrapped in silver foil. He handed it to Tyson. Liz screwed up her face and said, 'What on earth . . .' as

91

Tyson slit through the skin of his index finger and watched the blood well up. He dabbed it away with the clean swab that Fenton handed to him and checked his watch. Fenton and Liz watched in silence as Tyson continued to dab blood away. At length he said, 'There, it's stopping. See? Quite normal.'

Fenton let out a sigh of relief and said, 'Thank God. I thought for a moment that you were number five.' Now able to think of more mundane matters, he realized that he was now short of one blood sample.

'Perhaps Liz?' Tyson suggested, turning to look at her. She screwed up her face again before agreeing with more than a little reluctance. 'I hate needles,' she said as she rolled up the sleeve of her blouse.

'Look up,' Fenton told her before inserting the needle smoothly into the vein and drawing back the plunger. 'There now, that didn't hurt, did it?' Liz agreed that it hadn't. 'Just hold the swab there for a minute or so,' said Fenton, placing the gauze over the puncture mark, 'then you can roll down your sleeve.'

Fenton brought the tubes back to his lab and held them up to the window. One of them remained fluid while the other was clotting normally. Discarding Tyson's samples, he put the new tubes in the fridge to wait with the others until later. He would run them through the Analyzer in the evening when everyone had gone and Jenny had started her shift on night duty.

Fenton came downstairs to the main lab to see what lay in store for him and read through the request forms from the wards. 'I don't believe it,' he said out loud as he came across yet another request for a lead count. 'Twelve . . . fourteen . . . sixteen bloods for lead! What's going on?'

Alex Ross gave a thin smile. 'You've got Councillor Vanney to thank for that.'

'Vanney?'

'He's been opposing an extension to the ring road, and his latest tack is to whip up fear about lead pollution from car exhausts if the new road goes ahead. You know the sort of thing: IQ will drop by fifty points if you walk too near a Volkswagen Polo. He's been calling for the screening of all children living near the first stage of the road.'

'What's his real reason?'

'The more cynical among us might suggest that the new road would screw up a development of luxury flats that Vanney and Sons are building on the south side.'

'Turd.'

'He's a powerful turd,' Ross reminded him.

'Who are the "Tree Mob", Alex?'

Ross was taken by surprise. He visibly stiffened. 'What made you ask that?'

'The other night at the party you suggested that Saxon Medical had got special treatment because of the Tree Mob. Who are they?'

Ross put his hands to his forehead and said quietly, 'One day my big mouth will be the death of me.'

'I don't understand.'

'I've said too much already.'

'You can't leave me hanging,' Fenton protested.

Ross looked doubtful, then took a deep breath and said, 'There's an organization called the Cavalier Club which is currently well in with the establishment. Its emblem is an oak tree. It's supposed to represent the tree that King Charles hid up when he was hiding from the Roundheads.'

'But what's that got to do with Saxon getting preferential treatment from the Department of Health?'

'There are a lot of powerful people in the club. They scratch each others' backs, and what's more, they consider themselves to be above the law. Rumour has it their influence is growing all the time.'

'But a club?' protested Fenton.

'More a society really.'

'If you say so,' said Fenton. 'How come I haven't heard of it?'

'You were in Africa for a long while.'

Fenton found all this hard to believe until he remembered that the medallion that had fallen from Nigel Saxon's pocket in the car-park had had a tree motif on it. He didn't mention it to Ross.

Fenton nursed his dislike for politicians all through the procedure for lead estimation; it was the least popular test in the lab. True to form, his hands got covered in blood; they always did with lead tests. He was washing them for the umpteenth time when the phone rang and Ian Ferguson said, 'Tom, it's Jenny.'

Fenton finished drying his hands and took the receiver. 'Don't tell me,' he joked, 'you just called to say you loved me?' The smile died on his face when he heard Jenny sobbing. 'What's wrong? What's the matter?'

'I'm at the police station . . .' said Jenny, before she broke down again. 'They're holding me . . .'

Fenton couldn't believe his ears. 'Holding you? What are you talking about? You're not making sense.'

'The murders. The police think I did them.'

Fenton was reduced to spluttering incredulity. 'Is this some kind of joke? What are you talking about? How can they possibly think you did them?' He heard Jenny take a few deep breaths in an attempt to calm herself, then she said, 'It's little Jamie. He's dead. He bled to death! Oh Tom, I'm scared. Please come.'

The phone went dead before Fenton could reply; he clattered the receiver down on to its rest, then snatched it up again and called Jamieson.

'Nurse Buchan is at present helping us with our inquiries, Mr Fenton,' said the gruff voice at the other end of the phone.

'Come on, man! I'm not the bloody press. What's going on?'

'I am afraid I have nothing to add, sir.'

'Well, can I see her?'

94

'No you can't.'

'Is brain death a prerequisite for joining the Police Force?' snarled Fenton.

'I must warn you, sir, that . . .'

Fenton slammed down the receiver. His immediate thought was to rush round to the police station and demand to see Jenny, but the fact that he was in the middle of the lead tests prevented him from doing so. He realized after after a few minutes' thought that it would have been pointless anyhow. The police would not be impressed by histrionics. What Jenny needed was expert help, the help a lawyer could give. He went to speak to Tyson, who was equally shocked when he heard the news.

'Jenny needs a lawyer,' said Fenton. 'I wondered if perhaps you could recommend anyone?'

'Of course.' Tyson opened his address book. 'Phone this firm.' He copied down a name and telephone number on to a piece of scrap paper and handed it to Fenton, who returned to his own lab and dialled the number. They would send someone round to the police station.

Fenton found the lack of information was intolerable. Jenny had said that Jamie was dead but he had to know more; he had to find out when, where and how, and that might be difficult. Fenton's contacts with Jenny's family were few and far between, and not altogether cordial. Her sisters-in-law regarded Jenny as something of a scarlet woman for living in sin, as they saw it. Her brothers, although a little more tolerant of the situation than their wives, did not have much time for a man who did not work with his hands, and did not therefore conform to their notion of what a real man should be. But he had no alternative, Fenton decided. He would have to phone the Buchans; the number would be in Jenny's address book at the flat.

Fenton grounded the nearside foot-rest as he swung the Honda out of the hospital grounds and on to the main road. The machine's lurch served as a timely warning to him that he would be no good to Jenny dead. He forcibly restrained himself at every set of traffic lights.

The phone seemed to ring for ages before a woman with a strong north-eastern accent answered and Fenton announced himself. There was a silence, then the receiver was put down on what sounded like a wooden table. A few moments later a man said, 'Yes, what is it?'

Fenton recognized the voice as that of Grant Buchan. 'Grant? I'm phoning to say how desperately sorry I am about Jamie. But also something awful has now happened down here. They're holding Jenny in connection with Jamie's death.'

The expected outburst did not happen. Instead, Buchan said, 'I see.'

'What do you mean, you see?' Fenton exploded. 'Did you hear what I said? The police are holding Jenny! They think she had something to do with Jamie's death!'

Buchan was unmoved. He sounded as if he were under some kind of sedation as he said, 'My boy cut himself playing down the harbour. By the time he had covered fifty yards he was dead, every drop of his blood was on the stones. I can still see it in the cracks, it won't wash away.'

Fenton felt the man's agony. He rubbed his forehead and said softly, 'I'm sorry, believe me. I know what it's like to lose a child, but you must see that some awful mistake has been made. No one in their right mind could think Jenny was a murderer.'

After a long pause Buchan said, 'No, but my son died because his blood wouldn't clot. He had been poisoned with anti . . . anti . . .'

'Anticoagulants.'

'Anticoagulants. The method used by the Princess Mary Slayer.'

Fenton winced at the tabloid jargon.

Buchan continued, 'My laddie was never anywhere near

96

the Princess Mary Hospital, but Jenny works there and we stayed with Jenny when we were in Edinburgh.'

'You can't seriously believe that Jenny had anything to do . . .' Fenton broke off in mid-sentence. 'It's crazy!' he protested. 'The thought of Jenny being involved is just too ridiculous for words!'

'People get sick sometimes . . . sick in their heads.'

'No way,' said Fenton decisively. 'Jenny is not sick. Jenny is the sweetest, nicest, sanest person who ever lived. She did not kill Jamie; she did not kill anyone else. Let's get that straight.'

There was silence from Buchan.

Fenton was filled with frustration. 'Look, Grant,' he said, 'we can't talk properly over the phone. I'm coming up there.'

'I don't think that's a very good idea . . .' began Buchan.

'I'm coming,' said Fenton and put the phone down. He thought for a moment before picking it up again and dialling the lawyer's office. Yes, their Mr Bainbridge was still at the police station, and no, they did not have any further information.

Fenton paced up and down the flat like a caged tiger. He opened the drinks cupboard then closed it again without taking anything out. That wasn't what he needed. He opened another cupboard and took out his running shoes.

The pavements were wet but the wind had dropped as Fenton pounded out the first mile at a pace designed to replace tension with physical pain. Every time he found his mind straying to thoughts of the police or Grant Buchan, he lengthened his stride until the surge of anger was quelled inside him. By the end of the third mile his mind was calm and he had become more relaxed. He slowed to an easy jog and thought about what he was going to do.

He had told Grant Buchan that he was coming up to Morayshire but was that really the right thing to do? What good would come of it? What could he hope to find out? A sudden gust of wind caught the bare branches of the trees above him and made giant raindrops fall like diamonds under the streetlights. He moved off the pavement to avoid running directly beneath them, and the answer came to him. Jamie Buchan's death must hold the key to the whole affair. There must be a link between Jamie and the Princess Mary. The police thought Jenny was that link, but he knew she was not. Find it and he would have the answer to the whole nightmare. The sweat was trickling freely down his neck as he turned for home.

Fenton lay awake in the darkness watching the reflection of raindrops on the bedroom ceiling. The run had pleasantly stretched his muscles and a bath had relaxed him, but the flat felt so empty and lonely without Jenny. Where was she now? What were they doing to her? The police wouldn't give out anything other than the clockwork statement that they were still holding her. Sleep was out of the question and he still had a long night ahead of him before travelling North . . . But did he? If he rode through the night he could be there by morning. That would be better than lying brooding in the darkness. He dressed quickly, donned his leathers, collected a few odds and ends and tiptoed downstairs to rock the Honda off its stand.

Fenton kept the revs to a minimum as he turned in and out of the streets of Comely Bank at two in the morning; he had no wish to disturb the sleeping citizenry. He pulled out on to the main Queensferry road and headed for the Forth Bridge and the motorway.

SIX

The grey morning light was highlighting the white tops of the waves as Fenton reached Buchan Ness and stopped to rest his aching limbs. He coaxed the Honda off the winding road and paddled it with his feet over a stretch of shingle to lean it against the petrified stump of a long-dead tree. It made sounds of contracting metal as he walked stiffly over the scree to reach the water's edge and stretch his arms up to the colourless sky. He picked up a handful of pebbles and threw them aimlessly into the rough water, and seagulls screamed overhead in protest at the intruder. It was a cold, grey world.

The road traced the edge of the shore and wound between trees that were naked after a winter of rape by winds howling in off the North Sea. Fenton was relieved when the barren monotony of the landscape was broken by a neon sign advertising a transport café, open to service the early-morning fish trade. He swung off the road and followed the arrows.

The tea was hot and sweet and Fenton felt it travel all the way down to his stomach, making him think of sword-swallowers. He rubbed the back of his neck where the leather had been chafing and kneaded the backs of his thighs which were threatening cramp.

The road turned inland to cut across a stretch of barren headland and Fenton had to stop and check his map as he came to a junction with no signposts. He made a decision and turned right, and after a few minutes found himself heading towards the sea again. He stopped as he came to the top of a hill and looked down on the village where the Buchans lived. Pulling off a glove, he took a card from his top pocket and checked the address on it: 8 Harbour Wynd.

He let the bike freewheel silently down the hill and brought it to a halt on the cobblestones in front of the harbour. He let his foot rest on a pile of fish-boxes while he looked down at the smooth, oily surface of the water rising and falling against the slimy green stonework.

Three lanes radiated out from the hub of the harbour: one of them was Harbour Wynd. Fenton put the Honda up on its stand and walked slowly up over the cobbles to find number eight. The sound of the heavy brass knocker was surprisingly muted by the thickness of the door.

'Oh, it's you,' said Grant Buchan with no trace of pleasure in his voice. 'I suppose you'd better come in.' Fenton had expected no better.

'Who is it?' cried a woman's voice.

'It's Jenny's . . .' Buchan's voice trailed off as he sought a suitable description.

'Fancy man,' supplied the frosty-faced woman who emerged from the kitchen drying her hands on her apron.

Fenton's heart sank. He had met Grant's wife only once before and that had been when the whole family had been together. He remembered that then too she had maintained an air of prim disapproval. Mona Buchan stood in the doorway like an Angel of the Lord, hair tied back severely in a bun, shapeless cardigan buttoned up to the neck, eyes shining with self-righteousness from a fair-skinned face that had never known make-up.

'I'm very sorry about your son, Mrs Buchan,' began Fenton, ignoring the gibe.

'What do you want here?' she hissed. 'Haven't you and that . . . that . . .'

Buchan stopped the situation getting out of hand. He put his arm around his wife's shoulders and said, 'Easy, woman, make us all some tea, eh?'

Mona disappeared into the kitchen. 'I'm sorry,' said Buchan. 'She's very upset.'

'I understand.'

'But she's right. I can't see why you came here either,' said Buchan.

'Because the answer is here! It must be. Jenny didn't kill your boy. You must know that. The idea's just too ridiculous for words.' Fenton looked hard at Buchan, who held his gaze for a moment, then sighed and looked away. 'I just can't think straight any more . . .'

Mona brought in the tea. She clattered the tray down with a bad grace and turned on her heel. 'I'm afraid I have work to be getting on with,' she announced. The kitchen door closed again and Buchan continued, 'But why should the killer pick on Jamie? It just doesn't make sense.'

'I know,' said Fenton softly. 'I think Jenny must have been the unwitting link between the killer and your boy. That's what we have to find out.'

'What do you want me to do?' asked Grant.

'Tell me everything you did in Edinburgh, everyone you met, everywhere you went.'

Fenton took notes as Buchan spoke; not that there was much to record. The Buchans had gone from the train to the flat, from the flat to the clinic and back again. They had apparently met no one apart from the staff at the clinic, but the fact remained that at some time during these twenty-four hours Jamie Buchan had been poisoned so that a week later the blood would drain from his body and leave him a pale corpse on the cobblestones of his own village. If the answer did lie in the brief notes in front of him, Fenton could not see it. 'Did anyone give him sweets?' he asked.

'Only Jenny,' Buchan answered, making Fenton wish he hadn't asked.

'Do you think I could see Jamie's room?'

'He's in it.'

This answer shook Fenton to the core. He had not considered that the boy's body might be in the house.

'We got him back yesterday,' said Buchan quietly. 'Mona wanted him home once more before he goes away tomorrow.'

Fenton nodded silently, a lump coming into his throat at Buchan's distress. 'I'm sorry,' he said softly, 'I just thought that if I saw his things I might notice something that's been overlooked. But in the circumstances . . .'

Buchan stood up. Without saying anything he motioned to Fenton to follow him.

Fenton had to duck his head to accommodate the slope of the roof at the head of the narrow stairs before they entered Jamie's bedroom. The room was cold and smelled of dampness; old dampness, dampness that had been seeping through the thick stone walls for years. It had invaded the furniture and fabric, leaving a musty odour that Fenton associated with the seaside boarding-houses of his childhood. The little white coffin was bathed in pale grey light from the tiny dormer window that faced north to the sea; Jamie looked like a marble cherub. Fenton bowed his head and stood still for a moment in sadness.

'We haven't moved anything,' said Buchan.

Fenton looked about him. It was a boy's room — trains, boats, planes, an unfinished Lego model. The Millenium Falcon stood on its window-sill launching pad, ready to transport the plastic figures beside it to some far-off galaxy. Jamie's Jedi sword lay on his pillow. 'He was Luke Sky-walker,' said Buchan.

An anguished cry came from the stairs. The clatter of footsteps stopped as Mona Buchan stood framed in the doorway, her eyes burning with anger. Fenton was trans-fixed by the look of hatred on her face; white flecks of spittle pocked her lips as she turned on her husband. 'What in God's holy name possessed you,' she demanded, 'to let this — this animal near our son?' Buchan looked shaken. 'And you,' she hissed at Fenton, her voice a coarse rasp, 'how dare you.'

Mona Buchan's anger soared beyond the bounds of reason, and unable to contain herself any longer, she flung herself across the room, fingernails bared, blind to everything except Fenton. As she lunged forward her foot caught the edge of the trestle bearing Jamie's coffin and sent it crashing to the floor. Clad in his white shroud he lay there like a sleeping china doll among the toys.

Mona Buchan's rage evaporated. She collapsed to her knees and broke into uncontrollable sobbing as she rested her cheek against her dead son's body. Fenton knew he would never be able to forget the sight. 'Go,' said Grant Buchan. 'Just go.'

The Honda was the centre of attraction for a group of small boys when Fenton returned to the harbour, and their Star Wars gear suggested that they might have been friends of Jamie's. There was something familiar about one of the boys, thought Fenton, but he could not think what. Perhaps he was a relation of Jamie's. A brother? He could not recall whether the Buchans had had more than one child. 'Your name isn't Buchan, is it, son?' he asked.

'No, Mister. He's dead.'

Fenton got on the bike and fastened the chinstrap of his helmet.

'Can I have a hurl on the back, Mister?' asked the boy, resting his hand on the handlebars.

'Another time,' Fenton replied.

He did not look back as he reached the top of the hill above the village; he gave a cursory glance to the left for traffic then joined the main road to head for Fraserburgh at an easy pace. There he stopped at a harbour café, hoping that eating would alleviate the awful emptiness he felt inside, but it did not. He gazed out of the window at the boats nuzzling the quayside and saw only Jamie's lifeless body.

As he headed east on the coast road Fenton reflected on what his visit had achieved. Nothing, he decided, not a damned thing. Buchan had not told him anything that could possibly be of help in solving anything. Jenny was in as much trouble as she ever had been. He drew to a halt as he reached a point as far east as he would travel and took a last look at the grey northern water before turning south. It was cold but dry, and the wind would be behind him.

Jenny was in the flat when Fenton got back. They held each other for a long time before either spoke. 'I found your note,' said Jenny. 'Did you discover anything?'

'Nothing,' admitted Fenton. 'What's been happening here?'

'The police released me this afternoon but I've been told not to leave the city and the hospital has suspended me.'

Fenton could see that Jenny had been crying a lot: her eyes were puffy and red. 'Morons,' he said. 'Absolute morons.' He drew her even closer.

'The funny thing is,' began Jenny, half laughing, half sobbing, 'I can see their point of view. How could the hospital killer come into contact with Jamie unless it was me?'

'That's what we must figure out,' said Fenton with all the confidence he could muster.

'We're not terribly good at figuring things out, remember?'

'We'll do it.'

They lay still in the darkness, taking pleasure in their closeness, Fenton's fingers intertwined with Jenny's, his thumb gently tracing an ellipse on the back of her hand. Her shallow breathing was like music.

In the small hours of the morning Fenton lay awake while Jenny slept soundly beside him. She had been mentally exhausted, and reassured enough by his presence to fall into a deep sleep, her head still against his shoulder. For the first time in many hours she had felt safe, safe from the strange and the unknown; the overweight men in crumpled suits who smelled of sweat and down-market aftershave;

the men who sneered at everything she said; the red faces that shouted at her, mocked her, accused her. Surely these men could not be policemen? Policemen were quiet, well-mannered, helpful; they told you the time and gave you directions, patted children and inspired confidence, not fear. She had been terribly afraid; she had never known such fear.

The disorientation caused by being taken to a strange place full of hostile men had destroyed her self-confidence in one fell swoop. Her initial stance as an outraged citizen demanding her rights in a free country had collapsed within minutes, leaving her confused and afraid. A pleading note had crept into her voice as the ordeal had continued, and she had been filled with a desperate desire to please her inquisitors, to say yes to anything if it would breach the seemingly impenetrable wall of hostility. An innate strength of character stopped her from travelling along that road; but she had seen it and seen it clearly.

Fenton sighed in the still darkness of the room as once again his thoughts came to nothing. What was the connection, he asked himself, just what was it? One fact stared him in the face like an ugly mongrel: there had been no opportunity at all for the hospital killer to reach Jamie directly. Involuntarily he squeezed Jenny's hand as the unthinkable crossed his mind. Something was wrong with his train of thought, something basic.

An hour later, after much mental wrestling, Fenton came up with a new hypothesis. It was forced on him by the facts. There was *no* killer, *no* lunatic, *no* psychopath. It was a disease. A bacterium or a virus. A virus had dstroyed the clotting mechanism in the blood of all the people who had died. Why not? New diseases were being discovered all the time – Legionnaires' disease, Lassa fever, AIDS. The more he thought about it the more obvious and possible it seemed. The virus must be endemic in the hospital, lurking in unseen corners, just as the Legionnaires' bug had hidden in the showers of an American hotel. Jenny must have carried it home and infected Jamie. The fact that not everyone was susceptible to it would be typical of a viral infection. Everything pointed to its being a virus . . . except the death of Neil Munro.

The kraken of Neil Munro, burnt flesh peeling from his face, rose up from Fenton's subconscious to slow him down. No virus had pushed Munro into the sterilizer. A compromise was called for. Neil had been murdered, of that there was no doubt, but the others? No, it had to be some kind of infective agent. All he had to do now was prove it.

Jenny turned in her sleep and Fenton kissed her lightly on the shoulder. The question now was how he should go about substantiating his theory. Elementary. It was first-year student stuff. You isolate the thing and show it does what it does through controlled animal tests. But getting his hands on infected material was going to be quite a different matter.

He would need material from the people who had died — tissue and serum — and for that he would need top-brass help. That meant Tyson. Or did it? He was still smarting from the way he had made a fool of himself over the Dr Malcolm affair. He did not want it to happen again. Could he possibly do it alone?

Maybe it had been done already. Perhaps the Pathology Department had already screened tissue from the victims for infective agents. If that were so then his suggestion would be about as popular with Pathology as his last one had been with the police. That would be the last straw. He could just see MacDougal, the consultant pathologist and not the most patient of men, sneering at him and saying, 'Do you imagine that we're all stupid down here, Fenton?'

He glanced at the digital clock on the bedside table. Ten past four; four hours before he had to get up and go to the hospital, four hours in which to decide. Outside, the wind began to rise and moan through wires on the roof. The bedroom window rattled as it denied entry to the night. Fantasies of a commando-style raid on the Pathology Lab

106

led to visions of being caught and the implausible explanation that he would have to offer to the police. Inspector Jamieson's superior little smile appeared in the glow from the clock. There had to be another way.

The other way presented itself, and Fenton felt stupid for not having thought of it sooner. The Medical Records Department. He could simply go along and request the file on one of the victims. There might not be one for Susan Daniels or the Wilson woman, but there would certainly be one for the Watson boy because he had been a patient at the time. His file would contain a full post-mortem report and details of all the lab tests requested.

Fenton got up at seven and was in the lab by eight. He had left Jenny sleeping, partly because she needed the rest and partly to avoid any discussion about what he was going to do. He got straight to work on his excuse for the Medical Records people and thumbed through the daybook until he found the last entry for Timothy Watson, a blood-glucose estimation. He copied down details of the result and took a virgin report from Liz Scott's desk. Using two fingers and a great deal of concentration, he tapped out a stuttering copy of the original report, then altered the date stamp to match the date of the request in the daybook. He now had his excuse: a biochemistry report to insert into the Watson boy's file.

The Medical Records Department was situated in the administration block and smelt of dust and old cardboard. It had a blue-carpeted floor that deadened the footsteps of two young girls as they moved up and down narrow gangways between towering rows of patients' files. Cecil McClay looked over his glasses as Fenton entered through the swing doors and approached his desk. He continued writing and finished his sentence before saying, 'Yes?'

McClay managed to endow the word with the suggestion that Fenton was intruding, but Fenton had been prepared for it; he knew McClay of old. The man had been Medical Records Officer at the Princess Mary for over twenty years, and like many old-timers had assumed proprietorial rights over his department. To him medical records were an end in themselves. Outsiders wanting to see them were a nuisance to be discouraged whenever possible.

Had Fenton been on a legitimate errand, McClay's attitude might have incensed him, but as it was, he was politeness itself. He apologized for the inconvenience and asked if he might possibly take a look at the file on Timothy Watson.

'Your authority?'

'My own. I'm Fenton. Biochemistry. I have a report to add to the file. It must have been overlooked.'

'Leave it there. I'll see that it's entered.' McClay lowered his gaze behind the glasses.

'Actually, I'd really like to make sure that this is the only one we overlooked . . .' Fenton hoped his smile looked more genuine than it felt.

McClay considered for a moment, then swung round in his chair and said to one of the girls, 'Hilary! Watson, T., March three, Ward Four.'

The girl handed the file to Fenton with a look that promised more than a cardboard file should he choose to follow it up. He smiled and took it to a vacant desk.

The post-mortem findings were brief: Timothy Watson had died from loss of blood. Cross-reference was made to the haematology report, which described high anticoagulant activity in the sample and complete failure of the clotting mechanisms in the boy's blood. No mention was made anywhere of specimens having been taken and sent for bacterial or viral investigation. His idea was still valid. Everything was yet to play for.

Fenton looked at the shorthand on the back of the pathology report to discover what specimens had been taken at autopsy and how they had been stored. Four ticks under 'F' he dismissed as useless, because samples fixed in formalin would have lost all biological activity. There were two ticks under 'FR' for freezer; one was serum and the other heart tissue. Either of these would do for his purpose. He made a mental note of the reference numbers, closed the file and laid it gently on McClay's desk. 'Thank you,' he said. McClay grunted in response and did not look up.

The question of how to get his hands on the post-mortem samples occupied Fenton's mind for the rest of the morning. He knew a few people in Pathology but not well enough to ask for the samples. He would have to 'borrow' them, but how? Forced entry was out of the question. He was prepared to manipulate matters, use a little deception, generate 'misunderstandings', flirt around the edges of illegality, but not brazenly to cross the line.

The idea came to him as he washed before going to lunch. The Pathology Department had a washroom too. If he could find some reason to go to Pathology at around five-thirty he could sneak into it and hide until everyone had left. Then he could find the specimens at his leisure and let himself out. The idea became a plan.

At twenty minutes past five Fenton left the Biochemistry Department with his pulse-rate rising. There now seemed to be a dozen reasons for not going ahead with the plan and more occurred to him with every step he took towards the Pathology lab. He came to the green double doors and paused for a moment to steady himself. His mouth was as dry as the desert.

The sickly-sweet smell of formaldehyde engulfed him as he approached the reception desk and smiled at the girl technician standing there. She smiled back and read his coat badge. 'What can I do for you, Mr Fenton?'

Fenton held up the empty brown bottle he had brought with him from Biochemistry and said, 'I've run out of this stuff and the stores closed at five. Could you possibly let me have some until the morning?'

The girl took the reagent bottle from him and read the label. 'Of course,' she replied, and left him alone for a moment. Fenton looked anxiously over his shoulder to see the entrance to the men's cloakroom. It would be immediately to his right as he left. The sound of a door opening made him spin round in time to see the consultant Mac-Dougal leave his office and walk across the front of the reception desk. Fenton smiled; MacDougal ignored him.

The technician returned with a full bottle of reagent and handed it to him with a smile. 'There you go,' she said.

Fenton thanked her and promised that he would replace it in the morning. He left the reception area and side-stepped smartly into the cloakroom. It was empty. He breathed a sigh of relief: so far so good. He chose the end cubicle and sat down to wait, glancing at his watch. He did not lock the door, just pushed it almost shut, reasoning that anyone in doubt as to whether or not a cubicle was occupied would automatically use one of the other two. A locked door would be a sure sign of occupancy and might attract attention. If he were discovered he would simply flush the toilet and leave.

For Fenton the next thirty minutes seemed like years. The initial symphony of slamming locker doors and good-nights gave way to increasingly intermittent footsteps and distant door-closing. Just as he thought he might be alone at last, someone came into the cubicle next to his and stayed there for a full five minutes, forcing him into a raw-nerved silence; every intake of breath was a challenge to his self-control.

At last the toilet flushed and the door banged open. There was the sound of running taps, then the outer door bounced on its brake. Fenton was alone again. He had prepared himself for a thirty-minute wait after the last noise had died away. He checked his watch and began to reread the writing on the wall.

After half an hour Fenton tiptoed out of the cloakroom and into the reception area to find it dark and silent. No light escaped from under any door. He was alone . . . please God he was alone. The blood pounding in his ears told him that his nerves were already at fever pitch. He took a few deep breaths in a deliberate attempt to compose himself before following the signs to the post-mortem suite. There was enough light coming from the streetlamps outside to show him the way, which was just as well, for he had not thought to bring a torch.

He pushed open the blue door; inside it was pitch black. The post-mortem suite had no windows. He closed the door behind him and ran the palm of his hand up and down the cold tiling until he had found the light switch. Three strip lights groaned into life.

Fenton looked about him, his nose wrinkling at the heavy scent of the air freshener used to mask the lingering smells of death. The room was large, high and round. In the middle, two stainless-steel tables stood on their pedestals like traffic islands. They were free-standing; all the plumbing and the hydraulic lines for the tilt mechanisms had been run under the floor. Everything in the room was hard and smooth, predominantly stainless steel and tiling. There was nothing that would be harmed by constant sluicing.

The room might have been mistaken for an operating theatre at first glance, but the instruments on the wall gave it away: saws, hammers, drills, chisels; these were tools more readily associated with carpentry or butchery than with surgery. The spring balances and meat scales swung the analogy in favour of butchery. The precision of the paper-thin scalpel blade took a back seat in this environment, where the long, black, bone-handled knives on the wall performed their surrealist art on the cold tables.

Three heavily-insulated doors furnished with metal clamps fronted the body vaults. Fenton opened one, recoiling slightly as a waft of cold, damp air caressed his cheek. There were two occupants inside, hooded, shrouded, and identified by luggage labels round their toes. The small size of the bundles indicated that these were children. Fenton took one of the limp labels between thumb and forefinger and read it: Amanda Wright, aged twelve. He closed the door.

The large chest freezer looked as if it might contain what he was looking for, but he found the lid reluctant to open. He had to thump the heels of his hands against the clasp before the ice around the rim cracked and allowed the lid to rise with a groan. The large eye sockets of an aborted foetus stared up at him through a plastic bag, and he took a sharp intake of breath. Half afraid of what he would find next he began brushing away ice from the tops of plastic containers; a hand, an ear, the misty outline of a child's leg presented themselves. Fenton slammed the lid down on this hellish collection and rested his hands on it for a moment, breathing erratically. His impulse was to run, to get out, out into the night where he could walk in the rain, smell the grass, let the wind free him from this cloying warmth.

His anxiety subsided. He could think again. Where would they keep small specimens? His attention came to rest on a double bank of steel handles on the wall, lettered in alphabetical order. He went over and pulled out 'A'. They were freezer drawers: row upon row of little glass phials stored in numbered racks. He had found what he was looking for.

Using the reference number from the Medical Records file on Timothy Watson he found the correct serum sample and removed the phial, which he took to the sink and held under the tap until it had melted. Fenton then searched through a series of drawers and was lucky at the fourth attempt: clean sterile phials. He found a pipette and transferred a small quantity of the serum from the original phial into a fresh one. Then he replaced the original and closed the drawer with a click. It was over. He had got it. The compressor on the freezer shuddered into life and his heart missed a beat.

The thought that, should he drop dead from fright, he might well end up on one of the steel tables with his ribcage wrenched open and a hose sluicing out his chest cavity, put

112

wings on Fenton's heels. He switched off the lights in the post-mortem room and listened for a few moments before opening the door. The smell of the air freshener seemed stronger in the darkness. It threatened to choke him. The sounds were friendly enough; clicks from thermostats, hums from fridges, inanimate neutral sounds. He sidled out into the main lab.

The short wait in the darkness had accustomed his eyes to the gloom. Again he waited and listened before stepping out smartly into the corridor and containing his urge to run. He couldn't lock the door from the outside for he had no key; some poor soul was going to get a rocket in the morning for having left it unlocked.

The old villa was in darkness when he reached it. He unlocked the front door and switched on the light in the hall, taking comfort from the friendly, familiar smells of the solvents used in biochemistry. He checked the duty roster to find out who was on call. It was Mary Tyler. That presented no problem; no explanations would be necessary if she came in while he was still there. He took the serum sample from his pocket and fixed a self-adhesive label to it, adding the fictitious name Mark Brown. He put it safely away in his own freezer, donned his leathers and left.

SEVEN

When Fenton arrived home he found that a good night's sleep and a day on her own had done little to restore Jenny's spirits. Her smile of greeting lacked conviction and her lank hair and lacklustre eyes spoke of the strain she was under. He sensed that something else was wrong, but did not enquire, feeling that she would tell him in her own time. Half-way through their meal she said, 'I phoned Grant today.'

Fenton went cold.

'He told me what happened.'

'Jenny, I'm sorry. I should never have gone there.'

Jenny was close to tears. She said softly, 'It's all right. I know you were only trying to help. Grant knows that too. In fact, I think you managed to convince my brother that I didn't kill his son.' There was bitterness in her voice, and she covered her mouth with her handkerchief. Fenton got up and put his arms round her from behind. He put his cheek against her hair and rocked her gently from side to side.

When Jenny had calmed down Fenton told her of his virus idea. It was a candle in her darkness. 'Do you really think so?' she asked with more animation in her voice than he had heard for some time. Something persuaded her to have second thoughts. She added hesitantly, 'You're not just saying that, are you?'

Fenton was adamant that he was not and went on to give his reasons. Jenny found his enthusiasm infectious and with

114

very little prompting was able to add substance to the foundations of his argument. Despite this, and although desperate to believe it, she still felt compelled to play devil's advocate. 'But there *are* no viruses that cause uncontrolled bleeding, are there?' she asked.

Fenton countered the doubt by saying, 'There was no Legionnaires' disease either until a whole bunch of Americans dropped dead of it. Then people all over the world started recognizing similarities in cases that they had been seeing for years and dismissing as viral infections or pyrexias of unknown origin.'

Jenny accepted the argument and Fenton pressed home his case. 'What we're seeing is very acute haemophilia. Before you say it, I know that haemophilia is a genetic disorder but I can see no reason why a virus shouldn't be able to simulate the condition if it attacks the right cells.'

Jenny was sold on the idea, and asked Fenton what he planned to do.

'Get some material from one of the victims and find the virus,' said Fenton.

'But how?'

'I've already got it.' Fenton told Jenny his tale and saw her mouth drop open.

'But what if you'd been caught?' she said.

'I wasn't and I've got the sample.'

He would send it off for analysis under cover of a fictitious patient's name. He would make a special request for animal inoculation and ask for blood samples from the test animals. When he had evidence of the infective agent he would present it to Tyson.

'How long?' asked Jenny.

'Five days.'

With hope restored to her, Jenny's morale began to improve. She began to think of her return to work, of hearing the apologies, the assurances that 'not for one moment had anyone really believed . . .'

Fenton was pleased at the change in her – it was so good

115

to see her smile again – but he also felt a burden grow on his shoulders. What if the tests should prove negative? How could he bring himself to tell her? He knew very well that the repair to Jenny's psyche was only in the nature of a temporary patch. If the patch fell away the wound might well split open, and that could be disastrous, as he knew from experience. Life could so easily become a desert of depression, a limbo where time stood still. That mustn't happen to Jenny.

'More rain,' growled Fenton as he got up on Friday morning. He shivered involuntarily as he sat on the end of the bed, then rubbed his arms vigorously to combat the chill of the bedroom.

Jenny was not to be side-tracked with talk of the weather. She said, 'You'll get the report today.'

'Should do,' answered Fenton in what he hoped was a matter-of-fact voice. In truth he had thought about little else all night. His stomach was tied in knots at the very thought of it. Unwilling to look at Jenny in case she read his mind, he went to the window and drew the curtains back. 'I've had it with Bonny Scotland,' he announced, spitting out the words as he looked at the rain-lashed roofs. 'You've got to be a bit soft in the head to live here. Why don't we pack up and get the hell out?' He turned to look at Jenny.

'You will phone and tell me?' said Jenny, ignoring everything he had said.

'I'll phone. But whatever it says, nothing changes. I love you and you love me, and sooner or later this will all be sorted out. Okay?' Fenton's voice hardened on the 'okay' as he saw Jenny's gaze begin to drift away.

'All right,' she said softly.

Fenton was sitting at his desk when Liz Scott brought in the package. The yellow envelope on the outside said that it was the microbiology report; the box would contain the blood samples. He sat and stared at it for several minutes, anxious to know the truth but afraid of what it might be. He brought out a paper-knife and turned it over in his hand before committing it to the flap of the envelope and slitting it slowly and precisely open.

SPECIMEN REPORT: MARK BROWN
BACTERIAL SCREEN: NEGATIVE
VIRAL SCREEN: NEGATIVE

BLOOD SAMPLES ENCLOSED AS REQUESTED

Fenton felt as though a fist had hit him in the stomach. But after a few minutes of deep depression he saw an argument. The report was not conclusive. If there was a new bacterium or virus in the specimen then it might well require special culture conditions. In fact it almost certainly would, or it would have been isolated and described before. The real answer would lie in the blood samples of animals inoculated with serum from Timothy Watson. He opened the box and his agony was complete. Both samples had clotted perfectly. There had been nothing in Timothy Watson's blood to infect the animals. He had been wrong again.

Fenton pondered the consequences. He had built up Jenny's hopes for nothing. He could not have done a better job of pushing her towards a nervous breakdown if he had meant to. He crumpled the report in his fist and flung it across the room. Jenny would be waiting at home for his call. She would be pretending she was reading or dusting or cleaning or listening to the radio but really she would just be waiting, waiting for the phone to ring.

Fenton dialled the number. It was answered at the first tone.

'Jenny? The report hasn't come yet. Maybe this afternoon.'

Fenton felt worse than ever but he could not tell her, not like that, not over the phone. He needed time to think.

So there was no virus involved, no convenient infective agent to take the blame and clear up the mystery. What did that leave? A poison? That seemed unlikely, for too many people seemed to be immune; besides, you did not carry a poison on your person and pass it on inadvertently . . .

Fenton suddenly saw a crack in an otherwise smooth-walled enigma. Jenny must have passed on the agent to Jamie, and if it wasn't a bacterium or a virus she must have known about it! She must have given Jamie Buchan something she believed to be completely harmless, but it had not been. It had killed him.

Anger, superseding disappointment, erupted in Jenny. 'No, damn it! I did not give him anything. How many times do I have to say it? You're on the wrong track!'

Fenton felt the unspoken 'as usual' hang heavily in the air. He stopped badgering, and a silence fell that threatened to be louder than the argument. Keeping his voice well under control, he said softly, 'Jenny, you must see that this is the only logical explanation. You must have given the boy something you've forgotten about. Please. Think.'

'No! No! No!' Jenny's eyes blazed as she refused to have any more to do with the notion. Fenton made to put his arm round her but she turned away and stared intently at the fire. Fenton got up and went to the kitchen to make coffee. As he waited for the kettle to boil, he stood staring out of the kitchen window at the blackness, his hands in his pockets. Jenny had never turned away from him before. He felt angry, sad, sorry, ineffectual, stupid and, after a short while, cold. He poured the coffee and took it through.

Jenny didn't look up when he put the mug down beside her; she continued to stare at the fire. He sat down on the other chair and looked steadily at her left profile until she relented and turned towards him, then he broke into a half apologetic, half self-conscious grin. 'I'm sorry,' he whispered.

'Oh Tom . . .'

They held each other tight while the tears, the whispered apologies, the cheek-nuzzling tenderness, combined to soothe the wounds that they had inflicted on each other. A new silence ensued; this time it was a comfortable pool of serenity, and both of them were reluctant to speak lest they ripple the surface.

Fenton woke at three, his body damp with cold sweat. He sat bolt upright to free himself of the images of a nightmare; Neil Munro's face, a fountain of blood issuing from Timothy Watson's mouth and, through a red mist, the spectre of Jamie Buchan's dead face. A forest of arms had reached out towards him in his dream; Mona Buchan's arm had pointed and accused; Timothy Watson held out both arms in pitiful appeal; anonymous arms had reached out from a deepfreeze to wave like pond-weeds; Luke Skywalker had wielded a sword. This last image remained with him as he reeled into consciousness. In the darkness of the room he saw again the boy at the harbour, the strangely familiar boy with his hands on the handlebars of the Honda. 'Can I have a hurl, Mister? Can I have a hurl?' The image of the boy's face exploded into nothingness as Fenton realized that it had not been the boy himself who was familiar; it had been what he was wearing. He had had coloured plastic bands round both wrists: hospital name-tags!

Fenton shook Jenny hard in his excitement and coaxed her into wakefulness. She covered her eyes to protect them from the glare of the bedside lamp.

'Think, Jenny, think! Did you give any hospital name-tags to Jamie Buchan?'

An overture of confused sleepy noises gave way to silence as Jenny considered the question. 'Yes, yes I did.' Her eyes cleared with the recollection. 'I had a bunch in my uniform pocket. I gave them to Jamie to play with.'

Fenton stared at her in silence.

'All right, so you were right; I did give him something. I

gave him a few name-tags, but surely you're not going to suggest that he ate them and poisoned himself, are you?'

Fenton was not going to be ridiculed. He took both Jenny's hands in his and said, 'It's a start, and what's more it's a connection, a connection between Jamie and the Princess Mary. What else did you give him?'

Fenton's surge of confidence overwhelmed any argument that Jenny might have considered. She thought deeply before answering. 'No, I'm quite sure this time, nothing else.'

'Good, make some coffee, will you?'

Jenny's eyebrows arched but Fenton was deep in thought and didn't notice. He sat on the edge of the bed staring into space, tapping his right thumbnail rapidly against his gritted teeth. Jenny made coffee and brought it through. 'Your coffee, oh wise one.'

Fenton ignored the sarcasm if it registered at all. He took the cup and said, 'Well, if all you gave him were plastic name-tags, that's what must have killed him.'

Jenny, with less reason than anyone to scoff at suggestions which diverted suspicion from herself, felt forced to do so at this one.

Fenton remained adamant. 'If the name-tags are the only connection between the hospital and Jamie then they are the reason he died. It's logical, however unlikely it may seem.'

'How?' asked Jenny accusingly.

'I've no idea.'

Jenny shook her head. 'You said that you saw Jamie's friend wearing the armbands. He was quite healthy, wasn't he?'

'Yes.'

'Well?'

'I don't know, but I repeat, if the armbands were the only thing you gave to Jamie then they're responsible. Do you still say you gave him nothing else?'

'Nothing,' said Jenny.

120

'I'm going to talk to Tyson in the morning, but meanwhile . . .'

'Meanwhile what?'

'How long is it since we made love?'

'Quite a while.'

'That situation is about to end.'

'Do I have any say in the matter?'

'Not really.'

'Shouldn't we discuss this first . . .' murmured Jenny, her body beginning to respond to his touch.

'No,' whispered Fenton, 'I've already decided.'

Tyson listened patiently while Fenton spoke and did not interrupt, but Fenton could tell that he was failing to convince. Tyson's eloquent silence diluted his enthusiasm until a sense of the implausibility of what he was saying loomed up in him like guilt for some long-past sin. Tyson cleared his throat and began to speak. Fenton could tell that he was editing what he had to say for the sake of politeness. 'What you're really saying is that Saxon plastic kills people. Frankly, that is ridiculous.'

The words, coming from Tyson, carried the weight of a punch. Fenton tried to defend himself. He began, 'I know it sounds a bit . . .'

'Not a bit; a lot. It's just plain ridiculous. Saxon plastic has been through every test in the book and passed with flying colours. Do you know what tests any new health product must pass before it ever gets near a hospital?' Fenton did not but he could guess.

'Saxon plastic is safe. It is non-toxic, non-poisonous, non-flammable. It is safe when you heat it, safe when you freeze it, and safe when you are stupid enough to want to eat it. Now I know that you have been under great strain but this kind of nonsense is dangerous. We have enough trouble in this hospital without a lawsuit from Saxon Medical. Understood?'

Fenton sat in his lab silently licking his wounds. Nothing Tyson had said had made him change his mind; he clung to his belief like a terrier gripping a rag. He would just have to prove it on his own.

Fenton's lonely war was waged on a battlefield of paper as he read and reread every scrap of information he could find on Saxon Medical and its new product. He examined all the graphs and tables from the original trials and re-plotted the data in what turned out to be a fruitless search for flaws. Quite simply, there were none, and he had to come to terms with this fact after a week of silent evenings during which Jenny had plied him with coffee and kept what politicians like to call a low profile. As he admitted defeat and put down his pen to rub his eyes on Friday evening, he heard the sound of an ambulance siren floating above the wind and rain. It made him wonder if its occupant was bound for the Princess Mary. As it happened, she was.

The week had been special for Rachel Morrison because Wednesday had been her eighth birthday, a day she had been looking forward to for weeks because her father had promised her a bicycle. It had been waiting at the foot of her bed when she had woken that morning, all red, white, and shiny chrome. Her happiness had been complete — or almost complete, for the weather had been so bad that she had been unable to take it outside to ride it, but it was there and she could touch it and that was the main thing.

After school several of her friends had come to the house for a special birthday tea and they had laughed and played and eaten ice cream and meringues until they were exhausted. Rachel ate so much that she got a pain in her stomach; at least that was what her mother said; but the pain had become worse as the evening progressed, until finally her tears had convinced her parents that the doctor should be called.

By the time the doctor arrived the pain had moved down

and to the right, so that he had no difficulty in diagnosing acute appendicitis, and summoned an ambulance. There was nothing to worry about; appendicectomy was probably the simplest and most routine operation in the book. The following day Rachel Morrison died in the Princess Mary following a massive haemorrhage.

The fact that Rachel Morrison and Jenny Buchan had never met and that Rachel had been admitted to the Princess Mary during Jenny's suspension ended that suspension and freed Jenny from suspicion. Although they had not discussed the fact, both Fenton and Jenny had been aware that the deaths appeared to have ceased after Jenny's suspension. Now they spoke openly about it. Jenny was prepared to construe the pause as an unfortunate quirk of fate, but Fenton read more into it.

It now seemed obvious to him that there would be a pause in the deaths, for a pause would be bound to occur when all the susceptible people had died leaving a stable immune population. No one else would die until a susceptible person appeared on the scene again; a new member of staff, perhaps or, much more likely in the case of a hospital, a new patient. He blamed himself for not having predicted this earlier.

Jenny put a stop to his self-recrimination by pointing out that it would not have made the slightest difference. But should he tell Tyson? Predictions made after the event, he decided, were about as useful as three-pound notes. He would say nothing. With Jenny in the clear he felt so much better and more able to concentrate, so much sharper. He would find the link.

Jenny looked up from the newspaper she had been buried in and said, 'Listen to this. Someone called James Lindsay, aged forty-three, committed suicide after being dismissed from Saxon Medical for alleged theft. He threw himself under a train.'

'Poor devil.'

'Where is Saxon Medical?'

'On one of those industrial estates in Glasgow.'

'That would fit, it's a Glasgow address.'

Fenton took the paper and read the story for himself. When he had finished he said, 'He wasn't an executive with *that* address.'

'You know it?'

'It's near where I was born.'

'Is that the mist of nostalgia I see in your eyes?'

'No it isn't. They should have pulled the place down years ago.'

'Then what were you thinking?' asked Jenny.

'I was thinking that I might go to see Mrs Lindsay.'

Jenny was aghast. 'Whatever for?'

'Anything to do with Saxon Medical, I'm interested.'

Fenton went to Glasgow the following Tuesday. The Honda ate up the forty-odd miles between the capital and Glasgow in as many minutes, and Fenton was soon weaving his expert way through the derelict buildings and cratered sites that defaced the east side of the city. When he found the street that he was looking for, he pulled the bike up on to its stand and walked towards the tenement block, pulling off his gloves.

There was garbage everywhere, fish-and-chip wrappers, potato-crisp bags, rotting fruit, and the inevitable red McEwan's Export beer can. He flicked this last aside with his toe, thinking that one should be included in any time capsule as a representative artefact of Scottish life. There seemed to be one lying on the bank of every river and on the top of every hill.

The entrance to the close was stained with dried vomit, the protest of a belly too full of beer being asked to accommodate take-away food as well. Fenton thought of his father and his nights 'on the bevvy'. As always when he thought of his father, he experienced feelings of guilt and regret, for he had never really known him at all nor understood what had gone on in his head.

On the face of it, Joe Fenton had been a simple, rather uncommunicative man who had spent all his adult life labouring in the shipyards of the Clyde. He would work Monday to Friday, drink himself into oblivion on Saturday and lie in bed all day Sunday. His routine had never varied.

Although this lifestyle was by no means untypical of the area, Tom Fenton had always believed that there was more to his father's behaviour than the blinkered following of macho tradition. There had been something missing in his father's make-up, something he had often tried to define in the past but always without success. He had never known his father display any kind of enthusiasm for anything in all the years he could remember. It was as if he had lived his entire life on a pilot flame fuelled with enigmatic sadness.

Even when drunk Joe Fenton's thoughts, if he had any, had been concealed behind a moist-eyed smile. The burning political issues of 'red Clydeside' had left him cold, as had the titanic struggles between Rangers and Celtic. It was as if he had discovered some deep, dark secret at some early stage in his life; some awful truth so terrible that it made no allowance for the parallax of optimism and forced him to view his existence as one long inconsequential tunnel from birth to grave.

Tom Fenton had never known what his father's secret had been; whether he had found out the meaning of life or discovered that there was no heaven or hell, or whether for him there was just no point. The last possibility seemed the most likely. Joe Fenton had lived his entire life as if there had been no point to it at all. He had died the year Fenton had graduated, never having said much more to him than an occasional 'Aye son' in passing, a 'Guid fur you' when he had done well or a 'We'll hae nae mair o' that' when he had done wrong.

To Fenton's mother Rose, a simple, kind-hearted woman, Joe had been a 'good man', but within the parameters of marital behaviour in the area this simply meant that he had not physically abused her and had handed over his wage packet unopened on a Friday night. Conversation and companionship would have been alien notions from another world.

For some reason not totally clear to him even now, Fenton hoped that his father had been proud of him when he had graduated, perhaps because he feared in his heart of hearts that it really hadn't mattered a damn; it probably hadn't rated a mention in the pub. It may even have been an embarrassment.

His mind came slowly back to the present as he edged deeper into the mouth of the close, assailed by the competing smells of fried onions and cats' urine. As his eyes adjusted to the gloom he saw the iron gate that barred the way to the passage leading to the drying greens and was forced to smile at the nostalgia it evoked. It had been down one of these dark passages that he had received a great deal of his street education.

Levoy had been a popular game among teenagers in the area, a variation on hide-and-seek that had involved a great deal of hiding in dark closes with members of the opposite sex and not too much seeking. One girl some two years older than himself, whose name he now tried to remember, had taken it upon herself to see that he had not been bored during the long dark vigils. He recalled with fondness his early sorties into her underwear, his discomfort at being unable to unhook her bra, his ecstasy as for the first time a female hand had unzipped his fly and ventured inside. He remembered his bewilderment at being stopped when he had moved his own hand under her skirt to explore a magical maze of underskirts and suspenders. 'Sorry,' she had said, 'the flags are up.' Failing to understand and construing this as obligatory feminine modesty, part of the etiquette of back-close loving, he had pressed on to find his hand taken in a vice-like grip. 'Are you bloody daft or somethin'?' the girl had hissed. The harsh admonishment had dampened his ardour to the point where his proud member had begun to wilt but then the girl, realizing his complete ignorance of menstrual matters, had launched into a kindly explanation as to why he could not go 'all the way'.

With both his confidence and his erection restored, he had rewarded her by having an orgasm all over her dress.

Fenton climbed the dark stone spiral stairs, stooping down as he came to each door to examine the nameplates. He was half-way along the landing of the second floor before he reached 'Lindsay'. He paused for a moment to listen to the sounds of the close; harsh laughter from female throats conditioned by cigarette smoke and endless bawling at errant children; the bawling itself as yet another woman screamed out her frustration and inadequacy at her offspring. He pulled the doorbell and found it disconnected, so replaced the handle and knocked instead. The door opened a few inches to reveal the haggard eyes of a woman about five feet tall and those of a child some three feet below. 'I've told you,' she began, 'I'll pay you when I can. I just haven't got it right now.'

Fenton assured her that he was not there to collect money. 'Then what?' she asked.

'I'd like to talk to you about your husband.'

'What about him?' asked the woman suspiciously.

'Nothing bad, I promise. I just want you to tell me about him. Can I come in?'

'You're another reporter.'

Fenton was about to deny it when he noticed that the woman seemed pleased at the prospect of his being a reporter, so he smiled instead and she opened the door.

They sat down to talk in a small, sparsely furnished kitchen/living-room which impressed Fenton with its tidiness and neatness. It seemed almost an act of defiance against an ever-encroaching desert of filth and squalor.

'My Jimmy never stole a thing in his life,' insisted the woman. 'Someone planted that drill in his locker.'

'Why would they do that, Mrs Lindsay?'

'Because they wanted him out, that's why.'

Fenton's throat tightened as he saw the possibility of a management intrigue against James Lindsay because he knew too much about something.

'Who are "they"?' he asked.

'The men he worked beside.'

Fenton's heart fell. 'Why did his workmates want him out, Mrs Lindsay?'

'They were jealous because he was such a good worker. Jimmy said that when the company expanded to make the new plastic they would probably make him a foreman and we could move away from here.' The woman looked around with disgust at her surroundings; her eyes settled on a damp patch on the wallpaper. 'We were going to buy a bungalow in Bearsden,' she said mistily, 'and Jimmy was going to buy a Sierra. He said he'd get me a Mini for the shopping and taking the weans to school . . .'

Fenton thought he recognized the type. Jimmy had been either a dreamer or a drunk. He continued to probe gently, for the woman badly wanted to believe that her husband had been innocent . . . but he had not been, and this became more and more apparent with every answer. A familiar tale unfolded. Drink, gambling, moneylenders charging enormous rates of interest, threats, fear, desperation, and, in James Lindsay's case, suicide.

The woman started to sob quietly, while the child, who had not let go of her skirt for an instant since he had come, continued to stare at him and pick his nose unconcernedly. Fenton supposed that he must have seen a lot of crying over the past week or so. He looked for some way of changing the subject and his eyes fell on a photograph of a man in uniform on the mantelpiece. 'Was that your husband, Mrs Lindsay?' he asked.

The woman nodded then, blowing her nose and tucking the handkerchief into her skirt, she added, 'He was an Argyll. He looked so lovely in his uniform . . .'

Fenton sensed that the tears were about to start again and stood up. 'He was a fine-looking man,' he said softly. 'And a daddy you can be proud of,' he added, bending down to press a five-pound note into the child's hand.

Fenton restrained himself from taking an almighty kick at the beer can lying in the entrance to the close and compromised by flicking it aside once more with his toe. As he did so he suddenly became aware of two men who had been pressed up against the doorway. He spun round in surprise.

'Is this the wan, Bella?' asked one of the men, half over his shoulder to the darkness of the close.

Bella emerged from the shadows, a shambling mass of flab in stained apron and carpet slippers. She scuffled towards Fenton and chewed gum while she examined him. 'Aye,' she announced, 'that's the bastard.'

The questioner, a full head shorter than Fenton but squat and powerful, with a scarred face and nose that changed direction more than once, looked at him with granite eyes. His companion, an emaciated figure suspended inside a dirty black suit several sizes too large, stood one pace behind. His skin, a sickly yellow colour, was stretched over his cheekbones like the wing fabric of a model aircraft. He puffed nervously on a cigarette, holding it between the bunched fingernails of his right hand while his eyes darted nervously from side to side.

'I hear you were botherin' Mary Lindsay, pal,' said granite eyes with quiet menace. Fenton felt fear climb his spine like a glacier on the move. The memory of his last encounter with violence filled his head and the thought of enduring so much pain again was too awful to contemplate. 'I've been to see Mrs Lindsay, yes,' he said in carefully measured tones, filtering his voice to remove any inflection that could possibly be construed as antagonistic.

'Oh hiv ye,' said granite eyes, moving towards him slowly. 'Do you hear that, Ally? He's been to see Mrs Lindsay, yes.'

He exaggerated a sing-song middle-class accent as he said it. The yellow-skinned corpse quickly withdrew his left hand from the drapes of his jacket pocket and flicked his wrist to reveal an open razor.

'What in Christ's name is this all about?' asked Fenton, his mouth dry with fear.

Granite eyes smiled with no trace of humour. 'When will you bastards ever learn?' he hissed through gritted teeth. 'You canny get blood frae a stone. Mary Lindsay hisnae got any money, pal, savvy? Nae money!' His finger stabbed at Fenton's chest as his voice rose. 'So why dae youse bastards keep comin' round here? Are ye tryin' tae kill her like ye did Jimmy?'

Fenton could sense that granite eyes was working himself up into a frenzy and bringing the yellow-skinned corpse with him. This was not going to be any kind of warning. He only had seconds left. The fat woman stood idly by, chewing her gum as if she were watching television. In a moment she would change channels.

'There's been some mistake,' said Fenton hoarsely.

'You made it, pal,' hissed granite eyes, moving on to the balls of his feet.

Fenton bunched his stomach muscles and prepared himself for what he now saw as inevitable. Granite eyes was the big problem. The other one had the razor, but granite eyes was the real hard man and it would take more than one blow to take him out. He dismissed the notion of kneeing him in the crotch; granite eyes would expect that, for amateurs always tried it. He would go for a punch to the throat. If it connected the man would go down. If Fenton could then get in quickly with a couple of kicks he might stay down long enough for him to deal with yellow skin. With granite eyes out of the way, Fenton knew that he could take him, razor or no razor; in fact the man looked so ill that one blow might splinter his consumptive frame as if he were a matchwood doll.

Fenton looked into his opponent's eyes and was gratified

to find a flicker of doubt there as if he had suddenly realized that Fenton might not be the complete amateur he had taken him for and that he was also big. Fenton knew what granite eyes was thinking and took comfort from it. Correct, he thought, I've been away a long time but I know the game too. You don't realize it, but I know you . . . I've known you all my life . . .

'Stop it! Stop it!' cried a woman's voice from above, but Fenton did not look up; neither did granite eyes. They held each other's gaze, both afraid to give away any advantage.

'Leave him alone, Scobie! And you too, Ally! He's not one of them, he's a reporter!'

Fenton gave thanks to any god that happened to be listening as he saw granite eyes turn and look up. He turned back again and said, 'Is that right, pal? A reporter, eh?' He said it as if nothing at all had gone before and they had just been introduced. His smile revealed rows of rotten teeth. 'Doin' a wee story on Jimmy, are you? Exposing these moneylendin' bastards? Good fur you.'

'I'm doing my best,' Fenton lied.

'Well, ma name's Scobie McGraw and this here's Ally Clegg — two g's by the way.' The yellow corpse grinned. 'If there's anythin' we can do tae help ye only hiv tae ask.'

I don't believe this, thought Fenton. They want their names in the paper. He smiled wanly and said, 'Thanks, I'll remember that.'

'Right then,' said granite eyes. 'Is that your bike ower there?'

Fenton said that it was.

'Well, ye better get oan it then!' Granite eyes broke into bronchitic laughter at his own joke and turned to yellow skin and the fat woman for support. Fenton smiled weakly and started to walk towards the Honda.

'Just a minute, pal!'

The words hit the back of Fenton's neck like bullets. He turned slowly.

'Whit paper did ye say ye worked fur?'

'The *Guardian*,' said Fenton, giving the first name that came into his head.

'Jesus.'

Fenton continued on his way feeling as if he were walking on thin ice with a thaw in the air. He heaved the bike off its stand and mounted it as casually as he could, then pressed the starter as if it were the ejector button in a burning aircraft. The Honda growled into life and the sound was like a Beethoven sonata. He was moving and the motion was beautiful. The wheels were spinning faster, faster, bearing him away.

EIGHT

To Fenton's annoyance Jenny found the story of what had happened in Glasgow funny. She rocked with laughter when he told her of the feeling in his gut when he had first seen the open razor. 'It serves you right for prying,' she said.

'It was no joke,' Fenton protested. 'These things can cut you to the bone before you even realize it and you end up carrying the scar for the rest of your life, assuming there is a rest to your life.'

'I'm sorry,' said Jenny, 'it was just the way you told it. You know I couldn't bear it if anything happened to you.'

They sat down and Fenton told Jenny of his conversation with the Lindsay woman.

'So you're no further forward?'

'I suppose not.' Fenton leaned back on the couch and Jenny snuggled up close to him to play with the hairs on his chest through a space between two shirt buttons.

'What did you hope to find out?' she asked.

Fenton sighed and said, 'I suppose . . . I hoped to discover that Lindsay hadn't committed suicide at all; that he'd discovered something awful about Saxon plastic and been murdered to keep his mouth shut.'

Jenny rolled her eyes. 'That was a bit strong.'

'It was also wrong.'

'Then he did commit suicide?'

'There's not much doubt about that. He was up to his

neck in debt to backstreet moneylenders – and not the kind who were content to send him rude letters.'

'Poor man.'

'I think he must have been stealing tools from the factory as a way out of his troubles but when he was caught his position became absolutely hopeless; no money, no job, no nothing.'

'How will his wife manage?'

'The way women do,' replied Fenton quietly.

Saxon Medical featured again in the newspapers the following day, this time in the financial section. It was not a part of the newspaper that Fenton normally looked at but the word 'Saxon' had caught his eye. He read that rumours of a take-over involving International Plastics were rife in the city and a deal, said to be worth millions and founded on Saxon having obtained a licence for their new plastic, was in the offing. The new material, it was predicted, would revolutionize equipment in science and medicine. Saxon Medical, a small, family-based concern, was deemed too small to exploit the enormous potential of the new discovery and was now up for grabs to the highest bidder.

'Have you seen Saxon since the Sunday you helped him with the Analyzer?' asked Jenny.

Fenton hadn't.

'Then he doesn't know you think there's something wrong with the plastic?'

'No. Tyson told me to keep my mouth shut about it. You don't walk up to a manufacturer and suggest that his product is a killer without the slightest shred of evidence. You could become very poor that way.'

'Or worse,' said Jenny thoughtfully as she considered Fenton's experience with the fume cupboard.

'Or worse,' Fenton agreed.

'Did you tell Tyson about the fume cupboard?'

'No.'

'Why not?'

'The engineers who came to reset the fire-damper found the retaining clips in the flue. They said they were in bad condition. They could have failed of their own accord and caused the damper to close.'

'But the cyanide in the drain?'

'We use cyanide in the lab quite a lot. I couldn't prove anything. It could have been coincidence.'

'But you don't believe it was?' asked Jenny.

'No.'

Jenny's sigh was full of frustration.

Fenton said, 'I'm going to take a good look at the people who've died so far. Perhaps they have something in common, something that would point to why they were susceptible and others were not. It would help if you could lay hands on the ward files on the dead children.'

'I'll try,' said Jenny. 'Have you considered talking to Inspector Jamieson again?' she asked, sounding braver than she felt.

'No I haven't,' snapped Fenton, 'and I don't intend to.'

Fenton found a message lying on his desk when he got into the lab. It was from the Blood Transfusion Service and said simply 'Phone Steven Kelly'. He did so and had to wait for what seemed an eternity while someone at the other end went to look for him. He was on the point of putting down the receiver when Kelly finally answered. 'It's about the blood that Neil Munro asked for. Can I take it that you don't need it any more?'

Fenton had forgotten all about the request that Munro had made. He apologized for his long silence, adding truthfully that he hadn't yet come across any explanation of why Neil had asked for it in the first place.

Kelly accepted Fenton's apology with his usual good humour and said, 'So I can take the donors off stand-by, then?'

Fenton was puzzled. 'I thought Neil ordered blood from the bank?'

'No, he needed fresh blood. We had to send out postcards to suitable donors.'

'Was this the first time Neil had asked for blood?' asked Fenton.

'The second,' said Kelly. 'We had to call in a donor a week or so before he died. The blood was taken off in your lab as I remember.'

Fenton had a vague recollection of having seen Munro in the lab with a stranger at around that time.

'It's just that we sent out postcards to three people warning them that they might be called at short notice. Two of them have phoned to ask if that's still the case.'

'You can tell them no,' said Fenton, trying to think at the same time as he talked. 'Are you absolutely sure that Neil never mentioned what he wanted the blood for?' he asked.

'Absolutely.'

Fenton had an idea. 'Do you think you could give me the name of the donor who gave blood the first time? It's just possible that Neil might have said what he was using it for, especially if the donor came here to the lab and he had to make conversation.'

'Hang on.'

Fenton put down the phone and read back what he had scribbled down on the pad. Miss Sandra Murray, Fairview, Braidbank Avenue, Edinburgh.

It was a quarter-past seven before Fenton had finished the day's blood-lead estimations. As a consequence he had to alter the original plan to go back to the flat before going to Braidbank Avenue. Instead he would have to shower at the lab, eat in the hospital restaurant and go straight from there. He called Jenny to say that he wouldn't be home before she left for the hospital. She assumed that he would be working late at the lab, and Fenton said nothing to disillusion her.

The shower head cleared its throat and spluttered into life. Fenton shivered outside its spray until the temperature had settled down. The controller was faulty, so the water was either too hot or too cold unless it was adjusted with micrometer accuracy. Fenton made do with a tepid shower rather than risk anything worse.

He soaped himself and tried to remember what the stranger he had seen with Neil Munro had looked like, the woman he now knew to be Sandra Murray.

He turned the water off and stepped out to towel himself down, pausing briefly to hear whether or not the rain had stopped outside. There was no sound coming from the dark skylight above the washroom. No rain would be an unexpected bonus, but the fact that the wind seemed to have dropped as well made it all seem too good to be true. It was. He stepped out of the lab into a thick fog.

The Honda's headlight beam bounced off the swirling mist, creating a corona that slowed him down to a crawl as he edged out on to the main road. He wiped his visor more out of frustration than necessity. Bloody weather, he grumbled inwardly, for Edinburgh's weather seemed part of a personal vendetta being waged against him. The fog was a gambit to prevent him finding Braidbank Avenue.

He knew vaguely that Braidbank would be part of a well-heeled, comfortable sprawl of leafy avenues that fringed the lower slopes of the Braid Hills in Edinburgh so he headed off in that direction, slowly at first because of the fog, but gathering speed as he climbed out of the city and the atmosphere cleared. He turned off Comiston Road and began to work his way through the quiet backstreets.

The contrast between the Braids area of Edinburgh and the Glasgow streets where he had found Mrs Lindsay could hardly have been more marked. Braidbank Avenue itself was absolutely silent and exuded an aura of solidity and order. Twin rows of Victorian mansions stood like rocks of the establishment amidst mature and cultivated greenery.

They stretched out like troops guarding a royal route for two hundred metres or more.

There would be no Scobie or Ally to worry about here, no ineffectual bawling and screaming. This was where life's winners lived; these were the homes of people who were successful, either by profession or birth, where chequebooks and pens stood in for fists and razors, where quiet telephone calls removed troublesome intruders without obliging the caller to do so much as put down his gin and tonic or lift his eyes from the pages of *Scottish Field*. It was an open-plan fortress with no walls or gates, its garrison set apart by accent and attitude.

Fairview boasted a black, wrought-iron gate that squealed on its hinges when Fenton pushed it open. He closed it slowly to avoid any further histrionics but the latch still fell with a loud metallic clang when he turned his back. His feet crunched on the gravel and he felt sure that everyone within a two-mile radius must be aware of his presence, but he saw nothing stir within the house. He pressed the polished brass bell-push; this had no audible effect, but he waited just in case something had happened deep inside the dark temple. He was about to try again when the area in which he stood was suddenly bathed in light and a series of rattles came from behind the front door.

'Yes?' The silhouette of a large ungainly man now filled the doorway.

'I wonder if I might have a few words with Miss Sandra Murray?' said Fenton.

There was a silence which probed the verges of embarrassment before the man said, 'Come in.'

Fenton had to wait in the hallway while the outer and inner doors were secured with double locks and chains. Then he followed his host into a subtly lit room and accepted an invitation to sit down.

Now that he could see him more clearly, Fenton saw that the man was even more ungainly than he had taken him to be. He was very large, well over six feet, with narrow, sloping shoulders that stooped over the fat of his middle. His general untidiness was accentuated by the fact that his double-breasted jacket had been buttoned on the wrong hole, and his squint tie bore distinct signs of egg. Hair jutted out from his head at odd angles, and he peered at Fenton through metal-framed glasses which were perched on his nose like a see-saw at rest.

'What did you want to see my sister about?' he enquired.

'I'd prefer to speak to Miss Murray personally if that's possible,' replied Fenton.

'You can't,' said Murray.

Fenton waited for an explanation but none was forthcoming. He got the impression that Murray was enjoying his discomfort. 'Is she indisposed?' he asked. The word had been forced on him by the sheer elegance and quality of the room and its furnishings. No one could be merely 'sick' in such a house; they would have to be indisposed.

'No,' said Murray. 'She's dead.'

Fenton was shaken. He had been expecting some trivial explanation like flu or an evening class – not death. He noticed that his host was observing his reaction like an owl. Murray appeared to have engineered the shock deliberately. Fenton's discomfort grew. 'I'm sorry,' he said, wondering whether or not he should inquire further.

In the event Murray took the initiative. 'She was knocked down by a car,' he said. 'The bastard didn't stop.'

'How awful,' said Fenton.

'Were you a friend of Sandra's?'

Fenton confessed that he had not known her at all. He responded to Murray's exaggerated frown by explaining the reason for his visit.

'Another one!' exclaimed Murray, fixing Fenton with an unwavering stare.

Murray was making Fenton feel distinctly uncomfortable, but the significance of what he had just said superseded everything else. 'Another one? I don't understand.'

'You're the second person to come here from the Blood

Transfusion Service,' said Murray. 'Don't you people ever talk to each other?'

Fenton was annoyed. Why had Steve Kelly not told him that he intended visiting Murray himself? He apologized for the intrusion, explaining that he himself had no direct connection with the Transfusion Service but was a biochemist from the lab where his sister had kindly donated blood to help with a research project.

'Ah yes, with Dr Munro. Sandra told me about it.'

Fenton felt a sudden excitement creep over him. 'What did she tell you, Mr Murray?'

Murray's fingers scratched at his unruly hair and he screwed up his eyes as he tried to recall what his sister had told him. 'Something about a new plastic, I think. Dr Munro wanted to do some tests.'

Fenton had to make a conscious effort to control his excitement. 'Did she happen to say what kind of tests?'

'I'm sure she did, but it wouldn't have meant much to me. Sandra was the scientist in this family. I'm an artist. Science is a complete mystery to me.'

'I understand,' said Fenton, swallowing his frustration and trying to keep calm. 'But is there nothing you can remember?'

Murray lapsed into a dramatic trance. Fenton, outwardly calm, felt as if his head were full of broken glass. The seconds ticked by.

Murray eventually looked at Fenton out of the corner of one eye and let out an enormous sigh. 'I'm afraid not,' he said. 'But I do remember he wasn't happy with the stuff.'

Fenton hid his disappointment. 'No matter. Don't worry about it.'

He had fallen at the last hurdle but at least he now knew he was on the right track. He said, 'I mustn't take up any more of your time, Mr Murray, particularly as my colleague has already bothered you.'

'He didn't bother me,' replied Murray. 'He spoke to my sister.'

Fenton was confused. 'I thought he'd been here today.'

'No, this was three weeks ago.'

Fenton realized he had been jumping to conclusions. He had assumed that Steve Kelly had called to see Murray after their telephone conversation. But Kelly could not have been the caller three weeks ago or he would have said so. Someone else from the Blood Transfusion Service must have visited the house, but why? 'Was something wrong?' he asked.

'I don't think so,' said Murray, scratching his head again and looking more puzzled than ever. 'As far as I can remember the gentleman wanted to know the same sort of things as you . . .'

Fenton noticed the hint of an accusation in Murray's voice and set up a defensive screen. He said, 'I'm afraid things have been in a bit of a muddle since Dr Munro's death.' He apologized to Murray again for bothering him and got up to leave.

'May I offer you a drink before you go?'

Fenton declined politely; he had to drive, and if the fog was still around he would need all his wits about him. As the front door opened he saw that it was worse than ever.

Fenton opted for a bath as the quickest way of getting warm after being chilled to the marrow on the painfully slow journey home. He lay back and sipped whisky from a glass that he had placed on the soap shelf. There was a lot to think about before morning. For a start, why had Blood Transfusion run a check on a donor? Was this normal practice or had they some particular reason in the case of Sandra Murray? And why had Steve Kelly not told him? Surely he must have known? But this question paled into insignificance when he considered what he had learned from Murray about Neil Munro's interest in the plastic.

In finding out that Neil had suspected there was something wrong with it, he had not only uncovered the reason for Neil's preoccupation during the weeks leading up to his death but also found a possible motive for his murder. Someone had wanted to stop him looking too carefully into Saxon plastic; someone who must have known that he was beginning to have doubts about it, someone who had been close to Neil at the time and, of course, someone who had something to gain by covering up any discoveries.

There was only one candidate. The bloated face of Nigel Saxon swam into the steamy air of the bathroom. That would also confirm his suspicions over the incident with the fume cupboard. Saxon must have feared that he too would eventually discover whatever Neil had found out about the plastic. Saxon must have set him up with the acid and cyanide trap and then made an excuse to leave the room. True, he had dissembled well on his return, but that just served to show the devious cunning of the man.

'The bastard,' whispered Fenton as more began to make sense. Saxon and Neil had been working closely together over the new Blood Analyzer. If Neil had said anything to anyone about his fears it would probably have been to Saxon. Perhaps they had agreed to keep it between themselves if Neil had not been sure what the problem was. But when Neil had become certain, Saxon had killed him to keep it quiet. Millions, the newspaper had said; Saxon Medical was worth millions with a licence for the plastic.

Fenton's grip on his glass tightened as he came to terms with reality. He could not prove it. He still did not know what was wrong with the plastic and, when viewed coldly, the only additional evidence he had obtained lay in the word of an eccentric up in Braidbank who had told him that a dead man had told his sister, also dead, that he thought there was something wrong with it. Jamieson would just love that.

Perhaps he could get some kind of corroboration from the Blood Transfusion Service, thought Fenton. If he could speak to the person who had visited Sandra Murray, he could get a first-hand account of what she had said, and that might be good enough to convince Jamieson.

The bathroom had grown too full of maybes. The water was cold and his glass was empty. Fenton dried himself and rectified the situation of the glass. The flat still seemed cold.

Jenny got home just before eight in the morning and stifled a big yawn with the back of her hand, still holding her keys. 'Now I know what a whore feels like in the morning,' she sighed. 'What a night.'

Fenton listened patiently while she told him all that had happened during a busy shift. When she had finished he said, 'I went out somewhere last night.'

'Really? Where?'

Fenton put a cup of coffee in front of her and told her of his visit to Murray and what he had learned. Jenny looked shocked. Fenton had to prompt her. 'Don't you see? Neil thought there was something wrong with Saxon plastic too!'

'But what?' asked Jenny.

Fenton admitted that he still didn't know but pointed out that just to have his suspicions confirmed by what Neil had believed was a step forward. 'And it provides a motive for his murder,' he added. 'This is what connects Neil's death to the others.'

'Saxon!'

'Saxon,' Fenton agreed. 'He was working closely with Neil and he had everything to gain from the plastic getting a licence. It had to be him.'

Jenny could find no real reason to argue. 'If you're right this is absolutely incredible,' she said, 'but you could still be wrong.'

'I know, I know.' Fenton got up to refill their coffee cups.

'Why did Neil use this Sandra Murray as a donor?'

'I don't know,' confessed Fenton.

'You people generally use each other when you want volunteers, don't you?'

'I suppose he wanted a different blood group,' said Fenton almost automatically, then both he and Jenny saw the importance of what he had said at the same time. 'Could that be it?' he wondered. 'Different blood groups? People in one group are susceptible while others aren't?'

Jenny broke the spell of the moment by beginning to rummage through the black leather bag that rested on her knees. She pulled out a cardboard folder and handed it to Fenton, saying, 'These are the details you asked me to get on the child victims. I only managed to get the one; this is the ward file on the Watson boy.'

Fenton flicked open the cover and traced his finger down the page till he found what he was looking for: 'AB'. So the boy had been blood group AB, which was quite rare. If Sandra Murray had been in the same group, he was in business.

Fenton nearly bowled Ian Ferguson over as he came into the lab and rushed up the stairs, speeding himself up with strong pulls on the bannister. The young biochemist half turned to receive an apology but was disappointed; Fenton pressed on regardless and shut his lab door behind him.

With his white coat only half on, Fenton dialled the Blood Transfusion Service and asked to speak to Steve Kelly. Kelly answered while Fenton was still holding the receiver between shoulder and cheek in order to get his left arm into the coat.

'Good morning. How did you get on?'

'Just tell me one thing. What group was Sandra Murray?'

'Is that my starter for ten?'

'It's important.'

'All right, hang on.'

Fenton drummed his fingers on the desk while he waited impatiently for Kelly to return.

'She was B positive.'

Fenton swore.

'Are you always this sweet in the morning?' Kelly asked.

Fenton apologized, and explained that a pet theory had just died.

'Want to tell me?'

'Some other time. You didn't tell me that someone from BTS had interviewed Sandra Murray.'

'What are you talking about?'

Fenton repeated what Murray had told him.

'No way,' said Kelly.

'I don't understand.'

'He must have been mistaken,' Kelly went on. 'No one from this department would have gone there because we have no interest in what the blood is used for. As far as we were concerned we had received a request from Biochemistry for fresh group B blood. We did the paperwork and complied with the request. That was the end of it.'

Fenton's spirits hit the floor. He started to say something but felt too dejected to go on. He managed to summon up enough energy to thank Kelly for his help, then put the phone down.

It had started to rain again. Fenton idly tapped his pencil end over end as he gazed at the drops on the window and faced up to the latest question. If no one from Blood Transfusion had gone to see Sandra Murray, then who had? After a moment's thought Fenton found the obvious answer. Neil Munro's killer. The killer must have gone there to find out how much Sandra Murray knew, and when it had turned out to be too much he had arranged for her death as well. The hit-and-run accident hadn't been an accident at all.

Almost afraid to face up to this latest possibility, Fenton played with the information in his head. It was a piece in a puzzle; he turned it round and round and tried to make it fit. A mistake! The killer had made a mistake. For Murray might have seen the man who had visited his sister pretending to be from Blood Transfusion, and if that were so, he could identify the killer. What was more, if Murray described Nigel Saxon then he would have enough to take to the police. They could nail Saxon without actually knowing what was wrong with the plastic.

Jenny telephoned at eleven saying that she couldn't sleep; she had to know about the blood group theory.

'Wrong again,' confessed Fenton. 'Sandra Murray was group B, not AB.'

Jenny made disappointed noises. 'It might still be worth checking further,' she said.

'Maybe,' Fenton agreed without any real conviction, 'but there's something else.'

'Oh yes?'

'I think that Sandra Murray was murdered. I think that Neil told her something was wrong with Saxon plastic and the killer found out. Her death wasn't accidental at all. She was murdered just like Neil.'

There was a short silence before Jenny said quietly, 'Tonight, Tom, tell me tonight,' then she put the phone down.

Fenton was irked by Jenny's failure to share his excitement but he tried to rationalize it. She'd been working all night and hadn't had any sleep, and she had a point. He wasn't short of ideas; the trouble was that none of them turned out to be right.

Ian Ferguson came into the room while Fenton was still deep in thought. Thanks to that and the fact that the rain was hammering on the window, Fenton did not hear him come in and was startled when he spoke. Ferguson apologized and said, 'Is everything all right? The way you rushed past me on the stairs I thought maybe something dreadful had happened.'

'Just the death of another theory.'

'Want to tell me?'

'There's not much to tell. I thought I'd discovered a fatal

flaw in Saxon plastic, something to do with patients' blood groups, but apparently I was wrong.'

'What made you suspect that?' asked Ferguson.

'A number of things. Neil Munro thought there was something wrong with the stuff too.'

'But this is serious. Have you spoke to Dr Tyson about it?'

'He assured me there was nothing wrong with the plastic.'

'How about Saxon themselves?'

'I have no evidence to back up my suspicions. I can't say anything.'

'I see,' said Ferguson. 'But surely there's something you can do if you think there's a problem?'

'I have to find out what's wrong with the stuff before I can do anything.'

'Is there anything I can do to help?'

Fenton thanked him and said he would let him know. He asked him not to say anything to anyone else for the time being.

When Ian Ferguson had gone Fenton considered his own reluctance to confide in anyone. The truth was that he did need help, for he was getting hopelessly out of his depth. The question was, who should he talk to? Who could he trust? He had been tempted to tell Ian Ferguson everything, but the fact that Ferguson had considered resigning from the lab when the going got tough had prevented him from doing so. He needed an ally without a question mark over his character. The matter resolved itself at lunch time when Steve Kelly came into the lab and plonked himself heavily down. 'Do you fancy a beer?'

Fenton sipped his beer, aware that Kelly was appraising him but unable to relax and talk freely.

'You're a man with a problem,' said Kelly.

'What do you mean?'

'I mean that you're so uptight about something that you're going to explode if you go on bottling it up. I thought you might want to talk about it.'

'I don't know what you . . .'

'All right, forget I spoke.' Kelly turned to concentrate on his beer.

Fenton considered his own obstinacy in the silence that ensued. Steve Kelly was as good as they came: solid, blunt, unpretentious. He had a bit of a weakness for the women, but in hard times a man could do a lot worse than have Kelly on his side. 'All right,' he confessed, 'there is something.'

They sat down to talk in one of the alcoves; the pub was still quiet before the lunch-time rush. Fenton told Kelly the whole story, and as he did so the first sunlight for many weeks, albeit weak and watery, rainbowed through the frosted glass and played among the dimples on the beaten-copper tabletops.

'And there you have it,' Fenton concluded, taking a sip of his beer while Kelly digested the facts.

'That is some story,' Kelly said at last, shaking his head. 'I didn't bargain on anything like this. To be frank I thought that you and Jenny might not be hitting it off or some such thing, but this . . . Jesus.'

'Now you know.'

'When are you going back to see Murray?'

'Tonight.'

'Want some company?'

Fenton found that he did.

NINE

The intermittent screen-wipe on Kelly's Ford Capri flicked away the drizzle like a cow's tail dealing with summer flies.

'I hope you gentlemen have a productive evening,' said Jenny as she got out of the car at the hospital gates.

'We'll try,' Kelly said.

'Good night, Jenny,' said Fenton softly, answering the look that was meant for him.

'Take care.'

The Ford turned off the main road and Fenton gave Kelly directions as he nosed it along the wet side-streets.

'You don't live up here if you work for the Health Service,' said Kelly, noting the size of the houses.

The headlights caught an elegant lady swathed in furs, out walking her dog.

'I suppose it just had to be a poodle,' commented Fenton as they passed.

'Very nice too,' murmured Kelly, who wasn't referring to the dog.

'Forget it,' said Fenton. 'You couldn't keep her in dog food. Take the next on the left.'

Kelly turned slowly into Braidbank Avenue and Fenton directed him to Fairview. He turned off the engine and restored satin silence to the night.

'How do we play it?' he asked.

'By ear,' said Fenton. 'Let's go.'

Kelly pushed open the gate. Fenton anticipated its squeal.

They rang the apparently silent doorbell and Murray appeared in the doorway. 'Yes?'

'It's me again, Mr Murray, Tom Fenton. I was here last night.'

'Yes?' repeated Murray.

'I wonder if we might have another word with you?'

Murray's face was contorted as he strained to see Kelly in the shadows. Fenton introduced them and Kelly held out his hand. Murray ignored it and turned round. 'Come,' he said and led the way inside.

Kelly shot Fenton a glance as they followed Murray indoors but Fenton pretended not to notice. Murray sat down in the chair he had been sitting in before, judging by the book and the half-empty glass beside it, and gestured to the two men to sit opposite as if they were candidates for interview.

Fenton noticed that the double-breasted jacket had been replaced by a more casual Fair Isle pullover whose already intricate pattern had been augmented with dried tomato seeds, custard, the ubiquitous egg, and some green stuff that defied visual analysis. Murray seemed to be in a constant state of agitation, searching through his pockets without ever seeming to find what he was looking for.

Fenton waited for a few moments, then coughed to attract Murray's attention. The pocket-searching stopped and Murray stared at Fenton without blinking until the latter spoke.

'We're puzzled about the man who came to see your sister, Mr Murray. Are you absolutely certain he said he was from the Blood Transfusion Service?'

'Yes,' said Murray without hesitation.

'Then you saw him?' asked Fenton.

'Yes.'

'Can you describe him?'

Murray produced one of his dramatic pauses before saying, 'Why?'

'I know this is going to sound strange, but the BTS says that no one from there called to see your sister.'

Another long pause; then Murray decided that the easiest course of action was to answer the question. 'He was of medium height and build, slim, fair, and somewhere in his middle twenties.'

Fenton felt once more a crushing sense of disappointment, for there was no way that Nigel Saxon could be described in these terms, not even by a loving mother. With unerring accuracy the slings and arrows of his particularly outrageous fortune had homed in on him again.

Fenton let Kelly continue the conversation with Murray while he wondered how to fit this latest piece of information into the puzzle, then he became aware that Kelly was asking about the fair-haired man. 'Is there anything more you can tell us about him, Mr Murray?'

'His tiepin.'

'What about it?'

'It was in the form of a small acorn.'

'And?'

Kelly said, 'And from little acorns great oak trees grow.'

'Precisely.'

'The Cavalier Club,' said Fenton.

'This may all be pure conjecture, of course,' said Murray, 'but worth bearing in mind.'

Fenton could not have agreed more.

Murray got up from his chair and crossed the room to a silver drinks tray. Without asking he poured out three whiskies from a crystal decanter and handed them round. He sat down again with slow deliberation, adjusted the glasses on his nose and said, 'Now you will tell me what this is all about.' It was not a request, it was a directive.

Fenton could see that the eyes behind the glasses had become cold and hard; the first indication of the inner man, he thought. It came as no great surprise, for he had already deduced that there must be more to Murray than the

151

bumbling eccentric he had seen so far. You didn't end up living in Braidbank by being a complete clown.

Kelly's look suggested that Fenton should answer, so he did, saying that they themselves were not at all sure what was going on but it did seem likely that the man who had come to see his sister was in some way mixed up in the deaths at the Princess Mary Hospital.

Murray looked at him like an owl contemplating its dinner. He asked slowly and quietly, 'Are you suggesting that my sister's death might not have been an accident?'

Fenton moved uncomfortably in his seat. 'It's possible.'

'Do the police know of this?'

'All we have at the moment are suspicions,' replied Fenton. 'The minute we have anything more we'll inform the police immediately.'

'You mean you haven't told them,' said Murray.

'Not yet.'

'Murder is not a game for amateurs, Mr Fenton.'

'We realize that, but in this case I think the professionals need all the help they can get.'

Murray conceded the point with a slight nod of the head. He said, 'I want to be kept informed of any progress you make, particularly if it concerns my sister.'

'Of course.'

'Spooky bloke,' said Kelly as they walked down the path to the gate.

'Spooky is the word,' agreed Fenton. He was glad to be out of the place. 'Tell me about the Cavalier Club,' he said. 'Or are you a member too?'

'I wasn't even a Boy Scout,' said Kelly, looking over his shoulder and pulling away from the kerb. 'I don't know that much myself, but what I do know I don't like.' He took the Capri up through the gears. 'As I understand it, it started out as a club for homosexuals in the city.'

'There's nothing unusual in that,' said Fenton.

'But this one grew into something else, something much bigger.'

'What do you mean?'

Kelly slowed down for some traffic-lights. 'It's difficult to define, but in every society there's a group of people who consider themselves above society in every way. I don't mean just in the legal sense; I mean in terms of morality and social convention.'

'You mean like the Marquis de Sade or the Hellfire Club?'

'That sort of thing.'

'In Edinburgh? Are you serious?'

'I'm afraid I am,' said Kelly with a seriousness that Fenton found uncharacteristic.

'So they're a group of weirdos. It's a sign of the times.'

'No, there's more to it than that,' said Kelly. 'This lot have power.'

The traffic-lights changed and Kelly moved off.

'How can they have power?' asked a disbelieving Fenton.

'The size and status of their membership decides that.'

'So there are a lot of kinky people around; that doesn't make them powerful.'

'Depends on who and what they are.'

Fenton was still reluctant to believe what Kelly was suggesting. 'All right, so you find the occasional judge who likes spanking schoolgirls' bottoms. That makes him vulnerable, not powerful.'

'Only while he remains one of a tiny minority. As soon as you get a lot of judges with the same taste, it gets uncomfortable for the schoolgirls.'

'You're serious about this, aren't you?'

Kelly stopped at another set of lights. He turned to Fenton and said, 'Let me tell you a story. When the club first started some local yobs thought they would go in for a spot of persecution but they miscalculated. The Cavaliers were experts in pain and violence, and the yobs came second – a poor second as it happens. One of them finished up in a mental home and hasn't come out. The others were too afraid to say what had happened to them, so no charges were ever brought.'

'Jesus.'

'He is definitely not a member.'

They drew to a halt outside Fenton's flat. 'What now?' said Kelly.

'A drink,' replied Fenton, avoiding the real question.

'A drink' became several and Kelly's wife phoned to ask if he was there. Fenton said he was and asked if she wanted to speak to him. 'No, no,' said Mary Kelly. 'As long as he's there with you, Tom,' she added, making her meaning plain.

Fenton came in somewhat unsteadily from the hall. 'That was Mary checking that you weren't screwing some nurse,' he said, diplomacy having been all but obliterated by the whisky.

'She has a point,' admitted Kelly.

'Damn right,' said Fenton, refilling their glasses.

'Hell, Tom, it's hard with all that pussy around.'

'The trouble with you, old son,' said Fenton, leaning forward in his seat, 'is that it's hard all the time.' Alcohol made the joke seem hilarious.

'Is Steve still here?' Jenny asked, when she got back in the morning. 'I saw his car outside.'

'No, he walked home last night,' replied Fenton sheepishly.

'I see.'

Fenton pretended that he didn't have a hangover and Jenny pretended she didn't know that he had. She made coffee while Fenton told her of the latest visit to Murray.

'But if it wasn't Nigel Saxon, who could it have been?' Jenny asked.

Fenton shrugged his shoulders and admitted that he had no idea, but he told Jenny of the tiepin that Murray had noticed.

'So there still might be a connection with Saxon.'

'Through this damned club. It's strange. Saxon doesn't seem to fit in, somehow.'

'I disagree,' said Jenny. 'I know all about the beer-drinking, rugby-playing, macho image he tries to create but that's the trouble: he tries too hard. Women get a feeling about these things. But this isn't helping; it wasn't Saxon who went to the Murrays' house.'

'True,' said Fenton, still trying to absorb this new impression of Saxon, 'but maybe he sent a friend.'

Jenny opened her mouth to ask something but Fenton stopped her. He said, 'Don't ask me what I'm going to do next. I don't know.' He kissed her lightly on the cheek. 'Have a good sleep.'

By eleven o'clock Fenton could see that the day was shaping up to be a bad one. Mary Tyler had gone off sick and in addition to the routine work that was coming in and the lead estimations, the hospital surgeons were performing a heart bypass operation and required constant biochemical monitoring of their patient. Fenton, being the senior member of staff on duty, carried responsibility for this.

When Fenton had been working for six hours without a break, Ian Ferguson came into his lab and offered to take over for thirty minutes.

'But you're busy too,' said Fenton.

'Just routine stuff. I'll stay behind this evening and clear it up.'

Fenton was grateful. He went to eat in the hospital canteen and was back within twenty minutes. 'I'm obliged to you, Ian,' he said to Ferguson.

'Think nothing of it.' As Ferguson got up to go he added, 'I meant to ask you yesterday. Did you ever find out what Neil Munro wanted the blood for?'

'Not yet but I'm getting warm.'

'Really?'

'He needed the blood for some kind of test connected with Saxon plastic.'

'If Neil was carrying out secret blood tests maybe that's what he needed the anticoagulants for,' suggested Ferguson.

'More than likely.'

'Do you think this is why Neil was murdered?'

'Yes.'

'I really think you should tell the police.'

'Not just yet,' said Fenton. 'I need a bit more proof.'

As she waited for her bus, Jenny huddled in the doorway of a small shop that had closed for the night. The angle of the doorway was such that she had to keep peering out to make sure that she would see the bus coming, but each time she did so the full force of the wind and rain assaulted her. She avoided the brunt of it by burying her chin between hunched shoulders and narrowing her eyes till they were little more than slits. She counted and recounted the change in her pocket as the time she normally had to wait expired and seeds of impatience germinated in the icy rain.

The comforting hulk of a double-decker bus loomed up out of the rain, spewing light and throwing up spray. Jenny held out her arm then stepped back smartly to avoid being splashed by the wheels as they approached the overflowing gutter. The driver noticed her uniform and said, 'Once again, eh?'

'I'm afraid so,' replied Jenny.

'What hospital are you at?'

'Princess Mary.'

'Rather you than me.'

Jenny took her ticket and moved to the back of the bus, thinking over what the driver had said. It annoyed her. The Princess Mary was a good hospital, one of the best in the world despite its antiquated equipment and lack of money, but to the public now it was the hospital that harboured the killer, a place to be feared. True, he had been less active lately, but then again the police had never caught him, had they?

As she looked out of the window, trying to see through the reflections, she pondered on Fenton's explanation for the deaths and realized how much faith she had been putting in it. Tom was surely right, wasn't he? There couldn't really be a psychopath stalking the hospital corridors?

The bus deposited Jenny on the 'quayside' outside the hospital and set up a bow wave as it pushed off from the kerb. Her attempts to tiptoe through the dark puddles were soon abandoned as pointless, and she squelched up the driveway with shoes awash. Her entry to the nurses' changing room brought squeals of laughter as she stood framed in the doorway, hair plastered to her face, creating her own small but ambitious lake.

Once she had dried out and her circulation had been restored to something resembling normal, Jenny walked along the main corridor to her ward. Outside, the rain lashed and battered against the tall windows which were now full of night-time reflections, and Jenny began to hum 'For Those in Peril on the Sea'.

'Good evening, Nurse Buchan,' said a tall, rather severe-looking woman as she entered the duty room.

'Good evening, Sister.'

'Twenty-three, including three new ones,' said the day sister, handing Jenny the patient list. 'You might keep an eye on them.'

'Of course,' replied Jenny, taking the list and scanning the names. She picked out the new ones; two were new admissions and one was a transfer from surgery. She flicked over the page for details of the transfer and read, 'Callum Moir, investigation of severe stomach pain, exploratory laparotomy, pyloric obstruction found and repaired.'

'He's asleep,' said the day sister.

'And the new ones?' asked Jenny.

'One is asleep but the other has first-night nerves; you know the form.'

Jenny nodded and signed the take-over form.

'Goodnight, Nurse.'

'Goodnight, Sister.'

Jenny began her rounds as the sister left, acknowledging the presence of the junior night nurse at the far end of the ward with a wave of her hand. Many of the children were already sleeping but she paused here and there to tuck in the occasional arm or leg freed by its restless owner.

She came to a pair of frightened eyes peering up at her from the mouth of their blanket cave. Jenny recognized the symptoms of first-night nerves; one sympathetic word from her and these full eyes would overflow. 'Ah, good, you're awake,' she began. 'I could do with some help. Would you mind?'

Surprise replaced fear on the child's face, for this was unexpected. Reassurance had been the odds-on favourite; he thought he might receive encouragement or even a gentle chiding, but a request for help? The surprised look still had not faded as his feet, now slippered, hit the floor.

'Good, now follow me.'

The slippers padded along behind Jenny until she stopped and pointed to the clipboard hanging at the foot of a bed. She said, 'I want you to read off these names to me as we come to them. All right?'

A nod.

'Well then?'

'An-gus Cam-er-on.'

'Check,' said Jenny officiously and moved on. Three more names and all thoughts of home and family had left the boy; he warmed to his new role as assistant to Night Nurse Buchan. Eventually he climbed sleepily back into bed.

The child recovering from surgery was sleeping peacefully in a side ward. Jenny placed her hand gently against his forehead and felt it to be quite normal. She checked the boy's notes; no medication was indicated and there were no special instructions. All that was needed was a good night's sleep. She tiptoed out of the room and closed the door behind her, a trifle more noisily than she had intended. She looked back through the glass panel. The boy had not stirred.

Midnight came and Jenny began to feel optimistic about the chances of a quiet night. She even said so to the junior nurse as they sipped illicit coffee in the duty room while the rain outside contined to pour.

'Brrr, I'm glad I'm not out in that,' said the girl, trying to draw the curtains even closer together to eliminate a persistent gap in the middle.

'Pity the poor sailors,' said Jenny.

'That's what my mother used to say.'

'Mine too.'

'Do you think he's out there?'

'Who?'

'The killer, of course.'

'Let's not talk about that.'

'Oh, I'm sorry, I forgot, I mean, I didn't . . .'

'Forget it.'

At one o'clock the phone rang. 'I thought it was too good to last,' said the junior nurse.

'Ward Ten, Nurse Buchan speaking . . . Yes . . . Yes . . . Understood.' Jenny put down the receiver and said, 'Admission in ten minutes, seven-year-old girl, burns to both legs, hot-water bottle burst.'

'Poor mite.'

'Prepare number three, will you?' said Jenny. 'I'll get the trays ready.'

On her way to get sterile dressings Jenny paused in the corridor to look through the glass panel at the surgical case. He was still sleeping peacefully, right arm outside the covers, fingers hooked over the side of the bed.

A distant siren gave early warning of the new patient's arrival, and the duty house officer came to the ward shortly afterwards. She had heard the ambulance from her room in the doctors' residency. 'Sounds like a bad one,' she said.

'Burns are always bad,' Jenny replied.

The junior held open the ward door to allow the trolley

to enter with its entourage of ambulance men, parents and policeman. Jenny signalled to the junior with her eyes and the girl ushered the parents away from the procession and into a side room where they would be plied with tea and sympathy.

Jenny stood by as the temporary dry dressings were removed from the child's legs to reveal a mass of livid raw flesh.

'Her mother used boiling water in the bottle,' said one of the ambulance men quietly.

'She's going to need extensive grafting,' said the house officer. 'We'll transfer her when she's stable, but in the mean time she's going to be in a lot of pain when she comes out of shock. I'll write her up for something.' She looked at Jenny and added, 'She'll need specialling as well.'

An hour later calm had returned to the ward. The girl had been sedated and installed in a side room under the care of an extra nurse who had been sent up to sit with her, the policeman had completed his note-book entry on the treble-nine call, and the ambulance men had returned to their stand-by quarters. The parents, stricken with remorse, had gone off to spend what was left of the night at home.

At 3 A.M. Jenny walked round the ward again, gliding quietly between the cots and beds in the soft dimness of the night-lights. All was quiet. She opened the door of the side ward to check on the surgery boy and found him still asleep, lying in the same position as before. As she closed the door it suddenly struck her as strange that he hadn't moved at all. He was sleeping, not unconscious, and everyone moves when they sleep.

Jenny had a sense of foreboding as she went back in again and approached the boy to put her hand on his forehead. He was cold, icy cold. There was a sound at her feet as if the contents of a glass were being spilled, but she knew that that could not be. She looked down to see a stream of blood pour from beneath the blankets and spatter over her shoes.

She felt faint but slowly pulled back the top covers to reveal a sea of scarlet.

Jenny buried her face in Fenton's shoulder and tried to find comfort in his arms. 'It was awful,' she murmured. 'He just bled to death in his sleep. If only I'd looked in sooner . . .'

'Don't blame yourself,' whispered Fenton. 'There was nothing you could have done.'

'You said it would be another patient,' said Jenny.

Fenton nodded.

'There's something else,' said Jenny. 'The boy had group AB blood like the Watson boy.'

Fenton held Jenny away from him in disbelief. 'But that's just too much of a coincidence,' he said. 'AB is a rare group.'

'Did you check up on the others?'

Fenton shook his head slowly and confessed that he had not. 'I thought when Sandra Murray turned out to have group B blood that we were on the wrong track.' He paused as a sudden thought struck him. 'But if all this *is* to do with blood groups, that's what Neil Munro's book is all about.'

Fenton felt excitement mount inside him as the letters and numbers in Munro's book began to make sense. CT did not stand for Charles Tyson, it stood for 'clotting time'. The figures in the columns were the times that samples of fresh blood took to clot in the presence of Saxon plastic. If he read the figure zero as the letter 'O' he found figures against it which tallied with the normal clotting time for human blood. The separate columns were simply repeat tests on the same samples of group O blood. Fenton found a similar set of entries against the letter 'A' and concluded, as Munro must have done, that there was no problem with either group A or group O blood, which would cover the majority of the population.

There was only one entry against the letter 'B', to which the initials SM had been added. Neil had clearly used Sandra

Murray's blood to test the behaviour of group B blood in the presence of Saxon plastic. He could have obtained blood of groups O and A from people in the lab, but for group B he had had to ask the Blood Transfusion Service. The figures for Sandra Murray's blood, although slightly on the high side, were within the normal clotting-time range. Underneath, Neil had written three dots followed by the letters 'AB'.

Munro had decided that the plastic affected people with group AB blood, which meant something in the order of three per cent of the population. That was why he had requested another donor from the Blood Transfusion Service; he had wanted to verify his conclusion.

Fenton picked up the phone and called Steve Kelly to get details of Munro's last request. Kelly told him what he was now already sure of: Munro had asked for a supply of group AB blood.

Fenton had interpreted everything in Munro's book except the numbers on the first page. As a last resort he considered that they might conceivably refer to a routine lab specimen number. He went downstairs to the office to check through the files and found that there was indeed a blood sample bearing the five-figure number in Munro's book. It had come from a patient named Moran and appeared to have been quite normal for all the tests requested.

Failing to see the significance of a normal blood analysis Fenton returned upstairs. He stopped when he got to the first landing as the name Moran rang a bell. It was the name of the patient whose sample had been a failure on the Saxon Analyzer during the trials. The failure had been put down to the fact that the specimen had arrived in the wrong sort of container, but when it had been checked on the routine analyzer it had given perfectly normal readings. It had been Saxon plastic at fault, not the specimen, and Neil Munro must have realized it. That was what had started his investigation off in the first place . . .

Fenton checked with Medical Records and ascertained

that the patient Moran had had group AB blood. More checking revealed that Susan Daniels had also had AB blood. A call to the records department at the Eye Pavilion told him that Jamie Buchan had belonged to group AB as well.

The conclusion was perfectly simple. Saxon plastic killed people with group AB blood. It destroyed the clotting mechanism. Susan Daniels had been constantly in contact with it through the samplers for the Saxon Blood Analyzer she had been testing. The patients had had Saxon plastic name-tags permanently against their skin, as had Jamie Buchan after Jenny had given him some to play with. The ward maid would have handled Saxon products every day in the ward. It made sense.

On the day that Neil Munro had worked out the problem with AB blood he must have told Saxon and immediately gone down to the Sterile Supply Department to have all Saxon plastic products withdrawn. Saxon must have followed him and pushed him into the sterilizer before he had had a chance to tell anyone.

It must have been Saxon personally, decided Fenton, for Neil had told no one else in the lab and he would have gone down to see Sister Kincaid as soon as he had realized what was going on. There would not have been time for Saxon to arrange for someone else to do his dirty work. He must have done it himself and for that, if Fenton was given half a chance, there would be something to pay.

TEN

Tyson was out of the lab at a meeting so Fenton called the hospital secretary, James Dodds, on his own authority. He was asked to wait while a lady with an affected accent checked 'to see if Mr Dodds was available'.

'Dodds here.'

'Fenton, Biochemistry. I think you may find this a little difficult to believe . . .'

Fenton was right: Dodds found it hard to swallow. He indicated his difficulty by making spluttering noises and other sounds of incredulity into the phone.

'You must withdraw all Saxon plastic products at once,' concluded Fenton.

'But are you absolutely sure?' protested Dodds.

'Absolutely. There's no madman on the loose in the hospital; it's the plastic.'

'But Dr Munro's death?'

'I'll be speaking to the police about that,' said Fenton, 'but the main thing is to stop the staff using anything made of Saxon plastic.'

'Of course, of course,' murmured Dodds. 'Right away.'

Saxon products were withdrawn from circulation. This was accomplished without much difficulty, for stocks in the hospital were generally low; the initial gift from Saxon Medical had dwindled down to a few weeks' supply. More were on order for when the products became commercially available, but now that would never happen.

Fenton wished that Tyson would return from his meeting.

He felt the need of moral support. Over the past two hours, ever since his conversation with Dodds, he had done little else but answer the telephone and deal with callers who wanted more details. He felt like the Caliph of Baghdad on a bad day, though he lacked the power to cut the heads off those who pleaded their case too strongly. If just one more person were to ask him if he was 'absolutely sure' . . .

'But are you absolutely sure?' asked Inspector Jamieson, making Fenton's foot itch. 'Yes, I am sure,' replied Fenton through gritted teeth. 'But for conclusive proof I've asked the Blood Transfusion Service to provide some group AB blood for us to test.'

'Who's bringing it?' asked Jamieson.

'Its owner. It has to be fresh blood. The donor will be coming here.'

Jamieson suggested that a police car should be sent to collect the donor so Fenton gave him Kelly's number. He passed it to his sergeant. 'See to it, will you.' He walked over to the lab window and looked out at the greyness. 'So we have a plastic murderer,' he said, still with his back to Fenton.

'So it seems.' Fenton could sense Jamieson's discomfort and understood it. The man had been hunting a non-existent killer and there would be no glory in this for him, no self-effacing media interviews, just another bumbling-copper story. But there was still the Munro death. Fenton thought he could read Jamieson's mind.

'I understand you have some ideas about the Munro death?' said Jamieson.

Fenton said, 'I think I know why he was murdered and I think I know who did it.' He brought out Neil Munro's notebook and said, 'I didn't understand this at first but I do now. It proves that Neil Munro knew there was a problem with Saxon plastic and, what's more, he had worked out exactly what it was.'

'And you think this is why he was killed?'

'The licence for Saxon plastic was worth millions.'

'To the Saxon Company,' added Jamieson.

'To Saxon the company, to Saxon the man.'

'Point taken.'

Charles Tyson opened the door and broke the spell. He came straight over to Fenton. 'I think I owe you an apology.'

'Let's just be glad it's over,' said Fenton.

'I should have listened to you earlier. I could kick myself.'

'You took the only line possible. Besides, I was out of my head with worry over Jenny at the time.'

Fenton's reference to Jenny had been for Jamieson's benefit. The policeman shifted his weight to the other foot but showed no signs of embarrassment. He said only, 'Perhaps you'll let me know when you've completed the blood tests.'

This was the kind of call Maxwell Kirkpatrick, senior clerk with the Scotia Insurance Company (est. 1864), had been waiting for all his life. His previous pinnacle of achievement in becoming secretary of the Grants Hill Church of Scotland Badminton Club (Monday Group) was now dwarfed by the fact that his blood group set him apart from mere mortals.

The white police Rover with the fluorescent orange stripe squealed through the gates of the hospital and came to a halt before the front door. Maxwell got out and looked up at the Latin inscription above the stone arch, a missionary zeal shining from his eyes. He didn't understand it but somehow it seemed right. The policemen fired a two-door salute and drove off, leaving Maxwell to enter the hospital alone. 'Good day,' he announced at the reception desk, in tones that suggested he might also collect cigarette cards and go train-spotting. 'I understand that – you need me.'

A few minutes later, Tyson took blood from Kirkpatrick and handed the full syringe to Fenton, who ejected half the contents into a regular test-tube and the rest into a Saxon plastic one. The click of the stop-watch sounded unnaturally loud in the quiet of the room.

As time passed Kirkpatrick found it increasingly difficult to maintain his expression of expectant interest. His smile began to pucker like that of a beauty queen held too long on camera, and his eyes moved backwards and forwards between Fenton and Tyson as he searched for clues from the preoccupied men.

'This one has gone,' said Tyson quietly. He tapped the side of the tube with his pen to make sure.

'This one hasn't,' said Fenton, who was monitoring the Saxon tube.

'Completely clotted,' said Tyson.

'Quite, quite fluid,' said Fenton.

'Game, set, and match,' said Tyson. He turned to Kirkpatrick and apologized for his rudeness. He explained what they had been looking for.

'Do you mean . . . there is no patient?' asked Kirkpatrick with an air of disappointment.

Tyson, sizing up the man, assured him that what he had just done would be instrumental in the saving of many lives. Kirkpatrick beamed. 'Just doing what little I could,' he said, looking modestly downwards.

'We're very grateful,' said Tyson. 'I'll ask the police to see to it that you are taken where you want to go.'

'Really?' Kirkpatrick's eyes opened wide. He had not reckoned on being returned to the office in a police car. This was an added bonus. Would they use the flashing light on the return journey? Would a constable hold the door open for him when he got out? By God, this would show that bitch in Accounts that Maxwell Kirkpatrick was not a man to be trifled with.

Tyson pulled on a pair of surgical gloves with traditional difficulty, and was taking the test-tubes to the sink when Inspector Jamieson arrived. He gently tipped the Saxon tube on to its side and let the blood stream out in a thin, even flow. 'You know,' he said, 'it's quite ironic really. This stuff

167

is probably going to turn out to be the most efficient anticoagulant known to man.'

'I think Neil had plans to investigate that,' said Fenton.

'Why so?'

'He had a range of standard anticoagulants and a bottle of solvent in a locked cupboard in his lab. I think he must have been planning to try and solubilize the plastic in order to test its anticoagulant capacity before he realized the significance of the blood groups.'

Fenton was intrigued by the amount of care that Tyson seemed to be exercising in dealing with the plastic test-tubes. As Tyson checked his gloves yet again for signs of damage he became aware that Fenton was watching him. He said quietly, 'Worked it out yet?'

The truth dawned on Fenton. 'The dirty tube . . . it wasn't a dirty tube at all. It was your blood. You have group AB blood.'

'Correct. I was lucky. I haven't had any reason to come into contact with the damned stuff for any length of time, but I don't relish coming that close again.'

'Any news about Mr Saxon, Inspector?' Tyson asked.

'Mr Saxon will shortly be helping us with our inquiries, sir,' said Jamieson, getting up to leave. Fenton screwed up his face at the official jargon, but he had his back to the policeman.

'I take it you and Inspector Jamieson don't get on too well?' asked Tyson when the door had closed.

'Something like that.'

'The business over Jenny?'

'I suppose so.'

'You may not like it but Jamieson was right to do what he did. On the face of it he had every reason to suspect Jenny, and what's more, the very fact that he saw the link between the deaths in the hospital and the boy's death up north means that he's good at his job.'

'If you say so.'

'I do. Now that we've established that, let's drink to the

end of this damned business.' Tyson opened a desk drawer and took out a half-full bottle of malt whisky. 'Fetch a couple of beakers, will you? Glass ones.'

Fenton lay on the sofa with his head in Jenny's lap and closed his eyes while she played with the curls of his hair.

'That's nice,' he murmured.

'Nothing is too nice for the hero of Princess Mary.'

'I just hope the police picked Saxon up.'

'You know, I still find it hard to believe that Nigel Saxon was the cause of all this,' said Jenny distantly.

Fenton opened his eyes. 'What do you mean?'

'Well, he was brash and loud but basically I always thought he was weak, just like a big Labrador dog. I just can't picture him killing someone in cold blood. Can you?'

Fenton thought for a moment then said quietly, 'I agree, but he must have done. Unless you have a better idea?'

Jenny shook her head. 'No, but there's something not quite right about it . . .'

'What do you say we concentrate on something else?'

'And just what could that something be?' asked Jenny with a smile.

Fenton drew her to him and left her in no doubt.

The atmosphere in the flat might have been considerably different had Fenton known that while he was making love to Jenny, Nigel Saxon was not safely in police custody. In fact, he was not even in the country, for he had taken an afternoon shuttle flight from Glasgow to Heathrow and subsequently boarded a flight bound for Greece.

Fenton was furious when he heard the news from Charles Tyson and immediately blamed Jamieson. 'All he had to do was pick him up. I suppose he gave him a lift to the airport and carried his bags into the terminal.'

'It wasn't the Inspector's fault,' said Tyson calmly.

Fenton looked sceptical.

'James Dodds phoned Saxon Medical after you called him

169

yesterday. He saw no reason not to and thought that the company should be made aware of the problem with their product. He called them before he called the police, so Nigel Saxon knew the game was up even before Inspector Jamieson had been informed.'

'I'm sorry,' said Fenton. He left Tyson's room and closed the door quietly. His thoughts returned to Saxon and his anger was reborn. He tried to swallow it, but it lay in his stomach like a lead weight.

Press and television coverage of the end of the 'Princess Mary Affair' was extensive, and raised a number of issues for ambitious politicians to exploit. Was the screening procedure for National Health Service products adequate? asked the opposition. Perfectly so, replied the government of the day. Clearly not, hollered the opposition. Once again the government had been found lacking. The air vibrated with the sound of stable doors being slammed. The thalidomide tragedy was resurrected. Why had we not learned our lesson? The American Food and Drug authority had banned thalidomide in the United States; the odds were that they would have spotted the problem with Saxon plastic as well. Nonsense, retorted the Health Department. Cover-up! cried the opposition. Heads must roll! bayed the press.

'Ye Gods, it's all so predictable,' complained Jenny as she put down the evening paper. 'If one says black the other says white.'

The financial press had a different set of priorities. It paid lip service to the 'awful human cost' but it was the financial mess Saxon Medical had created that really captured its imagination. Had the money involved in the take-over actually changed hands? If the licence had been sold by Saxon, had the responsibility been transferred with it? Would International Plastics be liable to lose millions, not only in the loss of the product, but in lawsuits brought against them by the relatives of the victims?

Speculation along these lines had already done damage to International's share prices, but the company said nothing in public. It was not too hard to guess what they were saying in private. Fenton supposed that cohorts of lawyers would be working round the clock in an attempt to shed blame.

Saxon Medical took a different approach, simply shutting up shop and going to ground. John Saxon, Nigel's father and founder of the company, walled himself up in his Georgian mansion in a Glasgow suburb and refused to see anyone. The work-force had been paid off, and Nigel, of course, was in Greece.

No public mention had been made of any police interest in Nigel Saxon, and as yet no enterprising journalist had sought to forge a link between Neil Munro's death and the Saxon plastic tragedy. This gave Fenton an idea. It occurred to him that a conviction against Nigel Saxon would be of monumental importance to International Plastics. If the company could establish that Saxon had known about the defect in the plastic before the licence had changed hands, the deal would surely be deemed to have been fraudulent. It was very much in International's interest that Nigel Saxon be brought to justice. International knew nothing of any criminal involvement in the Saxon plastic affair. What would happen if he were to tell them?

Fenton thought about this for the rest of the afternoon and began to like the idea. Surely in the circumstances International Plastics would mount their own investigation, employ the best agents in the country to track down Saxon, ferret him out, bring him back?

There was, of course, Interpol. Fenton had been brought up on films where Interpol was brought in, but he could not recall a single real-life incident where it had played a major successful part. Once across the channel it seemed that villains were home and dry. Even the occasional international arrest seemed to flounder in a welter of legal wrangles and territorial jealousies. The more he thought about it the more convinced he became that a private operation based on sound mercenary principles stood the best chance of making Saxon pay for what he had done.

To Fenton, International Plastics was a name from the newspapers. He had no idea where the company was located and no notion of how to go about approaching it. The trouble with large companies, he felt, was that so few people of importance seemed to be accessible within them. They always surrounded themselves with small fish, who in turn surrounded themselves with even smaller fry. Fenton could see himself splashing around for some time, being shunted from one two-metre office to the next and having to explain to men with frayed collars and cuffs that what he had to say was not for their ears.

That in itself would be a problem, for suggesting such a thing even obliquely to a minion would be tantamount to an Israelite's expressing agnostic tendencies while crossing the Red Sea. The resulting maelstrom of obstruction and red tape could be fatal to the spirit.

Fenton told Jenny what he had in mind. She exploded. Fenton had never seen her so angry. He reeled as her temper caught fire like a stick of dynamite. 'How dare you?' she blazed. 'Is there no end to your arrogance?'

Fenton sat wide-eyed and speechless on the couch. He could not believe what was happening. 'Arrogance?'

'Yes, arrogance! You always know better. The police are stupid. Interpol's useless. Everyone is incompetent as far as you're concerned. Well, understand this: Nigel Saxon's arrest is a matter for the police, not you. Leave it alone! I've had enough. Do you understand? Just forget it or . . . or I'll leave you.' Jenny burst into tears and Fenton got up to gather her in his arms. 'All right,' he promised quietly. 'I didn't realize.'

Jenny banged her fist on his shoulder. 'I know, damn it,' she said, 'I know.'

Jenny's outburst had shaken Fenton but it had been what he needed. He now recognized that the hunt for Nigel

Saxon had become an obsession. It irked him so much that Saxon appeared to have got clean away with his crime that he had thought about little else for many days, to the detriment of everything else in his life. He promised Jenny that there would be no approach to International Plastics, no more talk of Nigel Saxon.

Jenny drew the curtains and turned up the gas fire as the wind got up outside. She switched on a small table-lamp and put an album on the stereo before joining Fenton on the couch. For once, the wind and rain contributed to the feeling of cosiness inside the room. Fenton's fingers played the opening bars of Beethoven's Moonlight Sonata on the back of Jenny's neck.

'Tom, I'm sorry.'

'Don't be. You were right.'

'I do love you.'

Fenton kissed her hair in reply.

The music, the warmth, the soft lighting and the hiss of the fire lulled them into a comfortable drowsiness. It was shattered when the telephone began to ring. Jenny got up to answer it and padded out into the hall in her stockinged feet. She came quickly back and stopped in the doorway looking ashen. 'It's for you,' she said. 'I think it's Nigel Saxon.'

Fenton rose like an automaton. He felt cold all over as he sidled past Jenny into the hall and picked up the receiver. Slowly he said, 'Fenton.'

The dialling tone filled his ear and brought instant relief. He let out the breath he had been holding and put down the phone. 'No one there,' he said, knowing that Jenny was standing behind him.

'It was him. I know it was.'

'Maybe a wrong number, someone who sounded like him.'

'He asked for you by name. Saxon has a distinctive voice and he phoned here several times to ask how you were when you were in hospital. It was him,' said Jenny in an unwavering monotone.

'But why? Why phone me? He knows Neil was a friend of mine. I'd be the last person in the world to help him.'

'I don't know why. I only know it was him.'

Fenton rubbed the back of his neck.

'What are you going to do?' asked Jenny.

'Nothing I can do,' he replied.

In spite of their efforts to re-create the earlier peace of the evening the phone call had ruined it. The warmth, the music, the cosiness were still there but the mute telephone rang in their ears. They had gone to bed and were just on the point of falling alseep when it rang for real.

'I'll get it,' said Fenton, getting out of bed and hoping it would be anyone in the world rather than Nigel Saxon.

It was Saxon.

'You've got a nerve,' hissed Fenton.

'Just hear me out, that's all I ask.'

'Well?' snarled Fenton, continuing to listen against his better judgement.

'I know what you all think but I didn't kill Neil Munro. Believe me. I didn't do it.'

'Is that the best you can do, Saxon?'

'All right, all right, I know it looks bad. That's why I made a run for it, but I didn't do it.'

'Then give yourself up.'

'My feet wouldn't touch the ground and you know it. All the police want is a nice quick conviction to regain some credibility and I fit the bill. No, there's only one way I can prove my innocence.'

'Go on.'

'I have to give the police the real killer.'

Fenton paused before saying, 'Assuming that it isn't you, and I don't say for one moment that I believe you, how do you propose doing that?'

'I think I know who the real killer is.'

'Who?'

'I don't want to say just yet, but when I'm sure I may need your help. What do you say?'

Fenton was in a quandary. What did he say? What would Jenny say? Was Saxon lying and, if so, what was his angle? What did he have to gain? Could he be telling the truth? 'How long before you're sure?' he asked.

'A day, maybe two.'

'Two days, then I tell the police.'

'Thanks.'

'Where are you?'

The phone went dead.

Fenton returned to the bedroom, half afraid to meet Jenny's eyes. She said, 'It was him, wasn't it?'

'It was him.'

'Why? What in God's name did he want?' asked Jenny in exasperation.

Fenton told her.

Jenny held her head in her hands. 'Oh my God, what next?' She slapped down her palms on the bedcovers and looked up at him. 'Promise me one thing,' she said. 'If Saxon suggests any kind of meeting, you won't go alone. Take Ian Ferguson or Steve Kelly, or better still tell the police, but don't go alone.'

'I promise.'

Fenton fell asleep but woke at two and was unable to drop off again. He lay in the darkness listening to the sound of the wind but felt so restless that he was obliged to get up before he woke Jenny with his vain attempts to find a comfortable position. He pulled on a dressing gown and went to the kitchen to make coffee.

When he came through to the living room it was icy cold, so he relit the gas fire and huddled over it while he faced up to the old questions. A stream of doubts turned up again like unwelcome relations on the doorstep. Why couldn't real life be like a film, with a beginning, a middle and an end, and never any doubt who was good and who was bad? Things had just been on the point of resolving themselves when this had to happen. The arch villain had turned up claiming to be innocent and the big question now was, was he telling the truth?

'Are you all right?' came Jenny's voice from the bedroom.

'Sorry, did I wake you?' said Fenton.

'No, it's always the same when I get a night off. I wake up anyway.'

For two days the question had to wait. Fenton had almost decided to phone the police when Saxon called at seven on the second evening and said, 'I know who killed Munro and tonight we can prove it.'

The word 'we' rang out loud and clear in Fenton's head. He asked what Saxon meant.

'I want you to be here in the flat when he admits it.'

'Who's he? What flat?'

'I'm back in Edinburgh. I have a flat here that nobody knows about. Will you come at nine o'clock?'

Fenton felt distinctly uneasy. 'What's the plan?'

'I want someone here, quietly concealed in the flat, to witness what's said when my visitor comes.'

'All right,' said Fenton, feeling that he was jumping in with both feet. 'Where are you?'

'Do you promise? No police?'

'I promise.'

Saxon gave him an address in the New Town. The house number was 24a.

'Is it a basement?' asked Fenton.

'Yes.'

Fenton was scribbling down the address on the phone pad when he sensed Jenny at his shoulder. 'You haven't forgotten what you agreed?' she asked.

'I told him I wouldn't contact the police but I didn't say I'd be alone,' said Fenton. He picked up the phone again and called Steve Kelly. They arranged to meet in a bar near the west end of Princes Street.

* * *

'Whisky?' asked Kelly when Fenton arrived.

Fenton nodded and looked around to see if there were any seats free. There were not so they stood at the bar. 'What's going on?' Kelly asked, handing Fenton his glass and sliding the water jug towards him. 'I thought this thing was all over.'

Fenton fleshed out the story he had given Kelly over the phone and ended by saying, 'That's as much as I know.'

Kelly let his breath out through his teeth and whispered, 'Good God, how do I let myself in for these things?'

As they left the pub Kelly pulled up the collar of his overcoat and thumped his fist into the palm of his hand. 'God, it's cold.'

Frost hung in the night air and painted haloes round the streetlights as they walked east along Rose Street, once the haunt of the city's whores but now appropriated by fashionable bars and boutiques.

They had to step off the pavement as a crowd of young men, full of drunken bravado, spilled out of one of the bars. To judge by their clothes and accents they were from well-to-do families. One of them bumped into Kelly, who ignored him. Then he put his hand on Kelly's shoulder and said aggressively, 'Who do you think you're shoving?'

'Go play with your train set, Alistair,' said Kelly with a look that made the drunk back off.

'How did you know my name was Alistair?' asked the drunk, looking more confused than dangerous.

'It always is.' Kelly and Fenton walked on.

The streets quietened suddenly as they took a left turn and walked down into the New Town. Solid Georgian fronts guarded by black iron railings lined the road, presenting their credentials on brass plaques. Architect followed solicitor followed surveyor, interspersed with an occasional interloper from North Sea Oil and an occasional dentist for the private mouth.

'They say,' said Kelly, 'that on dark nights you can hear the dry rot sing.'

'Here it is,' said Fenton, looking up at the street sign. 'Lymon Place.' They were standing at the top of a steep hill that curved elegantly down to the left in quiet darkness. The pavement slabs glistened with frost.

24a was half-way down and shrouded in darkness. Fenton opened the iron-railed gate at pavement level and he and Kelly climbed down the stone steps to the basement area. They skirted round a blue-painted barrel which would contain bedding plants in season.

The brass knocker sounded loud and hollow but there was no reply. Fenton tried again and the two men waited in silence, their breath rising visibly in the freezing air.

'I don't think there's anyone there,' said Kelly, sounding less than disappointed.

'He said nine o'clock.'

Kelly checked his watch but said nothing. Fenton tried turning the handle of the door. It swung open with a surprising quiet ease, and the streetlights were reflected in a glass inner door. Fenton tried that too.

'Isn't this burglary?' whispered Kelly as it opened.

Fenton ignored the question and stepped quietly inside. 'Saxon?' he called out softly as he moved along the passage. There was still no reply.

'I smell burning,' said Kelly.

Fenton sniffed and agreed. There was a smell as if someone's hair had been singed.

The flat appeared to be completely empty. 'I don't get it,' complained Fenton after he had tried the last room. 'Why the hell did he ask us here?'

'What's this?' asked Kelly, tugging at a door in the hall.

'Cupboard?' suggested Fenton.

Kelly pulled it open and a yellow light shone up from the floor. 'Stairs!'

'A sub-basement,' whispered Fenton.

They made their way down the spiral stone steps, steadying themselves with their hands on the whitewashed walls.

'God, what a stink,' said Kelly as the burning smell

178

threatened to overpower them. Then he stopped short in front of a large door that had been covered in leather and inset with heavy brass studs.

'Try it,' said Fenton.

'I feel like Jack and the Beanstalk,' said Kelly as he turned the heavy ringed handle. The door swung slowly back to reveal a stone-floored dungeon which was lit exclusively by wall torches set in wrought-iron holders. In the middle of the floor lay the black smouldering remains of something they both barely recognized as the body of a man.

Fenton covered his face with a handkerchief and approached slowly. He knelt down beside the bundle as smoke rose from charred flesh like the pall from burning leaves on an autumn day, then recoiled in revulsion. 'He's . . . not dead,' he said, unwilling to believe what he himself was saying.

Kelly saw the smoke come from the man's blackened mouth in short, regular breaths. 'He must be,' he whispered. 'Is it Saxon?'

'Yes,' murmured Fenton, steeling himself to kneel down again. 'Saxon?' He looked for some part of the man that he could touch without hitting raw nerves, some way he could make contact, but it was useless. A groan came from Saxon's throat. 'Die, man, for God's sake, die,' Fenton whispered. As if in response a convulsion came from Saxon's throat. It culminated in a brief sigh and his head moved to one side.

'He's dead,' said Fenton.

'Thank God,' said Kelly. He looked round the room. 'Will you look at this?'

The dungeon theme had been pursued with meticulous attention to detail. The bare stone walls were decked with manacles and other articles of bondage. Whips of various sizes and materials stood erect in a long rack next to a table equipped with stirrups and iron wrist-clamps. The whole place was the embodiment in wood and iron of some mediaeval nightmare.

Kelly found a leather-bound book and opened it. It was a

photograph album. 'Jenny was right,' said Fenton when he saw the photographs. 'She thought that Saxon was bent; he sounded too macho, tried too hard, she said.'

'Bent is not the word,' Kelly replied, looking through the pages of the album.

'Takes all sorts, as my grandmother used to say.'

'So what happened here?' said Kelly, putting down the book and looking at Saxon's body. 'Some trick go wrong?'

'No,' said Fenton. 'His hands are bound. He couldn't have set light to himself.' He looked at the blackened corpse for a moment before starting to search round the room. He found a green jerry can and sniffed the contents. 'Paraffin,' he said. 'Some bastard shackled him, doused him in paraffin and started throwing matches.'

'Where does that leave us?' asked Kelly quietly.

'Up to our necks in something I'd rather you didn't make waves in,' said Fenton ruefully.

Fenton could see that he was in trouble no matter which way he turned. If he phoned the police he would have to admit that he had known the whereabouts of Nigel Saxon and failed to inform them. If he kept quiet and Jamieson found out later, the situation might even be worse. Jamieson might even suspect that he had been Saxon's killer, with revenge for Neil Munro as the motive.

'You're sure it's Saxon, aren't you?' Kelly asked.

Fenton nodded. 'I'm sure,' he said. 'Even like that, I knew him well enough to recognize him.'

'So what do we do?'

'Get out of here and pray that no one saw us come in.'

ELEVEN

Fenton and Kelly stood still for a moment in the quiet of
the basement area and courted the shadow of the wall while
they listened for sounds coming from above. When they
were sure that all was quiet, they quickly climbed the steps
to the pavement and started walking.

Like Christians cast into some Georgian colosseum they
looked furtively from side to side for signs of lions. They
saw nothing, but Fenton was far from convinced. He
imagined hidden faces behind every tall rectangular
window. He felt sure that their description was already
being noted and that hands were reaching for telephones.
He and Kelly suppressed the urge to run, but they were
filled with the nervous tension of thoroughbred horses held
under rein.

'Up here,' said Fenton, seeking the earliest opportunity to
return to noise and bustle. The lights of a white-painted pub
attracted them like harbour buoys, and the crowd inside
absorbed them into welcome anonymity.

'God, I needed that,' said Kelly, downing his whisky in
one gulp. Fenton ordered more and they began to take
stock of their surroundings. The pub's customers were
mainly young, fashion-conscious and noisy. The bar list
boasted sixteen different cocktails.

'Why, Steven Kelly!' cried a loud female voice suddenly
behind them. Fenton froze but he felt Kelly's eyes on him
before he turned round.

'Fiona Duncan, how nice,' said Kelly – failing his audition for RADA, thought Fenton.

'Whatever brings you here?' continued Fiona at the top of her voice. Kelly was struggling but Fenton realized that it didn't matter, for Fiona was hardly listening to the answers. She was only interested in her own performance. Fenton knew the type. Conversations were opportunities for self-projection, chances to display an ever-changing slide show of facial expressions to anyone who might be watching. The loudness of the voice was designed to swell that number.

'Tom, meet Fiona Duncan,' said Kelly, looking like a wet spaniel. 'She used to be a nurse at the Princess Mary.'

Fenton nailed Kelly with a glance before shaking hands with the loud girl. 'And where are you now, Fiona?' he asked politely.

'The Western General!' She announced it like the winning number in a raffle and her right hand waved a little cheer.

Fenton smiled, passing her back to Kelly.

'So what are you doing with yourself these days, Steve? Behaving?' asked Fiona.

Fenton saw the knowing look that passed between Kelly and the girl. He marked time with a fixed smile on his face until Fiona decided that she had to 'dash'. Her friends were waiting for their drinks. He almost felt the spotlight vanish as she moved her cabaret to the bar.

'Sorry about that,' whispered Kelly, looking sheepish.

'They should have doctored you at birth,' muttered Fenton.

Jenny welcomed them with a sigh of relief and a barrage of questions that made Fenton hold up his hands. 'You'd better sit down,' he said. He told her what they had found, trying to play down the gory aspects of the scene at 24a Lymon Place.

'But supposing he lies there for weeks before anyone finds him?' Jenny pointed out. 'Could our nerves stand it?'

The consensus was no. 'How should we do it?'

'Anonymous call,' said Kelly. 'I'll do it on my way home.'

The story was too late for the morning papers but the local radio station included it in its morning bulletins. Nigel Saxon, son of the owner of Saxon Medical, the company at the centre of the lethal plastic affair, had been found dead in a city flat and the police were treating the death as murder. There was no more. It sounded clinically clean and tidy, nothing at all like the hellish reality of what had lain in that basement. There was nothing to convey the sight, the smell. Fenton wondered how many other stories were deodorized every day, cellophane-wrapped and sanitized for the protection of the public. Did it matter?

The evening paper seemed to think that it did. 'New Town Funeral Pyre for Plastics Boss' concentrated on the charring and disfigurement of Saxon's body, managing to use the phrase 'barely recognizable' three times in the story. For the first time the police admitted publicly that they had been looking for Saxon in connection with their inquiries into the death of Neil Munro. The simple statement invited the public to draw their own conclusions. No mention was made of the sex angle, however, and Jenny suggested cynically that the police were going to sell it to the Sunday papers. She was wrong. The tabloids got hold of it the following morning and made a meal of 'Sex Secrets of New Town Basement'.

No 'secrets' were actually revealed, but the suggestion of homosexuality and the persistent use of the word 'apparatus' were enough to alter the nature of the crime for the law-abiding citizens of Edinburgh. Outrage at the murder became muted. The unspoken view that this was an affair that God-fearing folk were better off not knowing about became prevalent.

Fenton could not help but feel that the police had orchestrated the whole thing, and it had worked. The pressure was off them, for to all intents and purposes they had tracked down Neil Munro's killer and he was dead; this was better than a conviction for the ratepayers. As for Saxon's killer, they would go through the motions, but there was very little pressure on them this time. No one cared about Saxon or his seedy society.

So Fenton assumed. He had to change his mind when the police issued the descriptions of two men that they wanted to interview in connection with New Town murder.

Fenton held his breath as he listened. Two men aged between twenty and thirty; one was six feet tall and dark, the other slightly shorter with fair hair and broad shoulders. Both had been seen leaving the area of the basement flat on the night in question.

Fenton's first instinct was to phone Steve Kelly but he talked himself out of it, deciding that it was a panic reaction. Kelly phoned him. There was nothing really to say.

Kelly phoned again in the evening soon after eight, just as Jenny was leaving for the hospital. 'We've got trouble,' he said, and Fenton's heart sank. Jenny paused in the doorway and said, 'Should I wait?'

'No,' said Fenton, 'just go. See you in the morning.'

Jenny threw him a kiss and closed the door behind her.

'What trouble?' asked Fenton.

'Fiona Duncan called me. She pointed out that the White Horse is very near Lymon Place and that I've got fair hair and broad shoulders.'

'Marvellous,' muttered Fenton, trying to think at the same time.

'I'm sorry about this.'

'I think we'd better go to the police before they come to us.'

'Do you think if I strangled Fiona I could ask for one other case to be taken into consideration?'

'I'll come round to your place,' said Fenton.

* * *

Fenton apologized to Mary Kelly for having got her husband into his present predicament but she was in a less than forgiving mood and her look came straight from the freezer. As they left Kelly gave her a peck on the cheek and said, 'See you later.'

Don't bet on it, thought Fenton. Gloomily they climbed into Kelly's car and set off for the police station.

'Good evening, sir,' said the desk sergeant, expecting a lost-dog story.

'I think you're looking for us,' said Fenton, feeling as if he were throwing away a key.

The sergeant stared at them until he saw a six-foot dark man accompanied by a shorter man with fair hair. 'Good God,' he said and lifted the telephone. Jamieson was summoned from home.

Fenton and Kelly were held separately during the wait, each accompanied by a silent constable. Fenton found his room oppressively quiet and free from distractions. It was furnished with only a table and four chairs and painted an institutional pastel green. At least the table creaked when he put his elbows on it; in this respect, it was more communicative than the constable. There was a vaguely unpleasant smell of disinfectant about the place, which conjured up visions of lice and filth and vomit and generally added to his feelings of unease.

'Any chance of a cup of tea?' he asked.

The constable mutely shook his head.

An awful thought struck Fenton. As yet, no one had asked for his name or any other details. Everything was being saved for Jamieson. It would be a surprise for him when he walked through the door. Fenton wondered what he would say.

'Oh Christ! This is all I need,' said Jamieson. 'Mr Smart-arse Fenton.'

Fenton struggled to adopt the right facial expression but couldn't find it. Aggression was definitely out in the circumstances, but contriteness went against the grain, especially with Jamieson. He settled for something along the lines of a British tourist being harangued by a foreign official in a language that he did not understand.

Jamieson finished his opening salvo and settled down to enjoying his work. He was going to play this particular fish for a while.

'Why did you do it, Fenton? Revenge? Was that it? He cooked your mate, you cooked him?'

Fenton spluttered out a denial, but the truth was that he hadn't seen the poetic-justice angle. Things were even worse than he had thought.

'How long have you been a practising homosexual, Fenton?'

Fenton clenched his fists.

'Is that why you got beaten up in that pub, Fenton? In the toilets, wasn't it?'

Fenton made for him. The constable dived in to restrain him while Jamieson just smiled.

Jamieson was in his element; he hadn't had so much fun for ages. He ran rings round Fenton, laughing away denials, playing him out, reeling him in, digging the hook in deeper, until at last he saw the fight in him begin to subside. It was always the moment he enjoyed most. He brought his face close to Fenton's and said threateningly, 'Let me tell you this, laddie. It gets very boring being taken for a mug by every half-arse who's seen *The Pink Panther*. You might just ponder on the fact that Nigel Saxon would be alive today if you'd contacted us as soon as he called you.'

Fenton and Kelly were released at a quarter-past midnight, a wiser and more sober pair. They compared notes as they walked down the High Street to collect Kelly's car. 'Do you know, he suggested I was queer,' complained Kelly. Fenton managed to summon up a smile in the darkness while a distant clap of thunder echoed over the roof-tops. 'Bloody rain,' he said.

Fenton went back to the Kellys' flat where Mary was waiting up. She seemed much happier to see Fenton this time and apologized for her earlier frostiness. Fenton said he understood.

'So what happened?' asked Mary.

'We got our bottoms smacked,' replied Kelly.

'That just about sums it up,' agreed Fenton.

Mary went to bed, leaving Fenton and Kelly drinking whisky and mulling over the events of the past two days.

'Did Saxon kill Neil Munro or didn't he?' Kelly mused.

Fenton tilted his glass slowly from side to side. 'It pains me to say it but I think he might have been innocent. I think he was about to shop the real murderer when he got killed for his trouble. The killer must have got wind of what he planned to do and turned up early.'

'The same man who called on Sandra Murray?' suggested Kelly.

'He could have killed Saxon, but not Neil. The killer must have been in the lab when Neil discovered the truth about Saxon plastic. It couldn't have been a stranger. And there isn't anyone in the lab who fits Murray's description of the fair-haired man.'

'Do you realize what you're saying?' said Kelly softly.

Fenton nodded. 'If Neil's killer wasn't Saxon, it must have been someone in the lab. Someone who primed the fair-haired man to ask the right questions. Someone who knew what happens when you add hydrochloric acid to potassium cyanide . . .'

The thought reduced both men to silence.

'But why?' asked Kelly.

Fenton shook his head.

'Did you tell the police about Sandra Murray's visitor?' asked Kelly.

'No, did you?'

'No.'

'Here we go again.'

* * *

It was very late and the streets were practically deserted as Fenton walked home. The temperature had fallen with the clearing of the skies, the air was still, and the stars twinkled brightly above him. As he rounded a corner he saw the source of the eerie white light that was lighting up the chimneys on the tenement roofs: a full moon hung in the sky like a communion wafer. A cat fled from behind a dustbin and dissolved in shadow.

Fenton fell into a troubled sleep but kept waking at almost hourly intervals until at four o'clock he got up and made coffee. He had gone through each male member of the lab staff in turn at least three times and had still failed to find any motive among them for killing Neil. He felt it was safe to eliminate all the females, for Neil's murder had demanded physical strength. The motive had to be linked to the Cavalier organization, Fenton decided. That was the link between Saxon and the fair-haired man. It seemed reasonable to suppose that it was also the link between Saxon and the killer in the lab.

Charles Tyson? He had defended Saxon plastic throughout and had done everything possible to dissuade Fenton from pursuing his idea that there was something wrong with it. What was more, Jenny had noticed that he had known what Ross had been talking about when he mentioned the 'Tree Mob'. He was also unmarried and never spoke of his personal life. But what about Ross himself? Ross had told him about the club in the first place but that might have been cleverness on his part, a ploy to make himself the least likely suspect . . .

Fenton gave up. The fair-haired man was the key to the puzzle. He must know who Neil's killer was. Fenton decided that he and Kelly must visit Jamieson in the morning.

The two men ran up the hill, keeping close to the wall in an effort to avoid most of the weather but meeting it head-on as they rounded the corner at the top. They had fifty metres or so still to cover before reaching the shelter of the police station.

'Do you think God has something personal against Scotland?' asked Fenton, shaking the water from his hair in the doorway.

'I think it's a character-building agreement he has with John Knox,' said Kelly. 'Let's face it, if you were having a good time you'd only feel guilty.'

Jamieson looked up from his desk as Fenton and Kelly were shown in by a constable who seemed strangely reluctant to let go of the door handle after opening the door for them. They had to enter sideways. Jamieson clasped his hands together under his chin and said, 'Don't tell me. Let me guess. You have a suspicion that the Queen Mother did the Brighton Trunk Murders?'

Fenton grinned painfully, conceding Jamieson's right to some revenge for his behaviour in the past. He told the policeman of his visit with Kelly to the Murray house and what Sandra Murray's brother had told them.

Jamieson knew the name Sandra Murray well enough. 'Hit-and-run death, up the Braids way?'

Fenton nodded.

'And you're saying she knew about the Saxon plastic problem?'

'Maybe not the details, but she knew that Neil Munro thought there was something wrong with it.'

'And that's what this fair-haired man wanted to find out?'

'It seems like it.'

Jamieson sucked the end of his pen in silence for a moment, then said, 'Did Murray tell you any more about this man?'

Fenton told him about the tiepin and watched Jamieson's expression change. The policeman put down his pen and rubbed his eyes with the heels of his hand before saying quietly, 'That lot.'

'You know them?' asked Fenton.

'Oh yes, I know them all right,' sighed Jamieson. 'We all

know them. The force is now full of senior officers who have tangled with that bunch and ended up giving road-safety lectures to five-year-olds.'

'You're serious?'

'I'm serious.'

Fenton looked at Kelly, who shrugged as if to say, I told you so.

'But you're the police. I thought . . .'

'I know what you thought,' interrupted Jamieson. 'You thought I could nip up to Braidbank, pick up Sandra Murray's brother and get him to identify the man?'

'Well, yes.'

Jamieson shook his head and said, 'Let me tell you what would really happen. Assuming Sandra Murray's brother was willing to co-operate, and if he knows anything at all about this mob he wouldn't be, we'd start making inquiries. A few days later I'd be directing traffic in Princes Street and Murray would be running for his life.'

'You can't be serious,' Fenton protested.

'I am,' said Jamieson. 'These buggers have so much power it scares me shitless.'

Fenton was shaken by the admission. 'So where does that leave us?'

Jamieson ran his finger round the inside of his collar and said, 'Now that you've told me this I am obliged to go and see Murray and ask him formally if he thinks he could identify the man. Frankly, I hope he says no, because if he doesn't there could be another hit-and-run accident in Braidbank within the week.'

Fenton was having difficulty in coming to terms with Jamieson's frankness, but he did have an idea and said so. Jamieson grimaced and Kelly smiled. Fenton said, 'Murray told me that his sister was the scientist in the family and that he was an artist. If he really is an artist, a brush-and-paint artist that is, he might be able to sketch the man for you and no one would ever know how you got on to him.'

'Sounds a good idea to me,' said Kelly.

Jamieson took his time but finally decided it was worth considering. 'If we could find out who the man was without his knowing it would give us time to build up a case against him. We could go in strong.'

Kelly suggested that he and Fenton should approach Murray and keep the police out of it in the man's own interest. Jamieson agreed but Fenton sensed that he was uncomfortable. He wanted to say something more but it was having a difficult birth. 'Gentlemen,' he began, tapping his fingertips together, 'with your agreement' – the words struggled over invisible barriers – 'I would like to keep this on . . . an unofficial basis for the time being.'

Fenton and Kelly waited for an explanation and it was even more laboured when it came. 'Frankly, once a report is written . . . I can't be sure who is going to see it.'

'I see,' said Fenton. He said it calmly but felt far from calm. 'Perhaps it would be better if we met on neutral ground next time?'

Jamieson nodded, relieved to see that Fenton had drawn the correct inference from what had been said and that no further explanation was necessary.

It was still raining heavily when they got outside so they made a dash for the car; it was still to no avail, for Kelly dropped the keys into the overflowing gutter in his haste to unlock the door.

'Did I dream that?' asked Fenton when they were inside.

'If you did I had the same one,' said Kelly.

Jenny looked aghast. 'But they're the police,' she protested. 'They don't say things like that.'

'That's what I thought too,' said Fenton, 'but I'm telling you exactly what Jamieson said.'

'Oh Tom,' said Jenny in exasperation. Fenton put his arm round her and tried to reassure her by saying, 'It's still a police matter. It's just that Jamieson wants to conduct it a little unconventionally.'

'When are you going to see Murray?'

'Tonight.'

Fenton and Kelly had decided to say nothing to Murray about any possible connection with the Saxon murder and not to mention the police at all. This was to be just a little follow-up to their previous visit.

'Actually I'm a sculptor,' Murray had said, 'but I think I can manage a rough outline.'

It had turned out to be easier than Fenton had thought it might be. He had the sketch in his hands and Murray had hardly asked a thing; in fact, the man seemed positively subdued. He wondered whether the whisky beside Murray's chair was to blame but abandoned that notion in favour of a box of pills that he saw lying open on the table. He sneaked a look at the label while Murray had his back turned for a moment and saw that it contained tranquilizers. They were a relatively mild brand but the alcohol was enhancing their effect.

Fenton looked at the sketch and admired Murray's competence.

'Thank you for your help,' he said, getting up to go.

'A drink before you leave?'

Fenton looked at his watch as a prelude to an excuse but the pathetic look in Murray's eyes made him change his mind. 'Thank you,' he said. 'Whisky for me.'

'Do you still think my sister was murdered?' Murray asked as he handed Fenton and Kelly their glasses.

'I think it's possible,' replied Fenton.

'I miss her, you know,' said Murray distantly. 'I never liked her much while she was alive but now that she's gone . . . I miss her.'

Fenton and Kelly exchanged embarrassed glances. Murray's eyes were fixed on the middle distance. He appeared not to notice their reactions as he continued, 'You see, she was the only person in my life who ever really cared for me and now she's gone . . .'

Kelly shrugged his shoulders in discomfort and Fenton

moved uneasily in his chair. Murray brought his gaze back to them and apologized for his rudeness. 'Another drink?'

As he and Fenton walked down the path to the gate Kelly turned and looked back at the house. 'Poor bastard,' he said.

The clock on the dashboard said eight forty-five and Kelly suggested that they contact Jamieson on the number he had given them. Fenton rang him from a call box on the edge of Braidbank. He looked down at the lights of the city while he waited for Jamieson to answer. The rain had stopped but water was still running down the gutters from the hill.

'Do you know a pub called The Gravediggers?' Jamieson asked.

'Corner of Angle Park?'

'That's the one, opposite Ardmillan Cemetery.'

'When?'

'Thirty minutes.'

'We'll be there.'

Jamieson arrived first. He got up as Fenton and Kelly came in and ordered a round. 'Any problems?' he asked as they sat down.

'None,' replied Fenton, reaching into his inside pocket to take out Murray's sketch and hand it over.

Jamieson pursed his lips as he gazed at it. 'Well, well, well,' he said slowly.

'You know him?' asked Fenton.

'I do, indeed I do,' replied Jamieson, still mesmerized by the sketch. 'That's Gordon Vanney, Councillor Vanney's son.'

Fenton thought that Jamieson looked as if he was being forced to remember something he would rather have forgotten and did not intrude. He and Kelly remained silent until the policeman began to speak in his own time.

'Four years ago,' said Jamieson, 'a girl named Madeline Gray took her dog for a walk on Corstorphine Hill; she was fourteen at the time. Four youths set about her. They stripped her, tied her up and raped her in turn. When they had finished they stuffed stinging nettles . . . into every opening in her body and left her, still staked to the ground.'

Fenton and Kelly listened in horror as Jamieson continued.

'When she could speak she named one of the youths as Vanney. She had recognized him because he lived in the same neighbourhood. We arrested Vanney but his old man got him out on bail.' Jamieson paused and sipped his drink as if the words were paining him. 'The very next night, while Madeline's father was out walking her dog, the dog ran off into the trees. It ran off with four legs and came back with three. Wire-cutters, the vet said. Two days later the leg arrived by post addressed to Madeline. It was in a flower box so her mother let her open it by herself. A note suggested that it might be her leg next if she didn't keep her mouth shut. She did and Vanney went free. The girl still isn't right, takes four baths a day.'

'What a story,' murmured Fenton.

'And you never traced the others?' asked Kelly.

'We never did. A pity, because before she stopped talking altogether, the girl told us that Vanney was just the one she recognized; he wasn't the ringleader. That singular honour went to a six-foot-tall, dark-haired youth wearing some kind of college or university scarf. He had a piece missing from his right ear lobe; she was very sure of that because she'd concentrated on it while he was raping her.'

'Four years ago, Inspector? You have some memory,' said Kelly.

'So would you if you'd seen that wee lassie,' replied Jamieson.

Fenton asked what Jamieson was going to do about the sketch.

'Watch and wait. Find out who his associates are. See who's an organ-grinder and who's a monkey.'

'You don't think Vanney could have killed Sandra Murray and Saxon?' asked Fenton.

'Vanney's a shit but he's small fry. Someone else always pulls the strings.'

'Any ideas?'

Jamieson shook his head and said, 'No, I haven't. We kept tabs on the bastard for a while after the Madeline Gray affair – you know the sort of thing; anyone farts in a built-up area and we pull in Vanney. But his old man pulls a lot of weight in this city. He started shouting harassment and we had to back off.'

'The same thing might happen this time,' suggested Fenton.

'No,' said Jamieson. 'This time it's unofficial, and personal.'

'You mean you're going to do it by yourself?' asked Kelly.

Jamieson nodded.

'Can we help?' asked Fenton.

Jamieson smiled faintly. 'Aye,' he said. 'Aye, you can.'

Fenton got to know Vanney well over the next week. The fact that Jenny was still working nights let him share evening surveillance with Jamieson, and leave that he was owed allowed him to do some daytime watching as well. Steve Kelly took over on the evenings that Jenny had off.

Vanney lived in his parents' house on Corstorphine Hill; it was a sprawling modern bungalow with large gardens and a gravelled drive that accommodated three cars. The Lotus belonged to Vanney junior. Each weekday morning he drove it to work in the city, leaving at eight-thirty and arriving at a merchant bank in the New Town at five minutes to nine. Lunch was from one till two and he ate it in a pub in Rose Street called The Two Shoemakers. He always ate with the same people: a tall, ginger-haired man with buck teeth and a loud voice and a short, squat, olive-skinned man who looked Italian, or maybe Spanish. They worked in the same bank as Vanney, but it seemed just to be a lunch-time friendship for neither of them featured in his evening social life.

Vanney had a girlfriend, which surprised Fenton, for he had assumed that any connection with the Cavalier Club implied homosexuality. It seemed that the club had broadened its horizons. The girl seemed likeable and came from a well-heeled background similar to Vanney's own. She was tall, nearly as tall as Vanney, and good-looking in a country-girl sort of way. Fenton liked her on sight and wondered what she saw in someone like Vanney; and vice versa if Vanney *was* homosexual.

Jamieson provided an answer to the second question. The girl's father was a director of the bank where Vanney worked. 'Vanney to a T,' he snarled, 'brown-nosing the boss's daughter.'

'What do you suppose her father thinks about it?' asked Fenton.

'Probably encourages it. Son of a prominent councillor, heir to a concrete shit empire; an excellent choice for his wee Denise. That's her name by the way, Denise Hargreaves.'

It seemed that Vanney followed a well-established routine. He and Denise Hargreaves saw each other twice during the week and again on Saturday: one disco, one trip to the cinema and dinner out at the weekend. He played golf with his father on Sunday and stayed in on Thursday. That left Monday and Wednesday.

TWELVE

On Monday Jamieson lost Vanney in town traffic and it was accepted as just one of those things, but when the same thing happened to Kelly on the Wednesday, the three men met to discuss tactics.

'Do you think he realized that he was being followed?' asked Fenton. Jamieson replied that he thought not, adding that Vanney had shown no sign of 'awareness'. Fenton himself had had no trouble following Vanney on the Tuesday, and the wrestling match that he had had with Denise Hargreaves in the car outside her house had not suggested the actions of a man who thought he was being watched.

'How did he get on?' asked Kelly.

'She slapped his face,' said Fenton.

'Good for her,' said Jamieson.

Jamieson and Kelly compared notes and found that they had lost Vanney at the same place in town. He had made a left turn out of Leith Street and apparently disappeared into thin air. 'He must have turned into a lane, or something,' said Kelly. Jamieson suggested that they should all attempt to tail Vanney the following Monday. Fenton would pick him up as he left his house, in case he chose to do something different, and the other two would wait near the top of Leith Street, the broad street leading down from the east end of Princes Street to the port of Leith, where they had lost him before.

On Monday evening Vanney left home at seven-thirty and Fenton followed on the Honda some two hundred metres behind, keeping at least two vehicles between himself and the Lotus at all times. The traffic was light enough at first and the only problem was the persistent drizzle.

Vanney appeared to be taking the same road as before into town and Fenton automatically assumed his route, an assumption that nearly caused him to lose the Lotus when he found himself trapped in the inside lane and Vanney decided to turn right. By the time he had recovered the Lotus had disappeared. He had to make a guess. Did he go down to the Grassmarket or up to the High Street?

Fenton bet on the High Street and gunned the Honda up Castle Terrace which wound round and up the side of the floodlit castle rock. The needle was touching sixty-five when he braked at the top of the Royal Mile in time to see the tail-lights of the Lotus as it sat waiting at traffic-lights. He freewheeled the bike down the steep cobbles, allowing a taxi and a Ford Escort to reach the Lotus first.

The lights changed and Vanney turned left. He was heading back towards Princes Street after going out of his way by nearly two miles. It didn't make sense, thought Fenton, unless of course he was taking routine precautions to avoid being followed on Mondays and Wednesdays.

As the traffic high above Princes Street began to flow down the Mound, a steep hill connecting the Old Town to the New, Fenton's pulse began to quicken. It looked as if Vanney was now heading for Leith Street. He hoped Kelly and Jamieson were alert.

Traffic at the east end of Princes Street was heavy as night-time commercial vehicles headed towards the main road south. Vanney was third in the queue at the lights and Fenton was seventh. An articulated lorry lay in fourth place.

The Lotus was three hundred metres ahead before the lorry had swung its tail out of Fenton's way and he had a clear road in front. He fought an impulse to twist the throttle. There was no point in appearing in Vanney's rear-view mirror like a bullet. He passed the lorry but held back as he saw the Lotus slow down for a roundabout. There were now four vehicles between him and the Lotus, an ideal number.

Fenton took his turn at infiltrating into traffic coming from the right and saw the Lotus turn off Leith Street to the left. This was where he had lost it last time. He leaned into the corner and straightened up to find that the Lotus had completely disappeared. There was a long straight road ahead but no Vanney. Fenton pulled into the side and cut the engine. He was relieved to see Jamieson come out of a shop doorway and walk towards him.

'All right. I give up,' said Fenton.

'Basement garage,' said Jamieson. 'Twenty metres along on your left. The door was already open. He just swung into it and the door closed behind him. The whole thing took less than five seconds.'

Kelly joined them from the other corner and said, 'It all looks pretty dead to me.' All three looked at the building. It was deserted and dark: no lights, no sounds.

'What now?' Fenton asked.

'We try to find out where Vanney entered the building. There must be an internal stair from the garage because he hasn't appeared on the street.'

Fenton volunteered to have a look and Jamieson agreed. 'Go in by the front door nearest the area of the garage.'

Fenton climbed the short flight of steps to the main entrance of the dark building. The door was unlocked. Inside, the cold and damp were accentuated by the blackness. It felt like a tomb. He examined the ground-floor doors as best he could, relying largely on light from the headlights of cars passing outside. They were filthy, and the grime on the locks and handles told him that they had not been used for a very long time. The smell of wood-rot was everywhere.

He searched for stairs that might lead down to the garage and found some, though he half wished he hadn't for they were completely dark. He stretched out his hands and touched both walls as he felt his way gingerly down them.

At the bottom he found himself in a passage that ran through the building. There was a scurrying sound nearby which made him lash out with his foot. The sound stopped but Fenton's pulse-rate was soaring.

Feeling his way along the wall he came to a door and groped for the lock. He couldn't see the rust on the bolts but felt it with his fingers as he tried to budge it. The tongue began to move and Fenton worked it backwards and forwards until at last it gave and clattered back against its stop, only slightly cushioned by a finger that had got in the way. He put his finger to his lips, simultaneously stemming blood and curses. He pulled the door open with his other hand and stepped out into a dark lane which ran along the back of the building.

There was a garage door to his right. Fenton looked at it and mentally plotted its relationship to the opening at the front where Vanney had entered. His heart sank as he realized the truth. The garage ran straight through the building. It had a front and a back door. Vanney was not in the building at all!

Fenton ran along the lane and round to the front of the building to tell Jamieson and Kelly.

'Did you check to see whether the Lotus was still there?' Jamieson asked.

'I assumed that he'd driven straight through,' confessed Fenton.

'We'd better check. He may have changed cars.'

Fenton and Kelly walked round to the garage door at the back. Unlike the modern metal door at the front, it was made of wood and rotting badly. Kelly knelt down to peer through at the bottom, where the wood had decayed into what looked like a row of rotting teeth. 'It's still there,' he announced. 'He changed cars.'

They agreed to watch in shifts until Vanney returned. One of them would stay near to the entrance of the lane while the other two could stretch their legs or get coffee at a café nearby.

Vanney did not get back until one in the morning. Jamieson was on watch when a green Mini slowed down and turned into the lane. He got a good view of Vanney at the wheel and noted down the number. The Lotus left shortly afterwards and ten minutes later Fenton and Kelly returned.

The three men agreed to meet again the following Monday morning near the entrance to the lane and follow the green Mini when it left. In the mean time they decided to abandon routine surveillance on Vanney, a move that proved equally popular with Mary Kelly and Jenny. Fenton wondered later about Jamieson. Was he married? The subject had never come up, and it was somehow not the sort of thing you asked him.

Spring suddenly came to Edinburgh. It flooded the city with a yellow sunshine, highlighting the rash of buds that had broken out on the trees in Princes Street Gardens. It made drops of rainwater from the previous night's downpour sparkle on railings like precious stones as Fenton rode to the lab through the morning traffic.

Heads that had spent most of the winter bent forward against wind and rain were lifted so that faces might receive the kiss of spring sunshine. Feet slowed as the lure of office central heating lost its grip on the imagination, and people stopped to speak to each other in the streets. They were smiling; the annual war was over and the survivors were glad to see each other.

The sunshine had even invaded Fenton's lab. It sought out the dust that coated reagent bottles and illuminated the intricacies of a large cobweb on the shelf. Now that he had seen it the dirt began to annoy him. He fetched a wet cloth and started to wipe each bottle individually. He was doing this when Charles Tyson came in. He said, 'I'd like to see you in my room in ten minutes if that's convenient?'

Liz Scott brought coffee into Tyson's office when Fenton

had joined him. As Tyson stirred his he said, 'I'm considering recommending to the Health Board that you be made official deputy head of department, Neil's position.'

'Thanks,' said Fenton.

'Don't thank me just yet. I said I was considering it.'

Fenton waited for Tyson to elaborate. He looked hard at Fenton and said, 'A senior position like this demands something more than just scientific ability. It requires a certain degree of diplomacy. It requires discretion, a willingness to operate within accepted guidelines. A willingness to drift with the prevailing current rather than a tendency to . . . rock the boat. Do I make myself clear?'

'Perfectly,' said Fenton, controlling his temper. He was being warned off and offered an incentive. The question was, what was he being warned off? Was it just his natural tendency to go to war with the hospital authorities that Tyson was concerned about or was it something more precise? He couldn't tell anything from Tyson's expression.

'Well?' said Tyson.

'I don't think I'm your man,' said Fenton. 'I reserve the right to play the game as I see it.'

'I see,' said Tyson, tapping the end of his pen on the blotting pad in front of him. 'Don't be too hasty. Sleep on it.'

Fenton got up to go.

'There is one more thing,' said Tyson.

'Yes?'

'I'm going to recommend to the board that Ian Ferguson be upgraded to senior biochemist. Do you have any views?'

'That's fine by me.'

'Good,' said Tyson. 'I hoped you'd say that.' He put down his pen and rubbed his eyes. 'I'll be glad when everyone can concentrate solely on their work again.'

Was that another warning? wondered Fenton. He searched Tyson's face but it was unreadable; he was concentrating on his papers again.

Fenton was checking the day-book in the main lab when

Liz Scott came in and told Ian Ferguson that Tyson wanted to see him. Ferguson made a face at Fenton and said, 'When the trumpet calls . . . ' Fenton smiled but said nothing.

The good weather lasted over the weekend, and Fenton and Jenny took their first real walk of the year. They went out to the village of Colinton and climbed up into the Pentland Hills to the south of the city. As they reached the top of Bonaly Hill they stopped to catch their breath and look at the view. Jenny was standing slightly lower down than Fenton, so as she looked north over the houses to the Forth Estuary, he looked at her. Her hair was like spun gold in the sun and her fresh complexion seemed to embody the spirit of the season. He stooped to kiss her lightly on the back of the neck and she raised her hand to touch his cheek. She did not speak.

'I love you, Jenny,' whispered Fenton.

Jenny still did not speak.

'All right, I don't love you.'

Jenny smiled and turned. She said, 'Tom, you will be careful tomorrow?'

Fenton reassured her and hugged her tightly from behind.

They walked through a pine forest on the way to Caerketton Hill and their feet were silent on a thick carpet of needles. Sunlight sneaked through the branches to create little pools of light on the floor of the woods.

On Monday morning Jamieson rang Fenton at the lab to finalize details about following Vanney. He and Kelly would tail the Mini in his car, an unmarked Ford Granada. Fenton was to follow on the Honda. If he felt Vanney had tumbled to the Granada, Jamieson would turn off, leaving Fenton to pick up the tail.

Fenton was glad that Jenny had already left for the hospital when he got home because he felt nervous and needed to be alone. Where would Vanney go? he wondered. Would they be any closer to discovering the truth about Neil's death by the end of this evening?

The butterflies in his stomach did not subside until the Honda had started and he had set out for Leith Street. Jamieson was already there when he arrived, although he was not late. The policeman handed him a two-way radio and gave him a crash course in how to use it in the five minutes before Kelly arrived.

Then, with ten minutes to go if Vanney was to be his usual punctual self, Fenton got back on the Honda and moved some two hundred metres away from Jamieson's car. He waited in a doorway watching the street.

Two minutes later, the Lotus swung into the street and nosedived into its garage. Fenton felt the adrenalin begin to flow as he began to watch the far end of the lane. The lights of the green Mini appeared at the junction; it paused, then turned left on to the main road. Fenton saw the Granada start on its way. He walked out from his doorway as if he had just emerged from the building and got on the bike. Settling at a comfortable distance behind Jamieson, he felt pleased at how smoothly it had all gone so far.

The Mini was making for the coast. Fenton hoped that it might take the main road south where there would be plenty of traffic to provide cover, but it was not to be. Vanney made a left turn at the edge of town and joined the old, winding coast road which meticulously followed the southern shore of the Firth of Forth. The Granada's head-lights would be in Vanney's mirror all the time, thought Fenton. The odds were that it would not alarm Vanney unduly, but he might feel obliged to prove to himself that he was not really being followed.

The test came as they entered the small coastal village of Port Seton. The Mini's left indicator began to flash and Vanney pulled in to the side and stopped beside some shops. Jamieson was obliged to drive straight past. Fenton stopped well behind the Mini. The street lighting was good. Vanney would have been able to get a good look at the Granada as it passed, maybe even taken its number. There was no way that Jamieson could take up the tail again.

It started to rain, and the sound of the drops hitting his leathers seemed unnaturally loud to Fenton as he sat motionless, waiting for the Mini to move off. It was a full five minutes before he heard the rattling-drain sound of the engine being started. Vanney moved off from the kerb and Fenton prepared to follow but held back until the Mini had left the edge of the village and disappeared round a right-hand bend. He did not want Vanney to get a look at him under the streetlights.

As soon as Vanney was out of sight Fenton gunned the bike to the edge of the village, then he took a risk. He throttled back and turned off his lights, reckoning that if he picked up the Mini quickly he could ride on its tail-lights. The rain on Vanney's rear screen would also help to obscure his presence.

Fenton could see red lights some two hundred metres ahead. With his heart in his mouth he accelerated to close the distance between himself and the car, knowing that the road between him and Vanney was an unknown quantity. One unseen pothole could bring disaster. He closed to within fifty metres and felt more comfortable now that the Mini's headlights were acting as pathfinders. The winding road did not allow the little car to move fast, which was just as well.

They had travelled about three miles when Fenton thought he caught a glimpse of something metallic off to his left, something in the sand dunes among the rough grass. As he passed the spot he saw that it was Jamieson's Granada, waiting with its lights out. Fenton wondered if Vanney might have seen it too but concluded not, for it was still raining heavily and the Mini's side windows would be speckled over. Vanney's view would be confined to the two semicircles cleared by the wipers.

Another two miles and the Mini's brake lights lit up the

night like Christmas candles, making haloes of pink rain. Fenton's foot shot to the brake pedal but he stopped himself in time; his own rear brake light would give the game away. Instead he clawed at the front-brake lever, full of apprehension as he concentrated on keeping the bike perfectly vertical. The slightest angle on the front wheel in these wet conditions would send it off like a bar of soap in the bath.

Fenton let out his breath as the Honda slowed to a walking pace and yielded to his control. Up ahead the Mini was turning off to the right, but not on to another road. It was entering what appeared to be the driveway of a big house. Fenton got off the bike and walked across the road to the entrance. 'Helmwood' said the letters etched into one of the stone pillars. He looked up the drive but there was nothing to be seen, and all he could hear was the murmur of the sea and the rustle of the conifers over the wall.

Fenton radioed the news to Jamieson who said that he knew the place. 'Move on a quarter of a mile. There's a beach track to your left. We'll meet you there.'

Fenton got into the back of the Granada and relaxed in its warmth; he had not realized how cold he was.

'Monkton's place,' said Jamieson.

Fenton needed more.

'Lord Monkton, ex-minister of state, pillar of the community. Power, wealth, influence, just the job for the Cavalier mob.'

'Shall we go take a look?' said Kelly.

Fenton detected a note of caution in Kelly's voice and recognized it as the reticence displayed by even the most law-abiding in the company of policemen.

'Why not,' replied Jamieson. 'There's no law of trespass in Scotland.'

They got out of the car into the salty night air and made their way up to the road. It had stopped raining but the grass and the trees were heavily pregnant with water and a conifer delivered its load over Kelly as he brushed against it.

'Sssssh!' said Jamieson as Kelly cursed.

Fenton had an advantage over the other two in that he was dressed for the occasion; inside his leathers and boots he was immune to the rain and proof against sand and mud. It was he who led the way back to the entrance to Helmwood, flattening a path through the long grass for the others to use.

The sound of an approaching car prompted Jamieson to say, 'Down!'

The three men crouched in the grass as a sleek Jaguar saloon slowed down and turned into the driveway. They had barely got to their feet when another car arrived. Fenton did not recognize the make but it looked Italian and expensive.

When all seemed quiet they stepped out of the grass and on to the tarmac of Helmwood's drive. 'I think we'd better stick to the trees,' said Jamieson.

'This side,' said Fenton, picking the place where the pine woods were less dense. The smell of pine resin made him think briefly of the day before, but this forest was different; it was hostile. The tall trees waved their branches threateningly against the dark sky as they made their way towards the chinks of light that advertised Helmwood.

'Must be having a party,' whispered Jamieson as they crouched in the shadow of the trees and counted the number of cars in the drive. 'I'd like to collect some numbers,' he said.

Fenton and Kelly waited while Jamieson sprinted across in a low crouch and disappeared among the gleaming machinery, notebook at the ready. It was ten minutes before he returned, slightly out of breath. 'This should keep the computer happy for a bit,' he panted.

'What now?' asked Kelly.

'A closer look?' suggested Fenton.

'All right, but let's take it easy,' said Jamieson.

'Do you hear music?' Fenton asked the other two as the wind dropped momentarily.

'I keep thinking I do,' said Kelly.

'There it is again.'

'Must be coming from the other side of the house,' said Jamieson. 'There are very few lights on this side.'

'We could circle round,' Fenton suggested.

They sank back into the trees and kept to the contour of the pine wood as they made their way towards the back lawn of the house. They could now see that a bank of windows on the first floor was brightly lit and the music seemed to be coming from there.

'What kind of music is that, anyway?' asked Kelly.

Fenton shook his head. 'Some kind of stringed instruments maybe.'

The size of the lit windows suggested that this was a very large room. 'A ballroom?' suggested Kelly.

'A ballroom with a balcony . . .' mused Fenton. He looked at Kelly and said, 'I can't see them coming out on the balcony on a night like this, can you?'

Kelly took his point and said, 'There's a fire escape running up the side of it.'

Jamieson pretended that he hadn't heard but Fenton and Kelly stared at him until he acknowledged that he had. 'All right,' he said. 'Let's take a look.'

Fenton climbed up the fire-escape ladder, followed first by Kelly and then Jamieson. He got to the top and swung his legs over the stone balustrade, then nestled down in a corner, taking comfort in the fact that there was no danger of their being overheard because the music and laughter coming from within were far too loud. The only problem would be the possibility of their being seen in the light that flooded out from the tall windows.

The music stopped and the hubbub began to subside. Almost imperceptibly the lights began to dim. 'Something's happening,' whispered Kelly.

'I wish we could see what,' answered Fenton. The lighting inside became lower and lower and Fenton decided to risk wriggling out along the balcony to a point just below one of the windows. Kelly bit his lip as he watched, then signalled that it was safe for Fenton to raise himself up for there was no one standing near the window.

Fenton raised himself slowly until his eyes were above the level of the sill, and his mouth fell open. He was looking at ancient Rome, at a palace of the Caesars.

Men clad in togas and sandals reclined on couches to be waited on by slaves bearing wine jugs and trays laden with food. At one end of the room three musicians sat with lyres. At the other centurions in full leather armour guarded tall double doors. Another centurion stood in the middle of the room carrying a standard. Fenton thought at first that it was a Roman eagle but then saw that it was not that at all. It was a golden tree, the symbol of the Cavalier Club.

Fenton caught sight of Vanney. He was sitting near the musicians and threw back his head to drain his goblet as Fenton watched. It was refilled almost immediately. Fenton crawled back along the balcony to join the others.

'A theme party?' suggested Jamieson.

'It looks too real,' Fenton replied. 'Everything, the mosaics, the marbles, the clothes, the trappings. They all look real.'

Before they had time for any more questions a fanfare sounded from inside and Fenton signalled that they should move out to the windows again. Jamieson joined Fenton at his window; Kelly took the next one along.

'My God,' murmured Jamieson.

A large square of rush matting was being spread out on the floor by four men dressed as slaves. When they had finished, one of the Romans, a tall, distinguished man wearing a purple-trimmed toga, raised his arm for silence.

'That's Monkton,' whispered Jamieson.

The double doors at the end of the room were opened to admit two wrestlers, naked to the waist, their bare torsos glistening with oil. They marched down the centre of the room and saluted Monkton by crossing their forearms across their chests. Monkton nodded and they began to circle each other on the mat. All lighting in the room had been extinguished apart from wall torches and candles. Spluttering flames were reflected in the sweat of the combatants as they struggled.

Fenton could not take his eyes away from Monkton's face. The man was in the grip of some terrible excitement. He was no longer the urbane man he had been at the beginning; his mouth quivered as he silently exhorted the wrestlers to greater efforts. His hand reached out almost absent-mindedly and gripped the thigh of the slave who stood by his couch. The boy, an effeminately pretty youth, winced as Monkton's fingers dug into his flesh, but he smiled as soon as Monkton looked up at him. Savagely Monkton pulled the boy's face down on top of his.

'Nice to see a return to Victorian values,' whispered Jamieson.

A few minutes later, as the wrestlers finished their bout to loud applause, Monkton and the boy left the room. Several other pairs also left. The lights were turned on and the music began again. The three observers crawled back along the balcony and into the safety of the corner.

Fenton asked Jamieson if he had recognized anyone else in the room.

'A few,' replied the policeman. 'Mind you, it's hard without their normal clothes. It took me ages to figure out who one of them was, although I knew the face well enough. Then I thought of him in a dog collar . . .'

'Did anyone see who Vanney was with?' asked Fenton.

'Couldn't see for the pillar,' said Kelly.

Jamieson nodded and said, 'We'll have to wait until he stands up.'

Once more the lights began to dim inside and they returned to their positions beneath the windows. Fenton saw that the absentees had come back and that Monkton was smiling, his features restored to distinguished calm. He raised his arm and the music ceased.

Four slaves marched towards Monkton carrying silver

trays laden with wine jugs and goblets and waited while he poured a little wine into each goblet. All the Romans in the room gathered in a large circle as the wine was handed out, then they raised their goblets in some kind of toast and drank in unison.

One of the slaves dropped his jug and it threw up a plume of red wine over Monkton's pristine white toga. Even in the dim lighting Fenton could see clouds of anger roll across Monkton's face. The slave prostrated himself on the floor but Monkton ignored him. He made some kind of signal to the man Vanney had been with, the man who had been hidden by the pillar all night. This man had his back to the windows. He was wearing an elaborate head-dress and carried some kind of silver baton in his right hand. A centurion approached him and took orders.

Fenton watched spellbound as a metal frame was brought into the room and dragged up in front of the man with the baton. Another signal and the slave who had dropped the wine was tied to the frame. One of the guards from the door approached and removed his helmet and cape. In his hand he held a whip.

The man with the baton spread the fingers of his left hand twice to indicate the number ten and the punishment began. Through the glass Fenton and the others could hear the sound of leather hitting flesh. The slave's teeth were bared in anguish and his eyes rolled as the skin of his exposed back was cut open. Blood mingled with the sweat of his fear.

After five lashes his torturer paused to adjust his stance and cover new ground. As the man raised the whip again Fenton got a good look at him and felt weak. 'He's the one who beat me up in the pub,' he whispered to Jamieson.

The slave appeared to have passed out. The Roman with the baton put his hand out to check, but as he did so the slave suddenly sank his teeth into the back of it. The Roman wrenched his hand away and raised his baton in anger.

Fenton waited for it to fall but it did not. The Roman regained his composure and spread his fingers to indicate another five lashes.

The unconscious slave was carried out and the blood cleaned from the floor. The lights went up again, glasses were replenished, and Monkton held up his hand for silence. 'To business, gentlemen,' he announced.

A murmur ran round the room, then it fell silent. Fenton saw that Jamieson had taken out his notebook. He smiled at Kelly.

'The figures, please,' said Monkton.

He stood to one side and another man, small and balding, with several long strands of dark hair combed individually across his scalp, got to his feet. He held a sheaf of papers in front of him.

'Halle-bloody-lujah,' whispered Jamieson.

Fenton and Kelly looked at him and the policeman said, 'That's Vanney senior.'

Vanney cleared his throat and said, 'Fifty thousand pounds from Theta Electronics for rating concessions on their new premises.' There was applause in the room.

'Two hundred thousand pounds from Corton Brothers for assistance with planning permission for their new housing estate and redefining of the green belt in that area.'

More applause.

'Forty-two thousand pounds for motorway maintenance contracts, fifty thousand pounds for housing stock maintenance contracts in the central region and a total of one hundred and eight thousand pounds for various supply contracts in the country as a whole.'

Loud applause.

'And now, gentlemen, an extra item. Twenty thousand pounds from Saxon Medical for our assistance in obtaining a Department of Health licence for their product. Despite subsequent "problems" I am reliably informed that the sale of the licence by Saxon to International Plastics will be deemed tomorrow by the courts to have been made in good faith.'

Vanney held his hands up and shouted above the hubbub, 'I think you all know who we have to thank for that!'

There was general laughter.

'This concludes my report.'

Monkton got to his feet again and announced an end to business for the evening.

Jamieson whispered, 'Let's get out of here.'

None of them spoke until they were back at the car, then Fenton said, 'I think I'm out of my depth.'

'You're not alone,' Jamieson told him. 'To do this right is going to take time but I'm going to get every last one of them.'

Fenton said, 'I wish I could have seen the face of the man with the baton. There was something familiar about him.'

'I thought that too,' confessed Kelly, 'but I'm damned if I can think why.'

THIRTEEN

Fenton drove home fast on the winding coast road. He needed some distraction from thoughts of the evening, and controlling the Honda at high speed demanded his total concentration. Bend after bend loomed up, ensuring that the bike was seldom upright for more than a few seconds before being swung over yet again. The road surface had almost dried out, leaving only the occasional puddle to be caught in the headlight and thrown up into the waving grass.

By the time he reached the outskirts of the city Fenton was both physically and mentally drained. He slowed down for the final roundabout and proceeded sedately along the well-lit tarmac until he reached the flat.

The gas fire burst into life and Fenton switched on the kettle to make tea before sitting down to think. Jamieson was right. It would take time to put the case together against the Cavaliers if he wanted to break the whole organization. An isolated prosecution would only put the Cavaliers on their toes and give them time to regroup. But he was off to a flying start with the names and figures he had obtained from Vanney's report. He knew exactly where to look for evidence of corruption and that was half the battle.

Fenton still had difficulty in accepting how widespread and powerful the Cavalier organization was. It was frightening, but his resolve to see Neil Munro's killer brought to justice was undiminished. The kettle started to whistle and he returned to the kitchen to make tea.

There had been no mention of Nigel Saxon at Helmwood and this was both disappointing and puzzling. It meant that he still couldn't be sure how Saxon had fitted into the scheme of things. If Saxon had been the originator of the plan to defraud International Plastics why hadn't he rated a mention at Helmwood? And if millions of pounds were involved in the fraud why was only the relatively paltry sum of twenty thousand pounds mentioned? Even if Saxon had finally turned traitor under pressure something surely should have been said, or was the elimination of a fellow member by murder too insignificant to merit comment?

A fitful night's sleep did not improve matters. Fenton was still in bed when Jenny came home. She opened the curtains.

Fenton said, 'Isn't it strange? You can't get to sleep all night, but the minute it gets light . . .' Jenny said she knew the feeling. She sat down on the edge of the bed to ask how things had gone.

Fenton told her everything and watched her face register shock and disgust.

'What's Jamieson going to do?' she asked.

'He's going to get to work on breaking them but it'll take some time to gather all the evidence.'

'And then what?'

'I don't know.'

'What about Vanney junior?'

'That's up to Jamieson.'

Jamieson phoned Fenton at around ten-thirty to tell him that things were well underway with the investigation into the corrupt contracts, and that the police computer, fed with the registration numbers that he had collected at Helmwood, had come up with some very interesting names.

'What about Vanney?' asked Fenton.

'With Murray's help and a bit of luck over the car we think we'll be able to nail him for Sandra Murray's murder.

With that facing him and being the little shit he is, he might spill the beans about the rest. Mind you, I still think it was Saxon who killed your friend Munro. He was the only one with a motive.'

'But if it really was Saxon how could he have hoped to blame it on someone else? Just coming up with a name would have been no good. The killer had to be someone in the lab at the time Neil discovered the truth about the plastic.'

'Saxon was probably in a blue funk when he phoned you and prepared to blame it on anyone whether it made sense or not.'

'Maybe,' Fenton conceded.

'People do strange things when they're desperate,' said Jamieson. 'Believe me, I've seen it all.'

Charles Tyson came into Fenton's lab just before noon and said, 'I've got a staffing problem. Ian Ferguson has just phoned to say that he's injured himself working on his car. The point is he was due to be on call tonight and I have to go out this evening. Mary Tyler has a meeting at the school and . . .'

'No problem,' said Fenton, 'I'll do it. I wasn't doing anything.'

'Thanks,' said Tyson.

By eleven-thirty that evening Fenton had cause to regret his generosity in agreeing to take over Ferguson's duty. He had been working almost non-stop since seven in the evening and now the acetylene gas cylinder had run out. He would have to bring up a new one from the basement and change over the reduction valve, a task best carried out by two people.

Cursing his luck, Fenton ran down the stairs and switched on the basement light. He wheeled the cylinder transporter over to a row of gas cylinders and rolled one out on its heel. With some difficulty he manoeuvred it on to the transporter and secured it with the catch chains before pressing the button for the service lift and waiting while the painfully slow motor brought it down.

As he came up in the creaking lift he heard a car draw up outside the lab and the sound of a key rattling in the lock. Fenton assumed it would be Tyson coming in to check on things after his evening out and was surprised to see Ian Ferguson appear at the head of the stairs while he was manhandling the transporter out of the lift.

'I thought I'd drop in and apologize for this,' said Ferguson, holding up his bandaged hand.

'You picked the right night to be off,' said Fenton. 'I've been running around like a cat with its arse on fire since seven o'clock, and now this.' He nodded to the cylinder.

'I'll get the spanners,' said Ferguson.

'What happened anyway?' asked Fenton.

'I changed my car on the strength of my promotion. I was checking the oil in it and the bonnet fell on my hand.'

'Nasty,' said Fenton. 'Anything broken?'

'No, just bruised.'

Fenton brought over the empty cylinder so that he could transfer the headgear and looked to see whether Ferguson had come up with a spanner.

'Will this one do? asked Ferguson, holding up a spanner, his back still to Fenton as he continued to look in the drawer.

Fenton's blood ran cold. He was transfixed by the sight, for in his head the spanner was transformed into a silver baton. The back view of Ferguson was the back view of the Roman with the baton.

Ferguson turned to see why Fenton had not answered. His smile faded when he saw the look on Fenton's face.

'You!' Fenton accused in a hoarse whisper. 'The knowledge, the motive and the opportunity. Neil told you about the plastic. It was you at Helmwood. There was no accident with the car. The slave bit you.' The look on Ferguson's face told Fenton that he was right.

Surprise gave way to arrogant resignation. 'Well, well, well,' said Ferguson quietly.

'You bastard, it was you who killed Neil!'

The spanner hit Fenton just above the left eye. He had been totally unprepared for it, and now the room burst into a galaxy of stars as he slid to the floor.

When he came round Fenton found himself bound hand and foot with the chains from the transporter. Ferguson was looking down at him with a sneer on his face. 'So you finally worked it out, Fenton,' he said.

'Bastard!'

'Tut, tut. You always were a bit rough, Fenton. Bright but rough.'

'Why? For Christ's sake, why?' asked Fenton, struggling impotently with the chains.

Ferguson looked as if he was enjoying Fenton's discomfort. He looked down at him like a parent patronizing a five-year-old. 'Money. What else?' he said.

'But how? What did you have to gain?'

'Saxon was in love with me,' said Ferguson. 'I played him along and made out that I loved him. It was too good a chance to miss. Everyone wants to fall in love with a millionaire.' Ferguson laughed at the thought. 'I arranged for him to become a member of the club and we helped him get his licence for a fee. He was pathetically grateful. The fat clown promised that when the deal went through with International Plastics, he would sign over half his share to me and afterwards make me the sole beneficiary in his will, just as if I were his wife.'

'And you had to kill Neil to make sure that the deal went through?'

'When Munro told me about the flaw he had found in the plastic that morning I saw all that money disappearing. I couldn't have that, now, could I? I took a short cut down to the Sterile Supply Department and waited till he arrived. You know the rest.'

'Was Saxon in it too?'

Ferguson seemed amused at the suggestion. 'Don't be ridiculous,' he sneered. 'That idiot knew nothing at all about it. He didn't have the nerve to play for high stakes.'

'But you did,' said Fenton quietly.

'That's what being a Cavalier is all about, Fenton.'

'Did you kill Saxon too?'

'The slow-witted clod finally twigged to what had been going on. I think he wanted to break off our engagement.' Ferguson laughed at his own joke.

Fenton felt sick but he had to know it all. 'Sandra Murray too?' he asked.

'She knew too much.'

'Don't you feel anything?' Fenton was furious with himself for not having suspected Ferguson sooner. Now when he thought about it he remembered that it had been Ferguson who had been on duty in the lab immediately before the incident with the fume cupboard and that Ferguson had been present to hear him volunteer to come in that Sunday to help Saxon.

'All that nonsense about wanting to change your job because you were scared . . .' said Fenton.

'I thought that was rather a nice touch,' said Ferguson.

Fenton saw his own death warrant in Ferguson's eyes and was desperately afraid. The thought that he would never see Jenny again was unbearable.

Ferguson looked around him and thought aloud. 'An accident with the cylinder, I think.' He said it as if he were thinking about the seating arrangements for a dinner party. 'Yes, that's it. You were changing the heavy cylinder all on your own when it fell on you and knocked you out. The lab filled up with gas from the leaking valve on the cylinder and there was a fire . . . an explosion.'

Through his fear Fenton saw that he had one chance. Ferguson would have to bend down to release the empty cylinder. If he could hit the transporter at just the right angle and just the right moment . . .

Ferguson bent down and Fenton's feet shot out to send

the heavy metal transporter crashing into him. One of the bars caught Ferguson behind the ear and he went out like a light. But for how long? The question bred new panic in Fenton. He was still tied up. What could he do? Could he risk trying to roll across the floor and down the stairs? What was the point? He wouldn't be able to open the front door even if he succeeded. The phone! If he could just get the receiver off the hook, surely he could dial three nines even with his hands behind his back.

Getting across the floor was more difficult than Fenton had anticipated; his frustration and fear grew with every second that passed. His mouth was drier than a desert as he finally succeeded in raising himself to his knees beside the table where the phone was, and a sudden groan from Ferguson almost panicked him into losing balance. It took four attempts to get the phone off the hook, then with a clatter it was done.

Ferguson groaned again and Fenton turned to see him move slightly on the floor. He managed to dial one nine, then slipped and cursed. Ferguson moved again and Fenton knew that it was hopeless. Even if he did manage to make the call Ferguson was going to come round long before the police could get to him. Despair threatened as he searched vainly for a way of injuring Ferguson more permanently.

Outside, a police siren started to wail. 'Please God, make them come here,' said Fenton out loud. To his amazement the siren grew louder and louder until it stopped outside the door of the lab and he heard car doors being slammed. He heard the front door being broken and the sound of heavy footsteps on the stairs. 'I'm in here,' he yelled as Ferguson struggled to his hands and knees.

Jamieson entered the room first. He was followed by two uniformed constables. He looked at Ferguson and then at Fenton in his chains, who was fighting to regain the power of speech.

'How?' stammered Fenton. 'Just how the hell did you know?'

Jamieson said, 'I didn't, really. The truth is we didn't get a computer report for one of the cars at Helmwood until twenty minutes ago because of a recent change of ownership. When I found out that the car belonged to one Ian Ferguson, and bearing in mind what you said about Saxon not being Munro's killer and how the murderer would have to be someone in the lab, I put two and two together. Ferguson wasn't at his flat so I put out an APB for the car. It was reported outside the lab . . . so here I am.'

Ferguson was now fully conscious. Jamieson bent down to caution him and place him under formal arrest. Fenton recounted all that he had confessed to.

'Is that a fact?' said Jamieson quietly.

'I'm saying nothing,' said Ferguson.

'Of course not, sir,' said Jamieson with a sneer.

Ferguson put his hand up to his head to feel the place where the transporter had hit him, and in doing so lifted the hair away from his ear. It had a piece missing from it. Fenton froze when he saw it and knew that Jamieson had seen it too.

Jamieson turned to the two constables and said, 'Wait downstairs.' The men looked puzzled but trooped obediently out and closed the door behind them. Without any warning Jamieson spun on his heel and swung his right foot into Ferguson's face. Fenton winced but Jamieson remained expressionless. 'That,' he said, looking down at the gasping Ferguson, 'was a wee something for Madeline Gray.'

When he could speak again through a mess of blood and teeth Ferguson spluttered, 'You won't get away with this, you bastard!' He turned to Fenton and said, 'You saw that, Fenton. You saw what he did to me.'

'Saw what?' said Fenton.

The winter was finally over.

Gerald Seymour

writes internationally best-selling thrillers

'Not since Le Carré has the emergence of an international suspense writer been as stunning as that of Gerald Seymour.' *Los Angeles Times*

HARRY'S GAME
KINGFISHER
RED FOX
THE CONTRACT
ARCHANGEL
IN HONOUR BOUND
FIELD OF BLOOD
THE GLORY BOYS
A SONG IN THE MORNING
AT CLOSE QUARTERS

FONTANA PAPERBACKS

Fontana Paperbacks Fiction

Fontana is a leading paperback publisher of both non-fiction, popular and academic, and fiction. Below are some recent fiction titles.

- ☐ FIRST LADY Erin Pizzey £3.95
- ☐ A WOMAN INVOLVED John Gordon Davis £3.95
- ☐ COLD NEW DAWN Ian St James £3.95
- ☐ A CLASS APART Susan Lewis £3.95
- ☐ WEEP NO MORE, MY LADY Mary Higgins Clark £2.95
- ☐ COP OUT R.W. Jones £2.95
- ☐ WOLF'S HEAD J.K. Mayo £2.95
- ☐ GARDEN OF SHADOWS Virginia Andrews £3.50
- ☐ WINGS OF THE WIND Ronald Hardy £3.50
- ☐ SWEET SONGBIRD Teresa Crane £3.95
- ☐ EMMERDALE FARM BOOK 23 James Ferguson £2.95
- ☐ ARMADA Charles Gidley £3.95

You can buy Fontana paperbacks at your local bookshop or newsagent. Or you can order them from Fontana Paperbacks, Cash Sales Department, Box 29, Douglas, Isle of Man. Please send a cheque, postal or money order (not currency) worth the purchase price plus 22p per book for postage (maximum postage required is £3.00 for orders within the UK).

NAME (Block letters) _____

ADDRESS _____

_____

_____